# LIVING BY HIS WILL

LYNNE STEWART

For Bernie

*Chapter 1*

*Now*

Athena flicked her lighter and lit a cigarette, only to immediately snuff it out on the wall next to the stair rail. She dropped it onto the sticky subway floor, where it joined the rest in an unsmoked cigarette graveyard forming at her feet. For a brief moment, she inhaled the last of the smoke as it swirled in the air, then turned her face away. She shouldn't have done that. She shouldn't have even bought the fucking pack of cigarettes to begin with.

"Fuck. Fuck. Fuck. Fuck," Athena whispered to no one. Sometimes, it just felt good to curse. It released something from inside of her that needed to get out.

Lighting the cigarettes was progress, believe it or not. It might not be exactly what her therapist had in mind when she said she wanted Athena to start breaking the rules, but a week ago, she couldn't even carry the cigarette pack around in her purse.

Now look at her. She was lighting up and everything.

Nathan hated smoking. Her pack-a-day habit was one of the first things to go when she agreed to be his. But Nathan was gone, and Athena had been given back her freedom, or so she kept hearing from her mother-fucking therapist. Exactly how much money had Nathan paid that woman to meet with Athena twice a week and listen to her whine about the world being pointless? Too much; that's how much.

Athena walked up the stairs and stepped out into the chilly night air. The moon was full, and the stars were twinkling above the streetlights. Most nights, she wouldn't even bother looking up, but that night felt different. Important. Something to remember. She took a deep breath of fresh air and exhaled slowly, heading down the deserted street. Without anything else to occupy her, Athena's mind wandered to places it shouldn't go.

Back to Nathan. Always back to Nathan.

He made that gigantic spot in her heart for himself intentionally, of course. Everything he did was intentional. Calculated. Measured.

When he was alive, he controlled every aspect of her existence, from what she wore to who she spoke to. The control had created her dependence on him. He totally got off on that shit, and so did she. But thinking about all that didn't help one bit. It just made her miss him even more.

It was a foregone conclusion that no one would ever make her feel that way again. Her therapist would tell her to be positive, that she'd find love again. It was implied that she could even find happiness in an egalitarian vanilla relationship, which made Athena's skin itch. No, thank you, Therapist Lady. She had no desire for anything that conventional.

Athena grimaced at the bright, buzzing streetlights. Being out at night alone was a thrill. Nathan had always forbidden her from doing anything like that. She wasn't allowed to take the subway at all, much less venture out on it after dark.

*Too many junkies that could damage my property*, he had said.

*Yes, sir*, Athena had said.

Case closed. But not anymore.

Taking the subway and walking at night were easy rules to break once she started her therapy sessions. Smoking cigarettes, picking out her own clothing, and relearning how to function alone in society? Well, those things hadn't come back to her so quickly. Don't bother asking why. Athena couldn't explain it, even if she wanted to.

Nathan knew it wouldn't be easy for her to move on and live without him. Of course, he was right about that, like he was right about everything. For the first few days after his death, Athena hadn't even bothered getting out of bed. She couldn't shower or even brush her teeth, for fuck's sake. Not out of mourning, but because she wasn't sure what to do. How should she dress? How should she choose what to eat? Where was she allowed to go? God forbid she ran out of body wash or something and had to go to the store. Without Nathan, all of it felt completely wrong, and staying in bed was the safest option.

Advanced-stage pancreatic cancer hadn't given Nathan much time to plan for his death. He had to be at least a little preoccupied with the news that he was going to die, but all he showed to Athena was his typical business-as-usual side. To her, he would always be the no-nonsense CEO who could move mountains in a single day.

Even with the pain, and the vomiting, and the sickness from the medications, he quickly set her up with a therapist to help her with the transition back to independence. He'd secured her housing and established a trust that distributed a stipend for her living expenses. For how long, Athena didn't know, but no one had indicated that she needed to go out and get a job, so it was quite possible that the trust was intended to last for several years at least.

No doubt, Nathan's other women had something similar to fall back on. Not that Athena was answering any of their group texts.

She knew she was coming off like a total bitch by

ignoring them, but she didn't have anything to say. They weren't "friends" and never had been. Soon enough, they wouldn't even be whatever it was that they were to each other before Nathan died. Tomorrow would probably be the last time she'd ever see them, for the reading of Nathan's will.

She could already picture exactly what it would be like. Her former master's other submissives would be there with her to hear his final wishes read aloud by his kink-friendly (and extra pricey) attorney. All of them would sit together in a room like the guy they had shared was a regular 45-year-old business executive, not the twisted BDSM-practicing polygamous individual he really was. That'd be weird, right? It'd have to be.

Athena wondered idly if they were all having the same problems. Were they having nightmares that this was all some fucked-up, twisted test? Were they worried that breaking all the rules would get them punished, too? Maybe they didn't care. Maybe they had already moved on to being with someone else. Now, that would be one hell of a test if Nathan was just waiting somewhere to see how loyal they were to him if they thought he was gone.

That was stupid, of course. Athena knew it wasn't a test. It was really the end. Nathan had sat down with each of his submissives individually to break the news when he received his diagnosis.

He had no doubt told Veronica first. She was his

legal wife, after all, and the one who had served him the longest. She deserved to know first. Athena wasn't sure how far down the totem pole she had been when it came to having that conversation with him, but that sort of thing didn't matter to her, anyway. She wasn't the one who tried to compare Nathan's time or affection between her and the others. If she tried to, she would break down completely. Even thinking about him being with the other women made her clench her teeth.

As stupid as it sounds, she mostly lived in denial and tried to forget that the other women in Nathan's life existed. That wasn't easy, given they all lived in the same apartment together, but she made it work because she wanted him. Belonging to Nathan was the reward. She didn't move into his house to join some twisted sorority, for Christ's sake.

Athena smiled, remembering the look he had given her when she had said as much at the dinner table one evening. She thought for sure he was going to warm her ass with a spanking right then and there over their meal. Veronica had saved her by playing it off as a joke, something Athena should have been more grateful about. If she owed anything to anyone in that room, it was Veronica.

She couldn't understand why the rest of them were so butt-hurt over her being aloof. It wasn't like Athena's feelings had changed over time, yet her detachment from the rest of the group had always been a sticking point with some of the other submissives. They felt like Athena was stuck up, that she wasn't committed enough because she didn't seek them out to paint nails or go shopping or whatever the fuck they did in the later hours of the afternoon if they weren't serving Nathan.

They didn't understand that her lack of enthusiasm for being around them wasn't because she wasn't committed to the lifestyle. Nathan had made that clear from the start: if she wanted to be his, she had to be all in. Fine. She had agreed to that readily when the time came for it. He wanted control of every aspect of her life. Her job. Her money. Her everything. He owned her. She was his property. She even had a fucking collar locked around her neck to prove it.

To Athena, wearing a collar had been the wildest, sexiest thing in the world. It still was, actually. So much so that she hadn't taken it off, even though Nathan had given her the key himself. He had instructed her to take it off when the time was right, assuming against all logic that the time would ever be right. Athena's fingers traced the dark leather strap and stainless-steel lock lazily. Not wearing it would be so weird.

Tomorrow, she'd see if any of the others had taken theirs off. Probably not, as there was always some level of competition amongst a few of them about who was more devoted to their master. Catty shit like that was to be expected, and the reading of Nathan's will would be a last chance for them to try and one-up one another. To be fair, Athena wasn't including Veronica in that assessment. While they hadn't always seen eye-to-eye, Veronica wasn't interested in competing with Nathan's other girls any more than Athena was.

She took the steps two at a time until she reached the door of her walkup Brownstone apartment. It was a converted unit that had begun its life as a massive home for some wealthy nineteenth-century family. More recently, it was restored and divided into several apartments, some one-bedrooms, and others, like hers, were studios. The other girls might live in bigger places, but Nathan knew her well, and the beautiful Brownstone was a perfect fit.

Athena unlocked the entrance that led to a shared hallway. From there, she fitted her second key into the lock of her own front door and disabled the alarm. She dropped her bag onto a chair, taking in the cozy space as though she was seeing it again for the first time. Her stomach grumbled, and suddenly, Athena was starving. She kicked her shoes off and padded over to the unit's charming little kitchenette. It was pretty basic, but it had plenty of space to make dinner for one.

That's all the space she needed now, anyway.

Chapter 2

*Now*

She didn't want to get sucked into feeling sorry for herself, so Athena pushed the ache of loneliness to the side. Dinner couldn't wait any longer; if she didn't eat soon, she'd skip another meal and violate her therapist's instructions about eating enough. Athena surveyed her options carefully, hating that choosing what to eat would require even more decision-making.

Some of the items stored in the mini pantry were staples for her. Things like tea, coffee, fruit, and veggies. Lean meat in the fridge and whole grains in the bread drawer. Other items still felt forbidden—like the snack cakes and instant ramen she snatched up like a junkie going through withdrawals when she went shopping at the supermarket. And the liquor. Definitely the liquor.

Nathan would have had a fatal heart attack over

seeing that stuff in her kitchen if the cancer hadn't gotten to him first. Her ass would have stayed bright red long after he had made her throw all those items out.

Still, she kept the two categories separate. One pile was her permitted food, another was the forbidden junk. So far, she hadn't strayed to that second pile. Was it finally the day she would cross that line?

Nope. She was still feeling guilty as fuck from lighting the cigarette earlier. She didn't need to deal with Top Ramen weighing on her conscience, too.

She opened the fridge and fished out some pre-cut veggies from a bag. Athena chopped them finely for a stir-fry. She plucked some chickpea noodles from the permitted pile of food, followed by spices and oil. The cutting board, which had been a gift from Nathan after she had "graduated" from cooking lessons with his wife, served as a platter for the finished bits while she prepped the rest of the ingredients.

Athena grinned, recalling how Nathan had insisted on her taking the cooking lessons. They were brutal, and she had tried to bully him into allowing her to quit more than once. But now she had to admit that those long hours spent with Veronica in front of the stove had been worth it. Not only could she follow pretty much any recipe, but she could also make Nathan's favorite dishes just from memory. Like the stir-fry, for instance.

The smell of soy sauce and ginger wafted through the air as she prepared the meal before dishing herself up a generous portion. The plates were beautiful, as was everything else that was already inside the apartment when she moved in. It was a force of habit to reach for more plates. She would normally grab a few for Nathan and the other women in the house, but she resisted the urge. Having only one plate to dish up punctuated how alone she was; a reminder that she was truly on her own.

With dinner ready (and little else to do), Athena carried her plate into the living area, a glass of wine in hand. Red wine was the only exception to Nathan's no-alcohol rule. Even so, she was only ever allowed one glass in the evenings with dinner. She sank into the designer leather sofa and grabbed the remote, flipping through the channels until she settled on a comedy.

It was a sitcom featuring a crazy big family. The squabbling characters remind her of when Nathan met her parents for the first time.

She had been nervous that day. Athena hadn't really believed him when he said he wanted to meet her family. She thought he was joking, mocking the fact that in their unconventional relationship, such things weren't necessary. But it turned out that he was very serious.

*You'll meet them as... what?* she had asked. *What*

*would I even tell them, Nathan? Hey, Mom and Dad, here's the man who owns me. We have kinky sex, just like he does with his wife. Sometimes we even fuck him at the same time.*

Nathan had snorted and shook his head.

*Just introduce me as your boyfriend,* he had said. *No need to scare the vanillas.*

Boyfriend or not, Athena was convinced that her parents wouldn't accept him. They were religious, very religious, but it's not like she had a choice about whether to bring him to her childhood home upstate. Nathan was the one to make that decision, and he made it long before he said anything to her about it. The knowledge that the situation was completely out of her hands had been a huge relief. Nathan wanted to meet her parents, and whatever the fallout was, it was his problem to worry about, not hers.

But all her hesitation turned out to be for nothing anyway. As soon as Nathan opened his mouth, Athena's parents were swept away with his charisma and charm. By the end of dinner, they were laughing just like the characters on the TV show. Athena was so at ease on the drive back to the city that she told Nathan she loved him.

She hadn't meant to. She wasn't sure how he would react to hearing that. Was their situation something that could include romantic love, or was that inappropriate? Veronica said she loved him, but that didn't necessarily mean it was the right thing for Athena to say.

Nathan had just reached for her hand. *Glad you finally figured that out, slave girl*, he said.

She didn't always love him. Sometimes she hated him, sometimes she regretted ever finding him. Or him finding her, rather.

Athena grew drowsy as the show went on, the wine and warmth of the room working their magic on her. Before she knew it, she was nodding off, and drifting to sleep on the couch.

In her dreams, she was transported back to the coffee shop where she first met Nathan. It was a small cafe that was more of a secondhand bookstore than anything else. The shelves were lined with a little of everything from fifth editions of classics to indie books from local authors. Most of the people who came in were regulars. It was a dive bookshop/cafe if such a thing existed.

Athena could see it all perfectly. Probably because she had been forced to relive the same scenario in dream form every night for weeks.

She was covering a shift for a co-worker (Melody), who had called out at the last minute to stay home with her sick kid. Athena wasn't even supposed to be working that day, but that didn't matter to fate, god, or whoever was in charge of people meeting each other. She was working at that moment for a reason.

Athena was steaming some milk for a latte when their eyes met. He wasn't a regular customer; she was sure of that, but something about him made it difficult to look away. She burned herself on the milk frother, getting lost in his gaze. He had smiled when she jumped at the sharp pain from the burn, and the trance was broken.

The weird thing was Athena couldn't decide what it was that made her instantly become a moth and for him to be a flame.

He wasn't like the typical guys she dated. Her usual type was artsy, with tattoos, a man-bun, and loads of student loan debt. For her to be interested, the guy would need to be some emotionally driven, almost hippy who liked that she matched their free-spirit vibes, right down to the ripped skinny jeans and clove cigarettes she always had on her.

Nathan stepped out of line at that point, finding a seat without even ordering a coffee. He didn't make it obvious to everyone else, but she could feel his eyes on her while she made every drink during the morning rush.

As the line moved, one of the younger men occasionally flirted with her when she handed them their order. It was nothing unusual, but it felt scandalous to have them show her interest while being observed by the new stranger so closely.

"Will I see you at open mic night, Athena?" Jared Rossi crooned. They had met a few years earlier in a creative writing class that she had taken at the nearby university. Neither of them left the neighborhood after graduation, and Jared came at least once a day, often extending the same invitation for her to hear him read his work at the bar down the street. Athena had never gone, but something about the man in the corner made her want to accept for once.

"I'd like that, Jared," she said, smiling. "What time is it again? Seven?" Surprise and eagerness colored his face. Of course, he hadn't expected her to say yes after all the times she had turned him down, and after seeing his reaction, Athena felt more than a little guilty about saying she'd go. She had no real intention of being there, but now that it seemed to actually mean something to him, she'd have to show up.

"Yeah, seven is great. They get things started around 7:15, so that will give us a chance to grab a drink beforehand. I'll save you a seat with my friends, okay?"

Athena gave a weak smile and nodded. Jared walked away, head held high, a man invincible.

She refused to look up and meet the stranger's gaze after that. The energy between them had shifted from magnetic to something more tense.

"I'm going on break," Athena said to the cashier. She couldn't remember what the girl's name was. Sammy? Or maybe Tammy?

Whatever her name was, she was new and didn't have her personalized apron yet. Sammy (or Tammy) nodded and turned to wipe down the counters before more customers showed up.

Stepping into the back alley, Athena texted her roommate, Harper, to see if she would be interested in open mic night, too. Harper worked as a receptionist at the hospital and was covering for the night shift. While they usually enjoyed having breakfast together, other times, the two of them didn't cross paths for days. It would probably be a few hours before she'd wake up and respond to the text.

Athena shoved the phone back into the pocket of her apron and fished out her lighter and the half-full pack of Djarum Browns.

Smoking was stupid, disgusting, and a waste of money, but it was also the thing that kept her anxiety at bay long enough to get through a shift of work and try to work on her own crappy art.

"That's the first thing that'll have to go. Just so you know."

Athena jumped, almost dropping the cigarette. The man from the coffee shop had followed her outside. Her heart beat hard in her chest, and alarm bells went off in her head. Only a creeper would be lurking in the alleyway. She glanced at the milk crate holding the back door open. It was between them, and she'd have to step toward him to get back inside the building.

"Can I help you?" Athena took a long drag from her smoke, grateful that her voice didn't shake and sounded more confident than she felt. She threw in a scowl for good measure.

The man gave her a knowing smile as if the simple phrase was an actual invitation rather than an attempt to get rid of him.

"You can," he said, taking a step forward. "But the question is, will you?"

Her breath hitched in her throat. She was frozen, completely taken in by his size next to her. Athena hadn't realized how tall he was from across the room, but now that they were within arm's reach of each other, it was impossible to ignore the way he eclipsed her.

Athena's eyes took in his neat haircut, skimming the dark suit that showed off his broad shoulders. He looked like a man who was used to getting what he wanted.

She had no idea at the time how true that was.

"Yeah, probably not. I'm on break right now, but there's another barista at the counter who will be more than happy to take your order."

"I'm sure she does a fabulous job, but I'd rather have you serve me." The man took another step forward and leaned in, making the already small alleyway feel claustrophobic. This time, when the warning bells started going off, Athena didn't ignore them.

She swallowed hard. "Look, I'm not sure what the fuck you're doing here, but if you don't back up, I'm going to scream."

"Such a pretty mouth for language like that," the man said. His eyes were on her lips like he wanted to taste them for himself.

*Fuck this shit*, she thought.

While he was distracted, Athena pushed him away, grounding the lit cigarette into his hand as she forced her way through. The odor of tobacco was strong in the air. It was impossible with such a minor burn, but she also imagined that the scent of smoke was mixed with the smell of singed skin.

The man grunted, then moved out of the way so she could easily escape him. Athena spun around, frowning. He was letting her go without even trying to stop her. Had she misread the situation?

The man grinned at her as if she hadn't just used him as a human ashtray. "I'm not trying to kidnap or assault you, Athena. I prefer my prey to be willing."

Her eyes widened. The man was psychotic. And he knew her name. How the fuck did he know her name? She hurried back inside, grateful when the door was locked firmly behind her.

The thought bothered her so much that she had difficulty concentrating for the rest of her shift. Thankfully, the man didn't return, or she would've had to call the police. Maybe he knew that since he seemed to know everything else.

It wasn't until she clocked out and removed her apron that the front of the uniform caught her eye. *Athena,* written clear as day in neat cursive, stared back at her.

Her name was embroidered on the front, just like everyone else who worked at the coffee shop. Athena groaned at her own paranoia and shoved the apron into her oversized bag. He knew her name from the apron. That was all.

Once again, she had overreacted, and now she needed a stiff drink to quiet her nerves. Athena began the walk home, where a nice bottle of tequila with her name on it was waiting. With the weird situation behind her, she didn't bother scanning the street as she left.

If she had, she might have noticed he was still there. Years later, they would joke and tease each other over their own recollections of that day. In her dream, Athena's subconscious intertwined both versions to recreate the scene.

She could easily imagine how he looked, patiently watching her walk home, all the while knowing he would one day make her crave him. Even asleep, it made her heart squeeze with grief. If only her dream self could turn around and run back to him. She'd jump into his arms and cling to him, refusing to let him go.

Maybe doing that would make it feel like he wasn't completely gone. But instead, she just kept walking home, like she always did.

## Chapter 3

*Now*

The next day, Athena woke up cold and stiff. Cold from not turning up the heat or grabbing a blanket, and stiff from sleeping on the lumpy sofa rather than walking the short distance to her bed.

She shook her head to clear it before sitting up and stretching her arms to pop her back. The grogginess was slowly replaced by an anxious sensation that settled in her stomach like a rock.

It was finally the day she'd hear what was written in Nathan's will. She'd been dreading it since he had passed away nearly two months earlier. The executor of his estate was the same attorney who helped him prepare the will and trusts for all the women.

Nathan had instructed the attorney to wait 60 days to gather all of them together, giving everyone time to grieve and adjust to an independent life before they received his final directive.

The extra time had been necessary. Athena wouldn't have been able to sit through a day like that right after losing him. She was still tempted to skip it, actually, but her therapist, Dr. Harlow, had insisted that going to the reading of the will would help bring her closure.

*Closure, my ass*, she thought. There would never be closure for her after experiencing a relationship like that. But, whatever. Let the shrink think what she wants. The sooner Dr. Harlow cleared her to stop coming in for sessions, the sooner she'd be rid of that obligation to her former master.

Athena quickly got ready for the day and grabbed her bag before heading out the door. After glancing at the time on her phone, she decided to take a cab rather than the subway. The generous monthly stipend from Nathan would allow her to always take a cab, really, but it still felt like a crazy indulgence when public transportation was infinitely cheaper and just a little less convenient.

What she didn't want was to get used to always having luxury, only to have it stripped away from her at some point. And living as basically as she could was one way of exerting some level of control after her world was turned upside down.

Still, there was no denying that Athena didn't have the extra time to waste that day, so she splurged and hailed a taxi to the curb outside the

Brownstone. As the driver weaved in and out of traffic, she tried to take her mind off what was to come by taking an inventory of the buildings they passed.

There was the coffee shop she used to work at, where Nathan and her first met. There was her dentist, there was her nail salon. Down that street, several miles away, was the apartment building she had lived in with the other members of Nathan's family until she moved out a few days after his death. Moving out was the one thing she forced herself to do right after Nathan died, and that's only because she knew that the Brownstone apartment was the one place she could be totally alone.

Finally, they arrived at the attorney's office, preventing her from compiling any other memories that hurt too much to recall.

She took a deep breath for extra courage as she walked into the office. It did little to help calm her nerves. She should have taken a shot of liquor before she left the house.

Inside the attorney's office, Veronica and the other two women Nathan had enslaved were already waiting for her. Teresa and Denise, sitting side-by-side as usual, looked young and beautiful. Just as she expected, none of them had removed their collars, either. She fought the urge to touch hers, wanting it to give her some strength in that moment. She paused to take in the scene, knowing she would want to remember it later.

Teresa was stunning. Tall, with artificially tan skin and light strawberry-blonde hair. She was the last to join their circle, causing Nathan to declare the family complete with its five members. Denise, on the other hand, was shorter than Athena, but they had the same porcelain skin. What distinguished them from one another, besides having opposite personalities, was their hair color and Athena's generous curves. Where she was soft, Denise was lean.

Nathan had explained it once when he caught Athena critiquing her figure in the mirror: one of them was not better, even if they were completely different. According to their master, none of them were more beautiful than any other. He wanted them all the same.

Athena usually didn't buy that kind of bullshit, but for Nathan, she suspended her disbelief. She surpassed an eye roll and nodded like what he said made complete sense. There was nothing else he could say that wouldn't have caused a civil war in his home, after all.

Nathan's determination for equality among the girls didn't stop the insecurities and pettiness entirely, though. Denise and Teresa were as thick as thieves when they weren't trying to compete for his attention. Maybe it was because he had taken them both as subs about the same time and had engaged in more threesomes with them than Athena had thought humanly possible. But then, what had she really known about group sex at all before meeting Nathan? All her sexual encounters up until that point had been one-on-one.

Even when she had joined in serving Nathan alongside Veronica, the times they had all wound up in bed together, she had needed a lot of direction on what to do. Her favorite threesomes were when she didn't interact with the other woman at all, and one of them rode his face while the other bounced on his cock, both lost in their own experiences and ignoring each other completely.

She shifted in her seat, remembering how hard she'd come in both positions. She was absolutely going to hell for thinking about deviant sex during the reading of Nathan's will, but something told her Nathan would have enjoyed her reliving those memories.

Athena glanced at Veronica, wondering if she ever thought about how it had been when it was just the three of them living in the house. As far as Athena could tell, it didn't cross the other woman's mind.

From Athena's perspective, it had been a really difficult transition to go from sharing Nathan with just his wife to being one of four in what felt like an overnight upset. If Veronica had felt the same way when Teresa and Denise moved in, she never showed it. Maybe going from two to four had been easy after the first adjustment when Athena was added to the mix. If so, Veronica had never complained about that, either.

Of course, Veronica also got off on sharing their master, so maybe it didn't make sense to compare their experiences at all. Maybe she thought Nathan taking more women was always a good thing.

Athena glanced up at the door when it opened, and Nathan's attorney entered the room. His smart suit and fresh haircut were like a walking billboard for success. The man was good at what he did, which is what had earned him Nathan's business and trust.

"Thanks for coming, everyone," he said, smiling at them as though there was nothing strange about a dead man having a wife and three concubines. "I know this has been a hard time for all of you."

Denise sniffed and pulled a tissue from her purse. Teresa rubbed small circles on Denise's back to comfort her. The attorney gave them a sympathetic glance before continuing with his spiel.

"I believe we have all met, but for the record, I need to proceed in a more official capacity. My secretary will join us to record the reading of the will, but she is just as discreet and sensitive to your lives and Nathan's alternative lifestyle as I am. Other than the necessary legal aspects, what happens here today stays in this room. Does anyone have any questions before I call her in?"

The four of them looked at each other and then back at him. They were ready to get this over with.

"Right," he said, nodding. Then he leaned over and pressed a button on the desk phone before speaking. "Sheila, we're ready for you to join us now."

A small, mousey woman let herself into the room. She was balancing a laptop and what looked like the world's biggest thermos, probably filled with coffee, in her hands. Athena was instantly jealous of it, kicking herself for not waking up in time to stop at Starbucks.

The woman set down her thermos and produced a voice recorder from her pocket. With a nod from the attorney, she flipped it on and set it on his desk.

"Today is March 14, 2024. We are gathered here in the offices of Schumer and Associates for the reading of the will of Nathan Garcia. My name is Alexander Schumer, and I am the executor of Mr. Garcia's estate. Can everyone else in attendance please state their first and last names for the record?"

"Veronica Garcia."

"Teresa Garcia."

"Denise Garcia."

"Athena Garcia," she added last. For some reason, Athena always went last, though she was first alphabetically and second in family order.

If the secretary was surprised that they all shared

a last name, she didn't let on. Taking Nathan's last name was expected of his submissives, even if he could only legally marry one of them. *It helps to remind you of your place in the family*, he had said.

"Wonderful," Mr. Schumer said. "Let's get started. Nathan wanted to keep this part as short and simple as possible, and I think you will all be happy with how his property is distributed."

The attorney rattled off some legal jargon, indicating that all of Nathan's property be distributed to the women equally, including the proceeds from their family home after it was sold. It, along with his other valuable assets, would fund the trusts set up for their benefit.

None of this was surprising to Athena. It had been discussed already. Nathan had never wanted children, and although Veronica could have easily claimed half of his estate herself as his legal wife, Athena knew she wouldn't contest Nathan's wishes. She had lived by his rule in everything for far too long to betray the man now, and her late husband would probably love to haunt her if she tried.

After the will was read, Mr. Schumer indicated that his secretary should turn off the recording. Athena reached for her purse, relieved that the meeting was coming to a close and she would soon be able to hide away in her apartment until her next therapy session.

"Ladies, please wait just a little while longer," Mr.

Schumer said tightly when Athena turned to go. "I'm sorry to keep all of you, but there is another document that Nathan wanted me to share with you. This document is not legally enforceable, but given the nature of your relationships, I'm sure you'll find it equally compelling."

Athena shared a glance with Veronica, wondering if she knew anything about it. No, Nathan's wife looked as confused as she felt. Athena didn't bother looking back at Nathan's other two former subs. If Veronica didn't know what this was, they wouldn't have a clue, either.

Mr. Schumer cleared his throat and unfolded the second document, reading Nathan's words. "Girls, I know the last few months have been hard on you. Believe me, it is difficult to imagine a time and place where I am not there with you.

"The four of you have given me the best life possible, and I have died a truly blessed and happy man. Just as you have sworn your lives to me, my life was promised to you, and I am thankful that we have remained together as a family until the end, a master with four beautiful submissives. However, you know me well enough to expect that I did not take your oaths lightly. You each wanted me to own you as human property, and I have.

"Now, my end has come, and while I am not there to reassure you myself, please find comfort in knowing that I am not abandoning any of you to be free women. Your therapists have helped you cope with grief, and the transition to living alone, but living a life without purpose is not a life I want for you.

"You swore a lifetime of service to me, and I'm holding you to it. I have never been one to share my property with others, but nothing about this is ideal. So, today, I am dividing up my inanimate possessions, as well as my living ones."

The four women were silent as the lawyer paused to let the words sink in. Athena felt the color drain from her face. *The fuck?*

"Is there more?" Veronica asked quietly.

"Yes, Mrs. Garcia. There is more," Alexander said, returning his gaze to the papers in his hand. "Regarding Teresa and Denise Garcia, I am giving you to an associate of mine, also living in the lifestyle. He has one sub pledged to him for a lifetime, and he admires the way you both were able to join our established family so easily. Given how close you are, I believe that having you serve the same master is the best course of action. He expects you to arrive at his home within 48 hours of the reading of my will. You can take whatever personal items you want with you. From there, he will manage the stipend I have left each of you to contribute to your support and maintenance for life."

Athena blinked slowly, trying her best to process

what was happening, but the lawyer was far from done.

"Veronica Garcia, you have been with me since we were young, and while you might not believe there is another man for you, I think you will be very happy living in service to our friend Daniel McNeil. He has never owned a submissive before, which is probably for the best. You can help him grow into the role, as you did with me. He also anticipates your arrival at his home within 48 hours, with the same financial plan in place as Teresa and Denise.

"Of course, that leaves Athena. Athena, I leave you to Donovan O'Malley, a relatively new friend I met at the lifestyle club, Safeword. He also does not own any subs, though I believe he has a collection of women serving him part-time. He will be a good match for your fire and help keep you in line. Unlike your sisters, you do not have a timeline to move into your new master's residence. Mr. O'Malley will approach you when he is ready. He has already taken control of your assets but has agreed to not touch the money in your account until after collecting you.

"I have been reassured that these men are prepared to honor a lifetime commitment with each of you and that they are worthy of your submission. If you find that not to be the case, please reach out to Mr. Schumer so that he can mediate or rectify the situation as needed. I hope you go on to serve these masters in my stead and know that I am giving you each my blessing to live full lives. All my love, until we meet again on the other side."

The room was so quiet that Athena could hear the beating of her own heart pounding away in her chest. None of the other women moved for several seconds, the gears in their heads spinning as one. Finally, Veronica cleared her throat.

"Was there anything else, Mr. Schumer?" she asked.

"No, Mrs. Garcia. That is the end of the letter." The lawyer paused, hesitating. "Of course, if you have any questions, or if I can assist you in any way, please let me know."

"I have a question," Teresa said. "What if we don't like these randos and we want out? Can we leave with our trust funds or what?"

Schumer shifted uncomfortably in his chair. "This is a highly unusual situation, Ms. Garcia, but the way Nathan set up the trusts stipulates that while you are to benefit from the funds, the men he referenced in the letter will be the ones deciding how the money is spent. Almost as trustees themselves, as it were."

"So, no then?" Denise looked pissed. Athena had to hide her smile at the turn of events. She never thought that any of them were with Nathan for his money, per se, but it was interesting to see who was more concerned about the money now that he was gone.

"I'm not saying that Ms. Garcia. I'm saying that it might involve a lawsuit, or at the very least mediation, to get everything straightened out should you not wish to follow through with Nathan's final instructions."

Denise crossed her arms and leaned back in her chair, huffing at the response. This clearly wasn't what she had planned, though the same could be said for any of them. Athena was sure that somewhere, somehow, Nathan was getting a kick out of riling everyone up about the trusts. He always did have a twisted sense of humor.

"What can you tell me about Donovan O'Malley?" Athena asked, breaking the strained silence.

Mr. Schumer nodded. "We met once when I delivered the news of this secondary document to him personally. Mr. O'Malley is a wealthy and successful businessman. He seemed cordial and... young."

He dug into his briefcase and pulled out a stack of papers that he placed on the table in front of her. "I have compiled some information about him, which I think you should be aware of before making any decision. Of course, I have similar files on the other potential partners, too."

Athena had already decided that the likelihood of her going along with this nonsense was about a zero percent chance, but her curiosity was winning out, and she wanted to know more about this random man Nathan was trying to pass her off to.

She had never even heard his name before. Not surprising, as Nathan rarely allowed her to visit Safeword with him, forever jealous of anyone else seeing her in the throes of passion.

He usually took Denise or Teresa (or both), never explaining why it was alright for people to see them cum and bleed all over the play floor, but not her. That was Nathan, in a nutshell: demanding exactly what he wanted, even if it defied all logic. Athena didn't have to like or agree with what he wanted. Her only job was to make sure he got it.

Honestly, though, being forbidden from the club made her even more interested in visiting the mysterious BDSM haunt. She wasn't interested enough to face the consequences of disobeying Nathan, but still. Athena wanted to know what went on in the dark corners of that place.

"Thanks, Mr. Schumer," she said, standing and gathering the papers he had set out for her. The other women seemed inclined to stick around, but Athena had heard enough. She turned to them, nodding a goodbye. "I hope everything works out for you guys."

Athena gave one last smile to everyone in the room and carefully shut the door behind her. The clicking of her heels on the tile floor echoed off the walls, another reminder of how alone she was now, just like with the plates. The signs were all around her now.

She hailed another cab to take her home, scared that a trip on the subway might result in losing one of the precious papers the attorney gave her. She had a lot of reading to do about this mystery man, but it didn't matter. There wasn't anything else occupying her time, anyway.

*Chapter 4*

*Then*

She really didn't want to go. She should've been working on a second glass of wine and relaxing in a tub filled with bubble bath in her crappy apartment. What had Athena been thinking, saying that she'd go to a lame open mic night?

It was too late for regrets, though. She was meeting Jared, and she'd be alone, as Harper already had a date lined up.

The filthy traitor.

At seven sharp, Athena pushed through the heavy wooden doors of the dive bar down the street from the cafe. Her eyes took a minute to adjust to the darkness after being out in the late summer sun.

There weren't a lot of people in the bar, especially for a scheduled event. It wasn't even clear if the other patrons were there for the show, as many of the tables around the stage were still fairly empty.

At least the small crowd size helped her find Jared easily. He waved hesitantly from across the room to come and join his table. When she did so right away, his face broke into a giant smile. Athena found herself nervous, too, as his awkwardness hit her. Whatever he was feeling, it was contagious.

"Glad you could make it," he said, pulling her in for a hug she hadn't anticipated. She hugged him back stiffly, feeling slightly uncomfortable but not wanting to make it weird by pulling away.

He smelled good. Clean, like dryer sheets. Her eyebrows raised as she noticed he had changed clothes since that morning. He looked casual but put together in his worn leather jacket and corduroy slacks.

"Glad I could make it," she said. "Thanks for inviting me."

"Guys, this is Athena," he said, turning to the others at the table. "Athena, I think you know Derrick, and the one on the end is Pete."

"Yeah, of course. Good to see you." She vaguely remembered Derrick from the same class she had with Jared a few years back. He had given off a good vibe back then, and the same feeling grounded her again at that moment. Pete grunted a hello but didn't look up from his phone.

Athena settled into a spot next to Derrick, slinging her purse over the back of the chair. He smiled easily at her, showing off a row of perfect teeth. "Do you want something to drink?" he asked.

"Yeah, sounds good," she said. "Whatever you're having is fine."

"Sure thing. Be right back."

Derrick walked back to the bar, leaving her with the other two men. She instantly wished she had declined the drink, as the energy at the table shifted as soon as he was gone. Pete's eyes remained glued to his phone, and he never acknowledged her, which felt rude and more than a little awkward.

Jared was frowning and seemed mildly upset that Athena had taken a seat next to Derrick on the other side of the small table despite there being an empty chair on his right. Whatever his expectations, he wasn't saying anything to her either, though that could be for the best. The unexpected hug made Athena want to give him a wider berth, especially after encountering the strange man in the alley that morning. She felt a little jittery about it still. Swearing off men entirely sounded more appealing every day.

With no one to talk to, Athena scanned the crowd. People-watching could be interesting, too. Especially in a place like this, where the customers ranged from young artists fresh from college to older locals who had probably been patrons since the bar opened in the 1970's. She fiddled with the cuff of her jacket, tempted to grab her phone, and mindlessly scroll through it, too.

Finally, the silence broke. "So, how have you been, Athena?" Jared asked, leaning across the table. "Whenever I see you, you're busting your ass with the espresso machine. We haven't had a chance to catch up in ages."

Athena forced a smile. "I've been good. Just working, making art, or trying to, you know?"

She accepted the drink Derrick handed her as he returned from the bar. Their fingers touched briefly around the cold plastic cup. The punch-like mixture of fruity alcohol burned when she took a sip.

All three of them nodded, agreeing. Yeah, they knew all about trying to force yourself to create something. No matter the medium, it was hard to tap into that creative vein day in and day out. For her, it was painting. Athena loved color and texture. She knew that Jared was a writer. Whatever Pete and Derrick dabbled in, the struggle was probably similar enough to commiserate with their version of writer's block.

"Thanks for coming out, everyone," a man said into a microphone as he stepped onto the wooden stage. "Tonight, we only have a few artists scheduled, but we are always open to anyone else who wants a moment in the spotlight, too."

The audience shushed each other, and there were a few scattered claps showing the host some support.

"Thank you, I truly appreciate it," he said,

grinning and taking a small bow. "Anyway, first up, we have a local favorite, Susan White. Please give it up for her."

The crowd mustered as much enthusiasm as it could for the young woman wearing the faux velvet mini dress. She smiled shyly as she took a seat center stage, but even then, her humility seemed like it was part of the act. She knew how good she was.

All around Athena, people seemed to hold their breath, anticipating what was coming next. She was vaguely aware of Derrick murmuring something about pitying anyone having to follow this act, but then she blocked everyone else out. From the first note, Athena was mesmerized. The rest of the room melted away as the soft croon of the woman's voice soothed all her irritation at coming out to the bar. It was worth it. This performance was worth it.

Athena shook her head, returning to the present as Susan White slipped from the stool and off the stage. The crowd's applause was still going strong long after she was gone, with the majority of people begging for more. She was too good to be preforming at a dive bar, but even that wasn't so unusual. It took the stars aligning for anyone to become discovered in the city.

"Alright, alright," the host said finally. "We could cheer for Susan all night, but we need to keep this going. Up next, Jared Rossi."

Jared cursed under his breath, clearly upset to be

going after Susan. Athena shot him a sympathetic glance and cheered a little louder on his behalf. His half-smile said it helped, at least a tiny bit.

Too bad his act needed more help than that.

He struggled through the first few lines, paper shaking. His face was beet red, and Athena died inside for him more than once. "I'm going to get him a drink. For after," she whispered to Derrick.

"Yeah, he's going to need it. It's his first time doing this, you know."

Athena frowned. "What? Jared's talked about this place for months."

"I'm sure he has. He's talked about you for months, too."

Derrick held her gaze for a second as if considering her in a new light before turning back to the stage. Athena blinked, then stood and walked to the bar. She made small talk with Jared in the mornings while making his coffee, but there was never anything more. Derrick must have misunderstood the situation.

She motioned to the bartender, glancing at the man sitting on the nearby stool. Athena froze when their eyes met, and a smile spread across his face.

"He didn't think you'd make it, I bet," he said casually. Athena gaped at him, so the man gestured to Jared bombing onstage. "The kid. He thought you were going to blow him off. He talked about this place to sound interesting, but he's not ready to share his work, and now he's living with his mistakes."

"What the fuck are you doing here?" Athena demanded, glaring at the customer who had cornered her in the alley only hours before. "Are you stalking me or something?"

He raised his eyebrows. "I didn't realize this was a private bar," he said.

"Right. Well, I've seen all I need for tonight, so I'll be leaving. Enjoy the rest of the show." She left the bar without ordering, wanting nothing more than to put some space between herself and the creep on the barstool. She was so distracted that she nearly ran into Jared as he exited the stage.

"Sorry!" Athena said, grabbing him by the arm to avoid tripping on her own feet. Her face burned, knowing that the stranger was probably still watching.

"Don't worry about it. Sorry you had to come out and see me tank." Jared steadied her but didn't remove his hand right away. His grasp felt warm through her sweater.

Athena gave him a weak smile as she pulled away. "You didn't bomb. It's really tough being in front of an audience. It takes some serious guts just to get up there."

Jared blushed, pleased with the compliment.

"Listen, I need to leave. There's someone from the cafe here, and I just don't feel like hanging out. He's a little... odd."

Derrick stepped in before Jared could respond. "Is someone giving you a hard time?" he asked, brushing his hand across her back possessively. "I drove here. Let me take you home."

"Um... yeah, that'd be great." Athena tried to ignore the glare Jared shot at him. Clearly, he had been ready to offer her a ride, too. To be completely honest, she was a little relieved not to have to ride with Jared. If Derrick was right about the whole crush thing, she'd much rather avoid the awkwardness of being alone with him for too long.

"Great. Let me settle the tab, and we'll get out of here," Derrick said.

For the first time since walking away, Athena glanced back at the bar. It wasn't necessary; she already knew he was still watching her. Athena felt his eyes burning holes into her skin. Sure enough, when their eyes met from across the room, she could feel his disapproval of something, probably that she was with friends and not able to be kidnapped and murdered.

Jared followed her gaze, frowning. "Yeah, I remember that guy from earlier today at the cafe. It's really weird that he's here tonight. Think you've got a stalker, Athena?"

She laughed uneasily like the same thought hadn't occurred to her a dozen times already.

"Listen, I'm happy to take you home," Jared said,

eyeing her meaningfully. "You don't really know Derrick... he's a nice enough guy, but it's probably best if you don't—"

"Alright, let's go," Derrick returned and shoved his wallet into his back pocket, taking her by the elbow. She frowned, wrapping her arms around herself to break contact with him.

She hadn't noticed before, but now she could catch the slight slur of his words. The last thing she needed was to get into a car with someone who was buzzed.

"Actually, I think I'll just get a ride share. Thanks for the offer, Derrick."

She pulled out her phone, hating the idea of spending money on an Uber but also not wanting to walk the short distance to the apartment alone at night, either. Not with a deranged customer following her, at least.

"Are you sure?" Derrick's voice rumbled low, almost hinting that she should reconsider.

"Yeah, no worries. My roommate will be home from her date soon anyway."

She pressed the button to order a car, which was picked up almost instantly. A driver's profile, Max with a Prius, filled the screen.

"Mind if I share it with you?" Pete asked, speaking for the first time. "I was going to get a cab. I'm just down the road a bit, too."

Athena nodded, stuffing the phone back in her

pocket. "Sure. Let's go outside to wait. It shouldn't be long."

She was eager to get away from the man's watchful glare. The walls felt like they were closing in on her with him so close by. At least with Pete there, it was unlikely that he would approach her again.

"If you're sure, Athena." Jared went in for a second hug, his eyes on Pete.

She returned it with even less enthusiasm than before. This time, Athena could smell the alcohol on his breath, possibly explaining why he lingered in the embrace a little too long. He and Derrick must have gotten an early start at the bar.

"Yeah, thanks for the invite. See you at the coffee shop." Athena turned and followed Pete outside, grateful to feel the fresh air on her face. She tried her best to ignore the look Derrick gave her as she left the bar. She couldn't quite put her finger on what it was, but it made her shiver in the worst way.

"He was pretty excited to see you here," Pete said, turning to her when they were alone. "Jared told us about you a few times... more than a few times, really."

"Mmmhmm." She didn't have anything to say to that. "I can see why. You're pretty cool."

She glanced down at her phone. Max with the Prius was still a few minutes away. Why was Pete suddenly so chatty?

"Smoke?" he asked, pulling a cigarette from the pack.

Athena shook her head, even though she would have said yes under normal circumstances. Right now, she felt trapped, like a cornered animal.

"He really has you spooked, huh?" Pete shuffled a little closer. "Don't worry. You're safe with me."

In hindsight, she should have taken her chances with Jared. But there was no way to know that until they were already in the car with Max, driving away from the bar to her home.

Pete was in the middle, way too close, despite there being plenty of room in the backseat. Athena was practically plastered to the window, begging Max silently not to drop her off directly in front of her building. Every fiber in her body was tingling with some sort of horrible spidey sense. Something bad was coming.

"Here you go," Max said, sliding into a parking spot next to the front door.

"Thanks," Athena mumbled, opening the door. "Can you drop him off at his place? You can add it to my charge."

"Nah, I'm just down the road. I'll get out here, too," Pete said, gripping the door to prevent her from closing it.

She hesitated. Could she ask Max with the Prius to wait until she was inside the building? Was that totally insane? It didn't matter. The driver was completely oblivious to her predicament. He was already checking his phone for the next ride and sped away as soon as Pete closed the door.

"So, this is your place? We're practically neighbors," he said, taking a step closer. Athena fiddled with her keychain, taking a step back.

"Great. Cool. I'll see you around then." She continued backing up, matching his steps forward.

"You know, I must've had more to drink than I thought. Would you mind if I crash on your couch instead of walking home?"

The thing was, he didn't seem drunk at all. His eyes were clear as they swept over her body, landing on her lips as she chewed on the corner nervously.

"Sorry, I have an early shift tomorrow. I can get another Uber for you if you want."

She hit the wall, unable to retreat anymore. She'd have to turn away from him in order to make it to the door, and Pete's grin grew as the same thought crossed his mind. His arms came up on both sides of her, boxing her in against the wall.

Athena closed her eyes, trying to calculate the best timing to knee him in the balls when headlights shone in from the street. A car door slammed shut, and Pete frowned, his eyes still on hers until they weren't anymore.

*Crack.* Pete was down in a second, moaning and crumpled in a ball. He clutched the side of his head, swearing and writhing on the ground.

In his place stood the man from the coffee shop. Their eyes met only briefly. He turned to Pete and pulled out a handgun, aiming it straight at Athena's would-be attacker. He released the safety, the click filling the air.

"If you ever come near her again, I'll give you more than just a concussion. Do you understand me?" His voice was eerily calm like he was having a normal conversation with a friend and not threatening a stranger's life.

Pete didn't answer. He flopped on his back, dazed and probably trying to piece together what had happened. He stilled when he saw the gun. Slowly, he lifted his hands above his head.

"I don't usually ask something twice." The gun discharged, hitting the ground inches from Pete's skull. He screamed, crying, and trying to shield himself from bullets. Athena's ears rang, and she raised her hands to cover them. The damage was done, but the pressure helped with the lingering pain.

"Stop!" she shouted, finally finding her voice. "Just... let him go, okay?"

The man glanced at Athena only briefly. "Do you understand, Leon? You stay away from her. If you see her on the street, you walk the other way. Got it?"

*Leon?* Why the fuck had Jared called him Pete?

Pete/Leon nodded and stumbled to his feet. Once

upright, he took off running, never once looking back. Now, alone with the stalker holding a gun, Athena wasn't sure if she was in a better situation or not.

"Did he hurt you?" The stranger moved toward her, scanning her body with his eyes.

She shook her head, unable to say more. Athena's attention stayed on the gun as he returned it to the inner pocket of his long overcoat. Her mouth was dry. She had a headache from the gunshot, and she wanted nothing more than to curl up, cry, and try to pretend none of this ever happened.

"Shhh... come here." His voice was so soft, so soothing, that it undid her. Against her will, tears started running down her face. He closed the distance between them and wrapped his arms around her.

Athena wanted to push him away, and she struggled against the hug for a brief second but then gave into it, heaving and sobbing out the emotions of being trapped against the wall, hearing the gunshot going off, fearing an entirely possible assault.

His body was warm and firm, athletic for a man his age. He was probably mid-forties, maybe a little younger. It was hard to tell as his facial features gave nothing away. They were timeless. Rugged. Hard.

It was difficult to concentrate on anything else when all she was thinking about was the gun hidden somewhere on his body. Athena prayed it wouldn't go off from their embrace. Then she prayed he wouldn't take it back out and use it on her.

It was a lot of praying for someone who didn't believe in god.

"It's alright, Athena. Don't worry. I've got you."

She snorted up a face-full of snot. Her cheeks were warm and mostly dry against his sweater. The fabric had absorbed almost all her tears, and she felt herself coming back down to reality. The catharsis of a good cry should never be underestimated.

With clear-headedness came a new fear. Athena froze, wondering if she should try to run for the door. Athena would never be able to unlock it in time, though. He would catch her long before she could.

"Your roommate isn't home yet," he whispered. "I'm going to help you get inside, draw you a bath, and then I'll leave. Understand, Athena?"

It wasn't a question, of course. It was happening. Short of calling the police after he left, there was nothing Athena could do about it. She nodded slowly, producing her key, and let them both inside the apartment building. He was several inches taller than her, but there was something else about him that seemed to take up the entire hallway. He was... a lot.

She fumbled with her apartment door key and forced herself to speak again. "Please don't try to come inside with me. Thank you for stopping him... whoever he was, but I want to be alone."

The man locked eyes with Athena. After a few beats, he reached up and caressed the side of her face. His hands were soft, but the unwanted contact felt like a slap. She worked hard to not flinch, and he gave me a small smile as though he knew she was trying to put on a brave front.

"Alright, Athena." He moved to take something out of his coat pocket, and for a horrible second, she thought he was going to bring out the gun again. Instead, he pushed a piece of paper into her hand. A business card.

"My name's Nathan. I'll call you in a few hours to see how you're doing," he said. "You might as well program my number into your phone now. If I call and you don't answer, I'll think that idiot is back for round two, and I'll come back, too. Understand?"

Athena scowled at the card and then at him. His confidence, the fact that he assumed she wanted anything to do with him, was unnerving.

Leaning forward, he whispered, "One day soon, I'll fuck that frown right off your pretty face."

Outrage and horror crashed over her. She had let the psycho into her home. She was going to end up raped and murdered, after all.

Nathan chuckled at her expression, the shock of his lewd promise leaving her speechless. Athena stayed frozen in place until she heard the click of the door closing behind him. She fumbled with the lock, deadbolting it and debating whether to call Harper and ask her to come home early.

Athena reached for her phone, ready to panic-dial her roommate, when it hit her. The most disturbing part of the whole thing was what the stalker had just inadvertently revealed.

How, after receiving absolutely no help or encouragement from her, did he already have Athena's phone number?

*Chapter 5*

*Now*

Athena owned way too much shit for a person living alone in a small apartment. Before Nathan, she had been pretty low maintenance, though she was also living as a young, starving artist who couldn't afford a more luxurious lifestyle. Nevertheless, she promised herself that soon she would begin paring down her wardrobe and cosmetics to only what she actually needed.

She tossed more bundles of designer clothes into a box, not bothering to take them off the hangers. It seemed pointless to go through the trouble of removing them just to hang the clothes back up again in a few hours.

It had been three weeks since the reading of Nathan's will, and she recently decided, over a few glasses of wine, that she wasn't going to wait around any longer for Donovan O'Malley to make an appearance. Part of her really wanted to tell him to go fuck himself in person, but the other part of her hated feeling like she was living in limbo, waiting for him to find the time to show up at her door.

It wasn't like she hadn't tried to contact him, either.

The day after hearing Nathan's final directive, she dialed Donovan O'Malley's office three times only to be dismissed with three different bullshit excuses. He was too busy to take her call. He was out to lunch with a client. He was otherwise engaged.

Finally, she gave up and had to leave a message with his secretary. The woman had practically sneered when Athena asked for him a fourth time, so she embellished her message a little just because she could.

"Yes, once again, my name is Athena Garcia. A-T-H-E- N-A G-A-R-C-I-A. Yes. That's right. I called earlier today. Please have Mr. O'Malley give me a call back as soon as he can. Apparently, my dead boyfriend has transferred ownership of me to him, and I'd like to deal with that sooner rather than later. I'm sure you understand."

The stunned pause on the other end of the line was a reward that Athena savored long after she ended the call. The thrill of doing something wrong without fearing punishment was both exhilarating and awful.

After all, what was the worst thing that Mr.

O'Malley could do to her? Cut off the payments from her trust fund? Make her leave the apartment? Show up at her door like the big, bad wolf? Athena didn't care about any of it. She was ready for anything, as long as it wasn't more waiting.

But, apparently, even an inflammatory phone call wouldn't be enough to inspire a response from Mr. O'Malley. By that point, any goodwill she had toward him had soured, and Athena knew she needed to make a change on her own terms.

She still had her personal bank account that was nicely padded from the steady stream of her trust fund deposits. The balance sitting in the account was more than enough to rent another place until the first few paychecks at her new job came in. Or, her old job, rather.

She was back on the schedule at the coffee house. The owners were still the same, thankfully, and they offered her a position as soon as she reached out to them.

The staff were new, though, so it also felt like a fresh start. No one was going to give her weird looks or ask a lot of questions about why she was back. Quitting to move in with some rich married guy had raised more than a few eyebrows among the old crew, and she didn't feel like explaining that her power exchange boyfriend was dead.

Athena closed the box she was packing and taped it shut. One major perk of having money was the luxury of hiring professional movers. Even if Donovan didn't cut her off, she fully intended to reject the trust fund money as soon as possible. It didn't feel right to continue withdrawing from it if she wasn't open to following Nathan's final wishes.

But in the meantime, she didn't feel guilty about using it to her advantage and hiring a team of movers was worth their weight in gold.

Regardless, Athena looked forward to having a paycheck again soon. Then she really could cut ties with this new "master" and get on with living her life, whatever that looked like.

She tried to imagine finding some vanilla boyfriend, getting married, having kids... to be frank, it all still sounded perfectly terrible. But so what? Maybe Athena wasn't sure what she wanted, but Donovan O'Malley wasn't it, and neither was living a life without working.

She smiled, imagining Nathan's face at the idea of her earning money again.

*Absolutely not*, he would say. *Your job is to be available to me. I'm not going to share your time with some low-level manager.*

Well, that wasn't the case anymore, and Athena wasn't going to waste away in the beautiful apartment that was just a cage in disguise, waiting for another man to take enough interest in her to come and visit. Especially since he wasn't even a man she had chosen for herself. It was almost like having an arranged marriage, but instead of her parents choosing a husband for her, her dead master was choosing her next owner.

When had her life taken such a weird turn?

A heavy knock made Athena jump. She dropped the pair of shoes she was holding and cautiously made her way over to investigate. The apartment was a secure building, and she should have had to buzz someone into the shared hallway for them to knock on her door.

The glass peephole revealed two men in grey jumpsuits standing on her welcome mat, both looking down at a clipboard. It was the movers, of course. She was being paranoid again.

Too many years living with Nathan and hearing about how badly he wanted to protect her from everything in the world had taken its toll on her nerves.

Athena removed the chain from the door and opened it for them. "Hey, thanks for coming. I'm done packing the kitchen and the living room. I have just a few more boxes waiting in the bedroom area."

The man closest to her nodded. "Sounds good. We'll start in the kitchen."

She shuffled back to her bed, for the first time hating that the apartment was a studio without actual separate rooms. It felt awkward placing her personal items into boxes with the movers standing right beside her.

She had to imagine they were used to this kind of thing, though. They probably didn't care what she was doing if she didn't create more work for them. They worked in companionable silence, and soon Athena fell into a rhythm of packing items, too.

The quiet caused her mind to wander, though. Was it wrong to take all this stuff with her if she was abandoning the plan Nathan had intended for her? Maybe she shouldn't take all the items from the kitchen. Or the bed. Or the table and chairs.

Those thoughts had occurred to her a few times over the past week, but her new place wasn't furnished, and the landlord said that this place had been decorated for her by Nathan. The items were Athena's to take if she was going to break the lease. There was no point in leaving them behind just to buy everything new all over again.

She fished out her phone and AirPods. Pandora lit up the screen, and she turned on some music to make the last of the packing more bearable.

Athena got into her own groove, wrapping picture frames in towels. She finally taped the last box shut when someone tapped on her shoulder. She spun around, panicked, and removed a Pod from her ear. It was just the movers again. She really needed to cut back on the caffeine.

"Sorry, miss, but someone downstairs told us to bring your things back up here. My buddy argued with him for a while, but it looks like our boss is siding with him. We'll leave you to it until you can get this sorted out, okay?"

Athena gaped at him, then at the wall of boxes stacked neatly in the kitchen. Sure enough, everything they had brought outside was back where she had left it. Next to the boxes stood a man, arms crossed, giving her an assessing look. He even had an eyebrow crooked skeptically as he took her in.

She knew instantly who he was, both from the pictures she found on the internet and her own intuition. Donovan O'Malley was standing in her apartment, preventing her from moving out. Athena's cheeks flamed, deeply embarrassed and pissed off at the same time.

There was another feeling, too. Something was familiar about him. Something about his eyes. Athena couldn't help but feel like she knew him from somewhere, but she had no idea where that could possibly have been. Surely, if she had met the giant of a man before, she would remember more than just his eye color.

"That won't be necessary," she said, turning her attention back to the man in the jumpsuit. "I'm moving out today, so please take those boxes back to the truck. I've already paid your company."

He refused to meet her eyes. "Sorry, ma'am, but I can't do that. I have my orders to leave everything here. I'm sure our boss will issue you a refund. Best of luck."

With that, he scurried away, making sure to leave a healthy space between himself and the man in the doorway. Not an easy feat with someone Donovan's size blocking a good portion of it.

Athena narrowed her eyes at the stranger, put her AirPod back in, and cranked up the volume on her phone. He had to pick up on those nonverbal signals, right? She was dismissing him, loud and clear. Turning, she finished taping the box and added it to the stack.

Her goal was to pretend that she was totally unbothered by his presence, as though his interruption and being abandoned by the moving team were part of her plan all along.

If she had learned anything from Nathan, it was that showing weakness was basically the same thing as waving a white flag when it came to dealing with dominant men, and she had no intention of bending to the will of this random asshole in a suit.

When she dared to venture a glance back at Donovan, his grave expression had changed to one of amusement. He was watching every move she made, and Athena felt horribly exposed despite the modest shorts and t-shirt she had on.

Could he tell her indifference was all an act? He was studying her, probably weighing his options for how to proceed, too. To her dismay, she felt a pang of desire and then an overwhelming amount of sadness. Nathan had given her that same look often, like she was a puzzle he was trying to piece together.

The best way to handle this would be to get the man out of her apartment, then she could start contacting another moving company. That's how you solve annoying, ridiculously tall, and handsome problems: one step at a time.

"Can you leave, please?" Athena said, removing the AirPod again. "I'm a little busy here."

"It looks like it," he agreed, running a finger lazily across a stack of boxes. "If I didn't know any better, I'd think you were trying to run away."

She snorted. "Hardly. I tried to contact you weeks ago. You didn't even bother answering, and now I'm moving on. But nice try, rewriting the narrative to suit you."

Donovan O'Malley barked a cold laugh, shaking his head. "Moving on, huh? Is that an option Nathan gave you? Some kind of an out from your arrangement if you were pissed off or throwing a temper tantrum?"

"Nathan never gave me an out," she said coolly. "Not that it's any of your business. Nathan's not here, and if he was, he'd kick your ass for me. He didn't have patience for pretentious jerks, and neither do I."

An uncomfortable silence hung between them, but not for long.

"Let me make sure I understand," he said quickly,

taking a few steps into the apartment. "You enter into a consensual, lifetime power exchange agreement with someone, and the last thing they tell you to do is just an opinion to you? What are you, some kind of fair-weather sub? A brat? Let me guess, you obey when you feel like it, and now that you don't feel like it, you're running away."

His grey eyes were dark; all traces of humor were gone. We were too close, just an arm's length apart. No, less than an arm's length apart, considering how tall he was. Athena straightened and glared back at him, silently daring him to take another step.

"It's a good thing I don't give a fuck what you think about me," she answered. "Just leave so I can find someone else to move all these boxes."

The uncomfortable twinge from before blossomed inside her and transformed into full-blown guilt. She could talk a big game, but Donovan's words hit home.

She had wanted to be a perfect submissive for Nathan, his perfect companion. The fact that she was denying his last request was something that had kept her up at night. She told herself it didn't matter. After all, she had tried to reach out to Donovan, and he hadn't responded, but now that he was standing in the apartment, that excuse fell flat.

As much as she hated to admit it, he was at least partially right in his assessment of her. She wasn't a sub prepared to do anything for her master. Her commitment to Nathan might be conditional.

Donovan's eyes searched hers, then froze. He found what he was looking for. Slowly, the features on his face softened. He tugged a curl free from Athena's loose messy bun, twirling it slowly between his fingers. She swallowed hard, torn between wanting to slap his hand away and the desire to lean into his touch.

Good lord. What was wrong with her? Some handsome jerk shows up, and she's practically ready to jump on him. She needed to get laid and soon.

"I said I would come collect you when I'm ready, Athena. That's exactly what you were told after the reading of Nathan's will, so having to wait for a little while shouldn't have been a surprise.

"I haven't touched the trust accounts, just as I promised, and when I come back for you, I expect you to have your head screwed on straight and be prepared to keep up your end of this bargain. Understood?"

"There's just one problem with that, Donovan," she hissed, finally pushing his hand away. "I've never made any bargains with you."

"I suppose that's one way of looking at it. You made a deal with your former master, and he made a deal with me. We are connected to the extent that you feel bound to honor your commitment to him." Donovan straightened, shrugging. "He made it sound as though you were obedient. Something of a joy to own, even. I wonder what he'd make of all this nonsense if he were here to witness it."

Athena struggled to find the right words or accusations or anything to shoot back at him, but she was at a loss. He crooked an eyebrow and turned, leaving the door wide open behind him. She stared around the nearly empty space as her confidence in what she was doing deteriorated by the second. What would Nathan have said about this? He wouldn't be thrilled, that's for sure.

And how the hell had Donovan convinced the moving company to abandon the job so easily? Exactly who was she dealing with here?

---

She tried calling eleven other moving companies. Eleven. And not a single one had any availability in the near future. At first, Athena thought maybe it was just some weird coincidence. Maybe the moving industry was slammed full of people all relocating at the same time, or they were short-staffed.

But then she started to notice that the companies were ready to help her until she gave them her exact address or her full name. Somehow, that always led to them backing out of taking the job.

Donovan O'Malley had gotten to them. She was sure of it. It seemed crazy that one random person could have so much control over her living situation, but being with Nathan taught her never to underestimate a dom trying to exert control over their sub. Unfortunately, it seemed as though Donovan was under the impression that Athena was his submissive. She was determined to rectify that as soon as possible.

Step one, unfortunately, was going to be resigning from the coffee shop. Donovan knew she worked there, as two of his goons had started shadowing her on a rotating basis. They would wait for Athena to lock up, follow her onto the subway for the ride home, and once she locked the door behind her, they would leave again. At first, she tried to convince one of them that he was tailing the wrong person. She had even threatened to call the police if he didn't leave her alone.

He had just looked up from his newspaper with a bored expression and said, "Take it up with Mr. O'Malley."

Athena certainly would have if the man ever returned her messages.

She didn't tell the mysterious bodyguards about quitting the coffee shop. The owners took it well enough, maybe because she hadn't been there long. Her new coworkers seemed the most put out over her leaving.

"I don't understand," a young barista named Amelia said. "You just started working here. Did you get another job offer or something?"

"Something like that," Athena yelled over the sound of aerating milk. She couldn't help but smile as she swirled a foam design in a customer's mug. Athena was going to miss working at the cafe. A lot.

'I don't buy it," Amelia said, shaking her head. "Does it have anything to do with the weirdos who come to see you every night?"

Amelia was smart. Of course, it had everything to do with that. "No, I just need something different. That's all."

And by something different, what Athena really meant was something downright terrifying. The only place hiring within a reasonable radius of her apartment was a nearby convenience store.

Her Brownstone faced a nice street with trees lining the sidewalks, but just two blocks over were some rundown buildings that included a 24-hour convenience store. One look at the bullet holes in the cement barriers and the ever-present police tower made it clear that the place had its share of unsavory customers.

She smiled to herself, almost giddy at how horrible it was. Working there would be the perfect way to get Donovan O'Malley's attention and his disapproval, all in one fell swoop. If she played her cards right, Donovan would be ready to break his end of the agreement within a week.

By Athena's estimation, it was an airtight way of

honoring Nathan's wishes while not having to put up with Donovan O'Malley for much longer. Her former master might have left Athena to him as "living property," but as far as she knew, there was nothing forcing Donovan to keep her if he decided she was just too much trouble.

And little did he know exactly how much of a headache she could be.

Chapter 6

*Then*

The morning after open-mic night, Athena tried to play it off like nothing had happened. She wanted to believe she had taken the Uber home, said goodbye to Pete/Leon in the car, and that the entire situation with Nathan and the gun had been some horrible nightmare. The bags under her eyes told a different story. She hadn't slept a wink.

At least she didn't have to do any heavy lifting during the morning conversation. Harper gushed over her date with a guy she had met at her gym, and she was satisfied with Athena's occasional half-assed laughs at her jokes. She was too excited about the new potential boyfriend to notice anything else.

"He's like 6'4" and has the ass of a god," she sighed, fixing a salad to take for lunch. As Athena's only friend with an office job, Harper was instantly more of a grown- up between the two of them, but the salad-making and morning workouts put her in a different class of human altogether. She was the kind of productive, slightly religious person Athena's parents probably hoped she would turn into. Together, they created an average person in their early twenties: kind of put together, kind of struggling to figure out the world. Harper brought the normalcy to the table, and Athena balanced her out by surviving mainly on coffee and cigarettes.

"So, when do I get to meet him?" Athena asked, taking a big bite of sugary cereal. It tasted like wet cardboard, but she forced it down anyway. She gave Harper a strained smile, and it was happily received.

"He's coming by tonight. Are you free?" Harper paused, studying Athena for the first time. "How was open-mic night, by the way? You look kind of horrible."

She shrugged. "I'm just hungover. The bar had wells on special."

"Hmmph. Maybe next time, drink some water before you pass out. Y our liver will thank you." Harper snapped her monogrammed lunchbox shut and slung her purse over her shoulder. "I'll pick up something yummy for dinner. Does sushi sound good?"

Athena's stomach flip-flopped at the idea of raw fish, but she nodded anyway. Hopefully, she'd be feeling better by then. She eyed her soggy cereal, knowing she'd pour it down the garbage disposal as soon as Harper left for work.

"Great! I can't wait for you to meet Josh!"

"Who's Josh?" Athena asked before she could stop herself. Of course, he's the guy Harper had been talking about for the past half hour.

"Okay, that does it. What happened last night?" Harper slammed her bags down on the counter. "Spill it. I'll know if you leave anything important out."

She pinned Athena with a glare that saw through any excuse she could come up with. Athena relented, taking a deep breath, wondering where to start. "It's nothing. There's just this guy. A weird guy. From work."

"Okayyyy." Harper leaned in, motioning impatiently for her to continue.

Athena sighed. "He was at the coffee shop and then showed up at open-mic night, too. I tried to leave early because he was weirding me out, but then another guy I shared an Uber with turned out to be an even worse creep, and the weirdo from the coffee shop showed up and kind of... scared him away."

Harper frowned. "Scared him away how? And how did the coffee shop weirdo know where you live? Did he follow you?"

"Probably? I don't know," Athena said. "He just... he threatened the guy who wanted to spend the night here, and then he gave me his card before he left."

Athena intentionally left out the part about how he somehow already had her phone number to call and check in. When he did call, she had picked up on the first ring, shouted that she was fine, and hung up, praying that was enough to keep him from returning to the apartment.

The plan had worked, but he had still sent her some laughing texts in response. She left those on read, hoping he'd get the hint and stop texting.

"Hand it over," Harper said, palm outstretched. Athena dug the card out of her back pocket and passed it across the counter. Harper frowned at the name, flipping it over a few times before sliding it back to her. "What does he want you to do with it? Are you going to call him?"

"Nope. I'll probably never even see him again."

"At least you have the day off," she said, collecting her assortment of bags again. "I'll try to get off a little early, but seriously, call me if you need anything. Or if he shows up here."

"Fine. Go," Athena said, shooing her out the door.

She wouldn't admit it to Harper, but she did double-check that the door was locked once she was alone. At least one of the two men from the night before had a gun, and she wasn't taking any chances with them barging in.

She thought about going back to bed, but she

knew she wouldn't be able to sleep. Instead, Athena grabbed a heap of blankets and shuffled out to the living room, building a nest on the couch like she was taking a sick day.

Athena flipped through the channels and settled on some old-fashioned cartoons. Between that and "breakfast," it was all too apparent that she was actually a ten-year-old living in the body of a 24-year-old woman. She snorted at the goofy humor on the screen, happy to be distracted.

Around noon, her stomach rumbled, angry at her for not even finishing the sad bowl of cereal. She needed something more substantial. Maybe something with protein, even. Athena was rummaging through the cupboards when a decisive knock sounded on the front door. She froze, staring at it.

"Open up, Athena." Fuck. It was him. Nathan-Garcia- the-stalker. She thought about pretending that she wasn't home, but it only took a few seconds for him to eliminate that option. "I know you're in there. You haven't left the building all morning."

She groaned inwardly, picked up her phone, and tried to decide if she should call the police. At what point was this considered harassment? He did save her from... something last night. Maybe she owed it to him to at least tell him face-to-face to leave her alone again. She wasn't interested in whatever he thought she wanted with him.

Athena padded over to the door and cracked it open. She was met with his bright eyes. They were crinkled around the edges. Amused.

And totally breathtaking.

"I need you to leave," she said. The statement didn't even sound convincing to her. Nathan didn't bother addressing it.

"Did you call in sick?" he asked, stepping around her and letting himself into the apartment. "I was worried when you didn't show up for work today."

"I, uh...I had the day off." *Why was she telling him that?*

"Fine. I can work around your schedule. Just send it to my secretary." Nathan shrugged his suit jacket off and started loosening his tie.

"I need you to leave, please," she said, glaring at the jacket and then at him. "I thought I was clear about that yesterday."

"Ha. Yeah, you were. Tell me, Athena, have you ever heard of power exchange relationships?"

"Have I heard of what?" she asked. "No. I don't know. Look, you need to leave."

She picked up his jacket and tie and opened the door. When he made no movement to leave, she balled up his things and threw them down the hallway.

"Go, fetch."

The humor vanished from his face.

"Retrieve my things from the hallway, please,

Athena.

Then, we can sit and talk about everything."

She looked from him to the door, then walked into the hall. She closed the door behind her and took off running, leaving him alone in the apartment. In hindsight, it's funny that she thought she stood a chance against him. Nathan would find her and take whatever he wanted, whenever he wanted. It was all part of his game. Cat and mouse.

To his credit, he didn't run after her that day. He waited at the table after making himself a cup of coffee. Athena walked to work to grab lunch, pulling her phone out to call the police, just to put it away again. The man, Nathan, didn't seem like someone who was concerned about the police. He probably had the resources to do whatever he wanted and make the police disappear into the background. At least, he gave the impression that was the case.

About a half hour later, Athena trudged back to her apartment. The best-case scenario would be to find him gone, maybe with a written apology on the counter. Something to make her believe that he regretted his actions and was never coming back. Instead, she was greeted with a stern glare and a lecture.

"You can't just run out of the building alone on this side of town, Athena. If you continue living here for the time being, you'll need to be more mindful of your safety. This isn't the best—"

"Just tell me what you want to say so you can go," she blurted, slumping into the chair across from him. "I'll listen for exactly fifteen minutes before I call the police. Consider that a thank you for helping me out last night."

Nathan's eyebrows rose. "Fifteen minutes of conversation is the reward for preventing a strange man from assaulting you?"

"I didn't know you were looking for compensation," she snapped. "It's fourteen minutes now, just FYI."

He threw his head back and laughed loudly, causing her to jump. "I like that. I like you, Athena."

She didn't respond. She didn't even move. She wanted to say something else about his time running out, but if he was really unhinged, another joke might push him over the edge.

"Okay. Since I am on the clock, I better talk fast. You know my name but not much else, so there's a lot we need to cover here." He leaned across the table. "Have you ever heard of power exchange relationships, Athena?"

"You asked that earlier, and the answer is still no. I haven't heard of power exchange relationships." Her words were clipped. They needed to move this along.

Nathan nodded. "I figured. They aren't exactly the norm, especially among your age group.

Essentially, power exchange relationships involve two or more people who reach a consensual agreement that one of them should have control over the other person.

"These types of dynamics also happen unintentionally, of course. A good number of relationships have some kind of power imbalance, but most of the time, that leads to unethical practices where someone takes advantage of the other person. Consensual power exchange is... well, consensual."

"Riveting. You have such a way with words. What does this have to do with me?" Athena imagined the fifteen minutes measured out as sand in an hourglass. She was eager to see the last of it run out.

Nathan chuckled. "It has to do with you because I practice that type of lifestyle. I'm the dominant person in my relationships, and I think you'd make an excellent sub."

She blinked, snapping out of the hourglass daydream. "A sub? What?"

"Sorry. A submissive is the partner who gives up control in the relationship. There's so much to explain. There's so much that we could explore together, really. It's been a while since I've introduced this to someone, and I'm making a mess of it. Maybe it'd be better for me to show you."

He stood and reached out a hand. Athena stared at it, then shot her eyes back to his. "Show me what, exactly?" "I want you to meet my wife. She lives as my submissive. I control everything in her life."

His wife? A submissive?

Athena stood and walked with him to the door. "I'm cutting our time short, and I changed my mind. You need to go now."

———

Nathan had laughed at Athena abruptly ending their conversation. He did as she asked and left, but not before pointing out that until they reached some kind of agreement, she was free to do as she wished.

Unless, he stipulated with a frown, you decide to put yourself in harm's way again.

That was laughable, that he thought what he wanted mattered to her at all. But a seed was planted, and Athena was curious to a fault. The moment Nathan was gone, she started Googling power exchange relationships to see if what he said was true.

Time passed quickly, and before she knew it, Harper was calling to remind her about their plans for dinner.

Fuck. She needed to get dressed and put the apartment back together. Harper and her new potential boyfriend would be there in less than a half hour with sushi.

Athena peeled out of her comfy clothes and hopped into the shower, scrubbing her body with her loofah. Her mind was still reeling over what she had read online and the conversation with Nathan. She was conflicted, at a moral impasse. Power exchange sounded fun. Maybe it would be something to try with a boyfriend to add a little bit of spice to the relationship, but Nathan was already married. She wasn't cool with being the other woman. A threesome might be interesting, but surely his wife wasn't really on board with sharing her husband long term.

A few weeks went by, and Athena researched a little bit more each day. Finding out about a totally different way of living was fascinating to her. And the more she learned, the more she wished that power exchange was something she could try firsthand.

For Nathan, Athena knew the ball was in her court. Finally, after a month of debating her better judgment, Athena pulled the business card out of her wallet and dialed the number.

Nathan picked up after the first ring.

"It's good to hear from you, Athena," he greeted her. "What can I do for you?"

"I, uh, read about power exchange relationships online," she said. Her mouth was dry. She couldn't believe she was doing this. "I think I'd like to try something like that, but not with you. I'm not interested in dating someone who's already married. I don't want to help you cheat."

"I'm not asking you to help me cheat, Athena. My

wife knows about this. It wouldn't be a secret."

She rolled her eyes. "Of course, she does. I'm sure she loves the idea of her husband owning another submissive, right?"

Nathan laughed. "Let's meet to talk about it, okay?"

So, they did. They met, and one thing led to another, and soon they were meeting regularly. Within a month, Nathan was spending a couple of nights a week at her house, showing her some of the benefits of submitting to him.

"Yes, fuck. Just like that. Right there!" Athena panted and squirmed, feeling her pussy tighten around his cock. He stuffed it in deeper, going harder, jiggling her tits violently as her face fell onto the bed.

"Shut up and take it, Athena. I'm going to shoot so deep in you, and I'm not even going to let you come. You love it, don't you? You love being my little whore. My little cum slut," Nathan said, pounding away. His cock twitched, and the warmth of his cum spread deep inside her. Even after he was done, he continued sawing into her, using his seed as extra lubricant.

Just like he said, she hadn't cum, but she felt exhilarated just the same. Another high had taken over her, something that made any regular orgasm seem pointless. She was floating. She might just fly off the fucking bed.

Nathan flipped her over onto her back, pulling out his dick and letting his cum run onto the sheets. He smiled at the excess that collected on the fabric and pushed some of it back inside her with his fingers.

"My cum goes inside you, baby. Don't waste any of that. Now, take me in your mouth and clean my dick off like a good girl." Athena obeyed without thinking, rounding her lips to cover her teeth when he rose to straddle her face. The saltiness of his cum filled her mouth, and he leaned down, resting his balls against her chin.

Athena's eyelids fluttered shut. She loved it. All of it. She tried to get him into bed as quickly as possible when he came over, effectively avoiding any other discussion.

She tried to pretend the rest of his life didn't exist, actually. The fact that he had a whole wife who was fine with him fucking other women was a major point of contention if she allowed herself to think about it for too long. The less time she spent focused on that, the better.

"Veronica should be here, seeing you covered in my cum," he murmured above her. Athena ran her teeth over him, a silent warning to stop talking.

Nathan chuckled. "Fair enough, Athena. You'll win that one... for now. No more discussing Veronica."

He came again like that, and she swallowed everything that he gave her. She was greedy for it, wishing it could all be hers.

"So, you'll agree to regular sex with me. Let me do practically anything with your body, but that's as far as it goes, huh?" Nathan asked afterward, his arms wrapped around her.

"I'm barely allowing this to happen, actually," she said. "You've almost outstayed your welcome."

He reached down to smack her on the ass. She feigned a yelp, even though it didn't even sting. She liked teasing Nathan. He made it way too easy.

"You want to know what I think, Athena? One of these days, you'll be begging me for more. I can spot a kinky girl from a mile away, and I knew as soon as I saw you in that coffee shop that one day, you'd belong to me."

Her mouth went dry. Why was what he was saying so... hot? Shouldn't she be turned off by the idea of belonging to someone? Especially someone with a wife? The sudden reminder of the other woman waiting for him at home had the same effect as taking a cold shower.

"I'm sure that line worked much better before you were married," she said, pushing him away.

Nathan shrugged, standing to get dressed. "It works about the same, actually. You and she are the only ones I've said that to, and I can tell you're turned on by it."

Athena huffed, tugging the blankets to cover herself indignantly. He frowned, yanking them back down.

"You don't have to be self-conscious about liking it, Athena. Veronica was turned on by it, too, and I like saying it to you. It just means that we're well suited for each other."

"Well suited for what, exactly?" she asked. "For fucking? Sure, as long as we don't talk too much and ruin it. But I'm still waiting for all the kinkiness you promised me, by the way. This has been hot, but not at all the mind- blowing orgasms you said I'd be having."

"Unfortunately, this is about all I have to offer you with the boundaries you've put in place. I'm a big believer in consent, Athena, and so far, you've only consented to a little bit of rough sex and some orgasm control. Don't worry, though. I have a feeling you'll be singing a different tune soon enough."

She snorted. "What exactly are you expecting me to want from you, Nathan? For you to marry me and become a full-blown polygamist?"

A smug smile filled his features, and he sat back on the bed. His hands continued to work at his tie, but his eyes were on hers.

"Sweet Athena, I expect you to offer me everything you have. Not just your body but also your possessions, your mind... everything. I can be a patient man. First things first, of course. You'll need to get over me being married, meet Veronica, accept my collar, and—"

"Accept your what?" Athena gasped. The internet hadn't said anything about a collar. What the actual fuck? Nathan finished knotting his tie and stood as though she hadn't interrupted him. "One day, Athena, you'll beg for me to own you in the same way I own Veronica. Until then, a little rough sex and some orgasm control is just fine."

He kissed her on the nose and tipped her face up to his. "Be my good girl. Come straight home after work, okay?"

Athena pushed his hand away. Nathan laughed, enjoying the sight of her naked body as she stood and got ready for work. She slipped into the bathroom, grateful for the privacy. She heard the front door close behind him, locking from the outside.

Athena frowned in the mirror, toothbrush in hand. She hadn't given Nathan a key. How had he managed to lock the door?

The day passed slowly, dragging on way longer than it had any right to. Jared hadn't shown his face at the coffee shop for weeks, either from embarrassment or something his friend "Pete" had said to him. That was yet another topic she hadn't breached with Nathan, along with questions like how he knew that jerk's real name and why he carried a gun.

Finally, at half after three, it was time for her to go

home. She hung her apron up and gathered her purse from the locker in the back.

"You seem like you're off in a hurry," Chantel said as we passed in the short hallway.

Athena shrugged. "I guess. Happy to have tomorrow off, at least."

It was a weird weekend. Usually, she was scheduled on Saturdays, but the owner was having some work done on the building, so everyone had the day off. Apparently, most businesses avoid closing on Saturdays, and the electrician they hired had cut the owner a good deal to do it then.

Chantel nodded. "I hear you. It's going to be so crazy sleeping in with my man. Or, you know, not sleeping." She gave a wink like Athena should know exactly what she meant.

Up until recently, she didn't. Athena only had a couple of boyfriends in college, and the dorms had a strict no- sleepover policy. And now, with Nathan being married, she would have thought there was no way she'd have him over at her apartment overnight. Surely, his wife would put her foot down about that.

But it turned out his wife didn't put her foot down about anything.

Nathan was at her apartment waiting with a dozen roses when she got off work. They fell right back into bed and stayed there all night. And all morning. And all afternoon. They fucked all over that room, in every position, using every imaginable trick to get him off. Athena was still experiencing complete orgasm denial, which was frustrating but also a little fun too.

It was a good thing Harper was mostly over at Josh's place, or she would have been concerned about them never coming up for air.

Athena did notice Nathan occasionally texting and smiling at his phone. She wanted to know so badly if he was messaging his wife, but that felt like a terrible thing to ask. Eventually, he caught her watching him and offered the information up himself.

"I know you don't want to talk about her, but Veronica says hi," Nathan said, putting his phone away. "She offered to bring us some food, but I told her that wasn't a good idea."

Athena nodded. Yeah, that would be a horrible idea. And yet... her curiosity was burning. Maybe one day she would work up the nerve to face Veronica, but then that would probably be the day she broke things off with Nathan. How could she possibly continue seeing a man after meeting his wife?

*Chapter 7*



*Then*

"If you want to be owned by me, you're going to have to suck it up and just meet her," he said during sex one day. They were four months in, and his prophecy was coming true. Athena was addicted to Nathan Garcia, and she didn't even know why.

He was good-looking, but not unreasonably so. Maybe it was his self-confidence or the dominant energy he gave off. He told her she was a natural submissive, that he was as drawn to her as she was to him. Given his insatiable appetite in the bedroom, she could see that being true.

Desperate to please him, Athena said she would meet Veronica in the heat of the moment. Nathan rewarded her compliance with the first in a long line of mind- blowing orgasms. It wasn't hard to tip her over the edge after all the months of orgasm denial. He was already inside her, pushing in deep and steady like she loved being fucked. His dick filled her just right, where the friction was constant without causing pain. He was thick enough to stretch her in ways other guys hadn't but not too large to make it uncomfortable.

He sped up his thrusting and growled in her ear, "Come now, and tonight you'll be making those noises for my wife, Athena."

She screamed. Yes! Yes, she'd make the same throaty gasps with his wife in the room, and as soon as she agreed, he told her to cum for him, and she did.

God, it felt so good. It was like something broke inside her, and all that was left after they were finished was lazy bliss. Her body hummed; her muscles relaxed. It was pure heaven.

"You've released all the built-up tension you stored inside from not obeying me," Nathan teased.

Or maybe it wasn't really teasing. With Nathan, it was hard to know for sure. Not that any of that mattered. What mattered was that Nathan called his wife as soon as he could get to his phone, promising her that both of them would be coming back to their house for dinner that night.

Athena tried to take it back, but Nathan wasn't having it.

"I don't make promises to my wife lightly, Athena. She's expecting us," he said. He was already annoyed with her for trying to get out of it.

Arguing any more wasn't going to go over well.

"Fine," she snapped, trying to match his irritated energy. "I'll meet her, and then we'll break up. That seems like the logical end to this."

Nathan chuckled. "Sure. Whatever you say, babe." He shrugged it off, completely unworried about taking her home. Unfortunately, none of their time together could have adequately prepared Athena for the visit. She knew as soon as she saw his building that she had made a horrible mistake.

His home was massive. It was in the ritzy part of the city, in a building with a doorman and a special elevator that required a private code. Athena didn't know enough about that side of town to guess how much it would cost to live in an apartment like that, but it had to be well into the millions of dollars.

No wonder he had made comments about the safety in her neighborhood. Compared to this place, she was living in a crack den.

Athena frowned as they stepped inside the elevator. "How did you end up at my coffee shop, anyway? You were a long way from home."

A smile broke out across Nathan's face, and he wrapped his arms around her from behind. "I was there for you, Athena. Do you remember going to the westside the week before? You were leaving the library, and I saw you as I was getting into my car. I was drawn to you, so I had my assistant follow you to work... and other places."

Her heart leaped into her throat as she struggled to react. Was that hot? Was it an invasion of privacy? The line between the two felt muddled more than ever.

"Don't overthink it," he said. He kissed her on the cheek as the doors opened to his foyer. Athena instantly felt underdressed as the space was decorated to the nines. Fresh flowers were perched on the hallway table, giving off a subtle scent that mixed well with the aroma of cleaning supplies and dinner cooking.

"Veronica! We're home!" Nathan called out as he hung up his jacket and took hers to add it to their closet.

"I'm taking the roast out of the oven, dear. Just a minute!"

Athena cringed at the sound of her perfect, crisp voice. She sounded cheery, excited even, like meeting your husband's mistress was something to put on the calendar, circled in red ink. Sorry, Linda, we can't attend your daughter's Bat Mitzvah on the eighteenth. That's the day my husband brings home his young mistress for me to meet. Yes, she's been told she will be expected to do something erotic. It's just so exciting!

Athena bit back a grin, causing Nathan to quirk an eyebrow. He grabbed her by the hand and led them into the very bright, very white kitchen. As promised, Veronica was setting a huge roasted animal carcass on the counter next to a fresh salad.

"Athena, it's so good to meet you," she said, wiping her forehead with the back of an oven mitt. Her hair was coiled on top of her head, and her dress was a simple black A-line, giving her a timeless look.

Her face was smooth, but Athena couldn't tell if it was from youth or some work she had done. They were clearly able to afford good plastic surgery if she ever wanted it.

Whether it was natural or not, the woman was gorgeous, and when Nathan left her side to greet his wife with a hug, Athena felt a sinking feeling in her stomach. Was it jealousy? Or regret, maybe?

"I'm sorry. This was a mistake," she said, turning to leave the kitchen. She opened the closet to get her jacket but froze when she heard footsteps running after her. Heels. It wasn't Nathan rushing up behind her. It was Veronica.

"Are you sure you want to leave, Athena? Please, don't go until we've had a chance to talk. We can sit together, just the two of us. Without Nathan."

Frowning, she turned to face the woman whose husband she had been fucking for the past several weeks. Why in god's name was Veronica trying to talk her into staying? She genuinely wanted to know.

So, she asked. "Why in god's name are you trying to talk me into staying?"

Veronica laughed. "Okay, I can see why you'd ask

that. Let's sit and chat, just for a minute, and I'll explain everything. If you still want to leave after that, I'll make sure Nathan lets you go."

She opened a door in the hallway, allowing Athena to take in the grandeur of the beautiful room when she switched on the light. It was an office or library, complete with walls of books and a fireplace. While the books on the shelves were real, the fireplace must be fake or electric, given the age of the building. Still, it looked warm and inviting.

Athena sighed and followed her in, making sure to close the door behind them.

"Sit, please," Veronica said, gesturing to the deep armchair across from her. Athena settled into the plush velvet cushions and stared at Nathan's wife, waiting for her to speak.

Veronica took a deep breath that morphed into a sigh halfway through. She kicked her heels off and propped her feet on the coffee table between them. She twisted a strand of hair between her fingers and looked off into space, almost as though Athena wasn't even there.

"Um, so... what did you need to tell me?"

She looked back at Athena, surprised. "Oh. Well, Nathan said I should stop you from leaving. He told me to talk you into staying. I was trying to think of what I might say to do that. I didn't have a chance to come up with any material, and he didn't give any suggestions of what to say to you."

Athena blinked and fell back farther into her seat. How was she supposed to respond to that?

After a few minutes, Veronica spoke again. "It might help you to know that Nathan really likes you, Athena. I think you being here with us would add to his happiness a lot."

"Okay... but there's more than just Nathan to consider in this, Veronica. How do you feel, knowing that I'd be...? I mean, that I am... sleeping with your husband? Isn't that horrible for you?"

And there it was, out in the open. She looked surprised at Athena's questions but probably not as devastated as most people would be. And at least Veronica didn't look like she wanted to murder her. That was a plus.

"He really hasn't explained anything to you, has he? Jesus, he can be so... okay, how much do you know about our lifestyle? Our relationship, I mean?"

"A little bit. Not very much," Athena admitted. "It's not something I really wanted to talk about, to be honest. Nathan promised me good sex. I was interested in trying some BDSM stuff that I had never experienced before, and I took him up on the offer."

All the words spilled out of her so fast. Once she started talking, she just couldn't stop, and Veronica nodded, encouraging her to go on, so she did. "He said he was married, and you were fine with him taking other partners. That's all I really wanted to know, that he wasn't really cheating on you with me. I'm not really in a relationship with him, anyway. What we have is casual. Short term."

She paused, creating space for Veronica to respond.

"Short term? That's... different. Nathan doesn't really do short term, you know?" No, Athena didn't know. The look on her face must have given that away. "Okay, let's start at the beginning. You mentioned BDSM stuff. Nathan and I are in a full-time, 24/7 power exchange relationship. He is the dominant one, and I'm the submissive one, as you probably guessed. Part of our relationship includes him having the option of taking other partners, while I only have him as a partner. Does that make sense?"

"No. Not even a little bit," Athena said. "I get the hotness of some power exchange, but what you're describing is totally different. You're saying that he can go and fuck literally anyone, and you have to stay here and wait around for your turn. Why would you ever agree to something like that?"

Veronica laughed again, like Athena was joking, but she stopped when she realized it was a serious question. "Oh. Okay, sorry. Let me explain. I agreed to this arrangement because it fulfills me and hits my kinks the right way. I like that Nathan has all the control, that he can follow his own urges while leaving me restricted. He told me that you liked orgasm control, so you have to understand—"

"He what?" Athena's cheeks reddened, and she felt her blood pressure rise to a boiling point. He had talked to his wife about the things she liked in bed. It felt so... violating.

"Fuck. Shit. Okay, sorry. Sorry, sorry, sorry. I thought you knew. Nathan likes to share information... well, it's not really important why. It's wrong that he told me that without asking you, but I don't think he meant to hurt you." They both stood. Athena stomped out of the room and into the elevator, not bothering to grab her jacket or say another word. He could keep it as a souvenir. Maybe they could fuck on top of it, discussing all the ways she had been a total idiot.

The Uber ride home was the most expensive fare in her life but having to ask for a ride home would have cost way more in terms of her dignity, so she opted for the ride share instead.

"Jeez, what happened to you?" Harper asked when she finally arrived home. It was raining, causing her mascara to run horribly. Her hair was a mess from the wind, and her clothes were soaked through since she didn't have her coat.

"Nothing. Men are jerks." Athena fumbled with her clingy, wet shirt, wrestling it off on the way to her bedroom.

Once free, she slapped it down angrily onto the

hardwood floor, the harsh sound satisfying to her as she glared around the dark room, pausing when she saw her bed. It was still unmade from that morning, her discarded panties tangled somewhere in the mess. The sheets probably smelled like sex, considering she hadn't changed them in a week. She and Nathan had made good use of them every day since then.

Athena hated the images that filled her mind of him holding her down and fucking her into the mattress, so she stripped the sheets off the bed and walked down the hall to the laundry closet. She tossed them into the washer along with her wet clothes. Satisfied and completely naked, she grabbed some soft pajamas and locked herself in the bathroom.

A hot shower helped at least a little bit. The familiar body wash scent and methodical routine of cleaning herself didn't make her forget Nathan's betrayal, but it was still soothing. Once she was dried off and into her pajamas, she returned to the living room to face Harper. She'd want to know what happened, at the very least. Athena was honestly surprised she hadn't pestered her for the story as soon as she came home looking like a drowned cat.

Athena froze when she saw him waiting for her.

"Hello, Athena. You left in such a rush that you forgot your jacket, so I wanted to return it to you.

Harper and I were just catching up. I didn't mean to stay so long."

She narrowed her eyes at Nathan and snatched the coat from his hands. He absolutely meant to stay that long and butter up her roommate. None of it was a mistake. It never was with him.

"Shoot, my mom's calling me," Harper said, phone in hand. "I have to take this. It was good to see you again, Nathan."

She scurried off to her room down the hall, leaving Athena alone with him. Her roommate had grown a little fond of him over the past few weeks when he was quick to recognize Harper's Star Trek references and backed her up when she said Athena should cut back on her hours at the coffee shop.

Chances were that her mom wasn't even calling, and she made the whole thing up just to force Athena to talk with him. Traitor.

"Well, you dropped my jacket off, so you can go now. Just give me your key first," she said, palm outstretched. Nathan raised an eyebrow. "Do you think that a lock would stop me if I really wanted to get in here, Athena?"

"That or the police," she snapped. "Hand it over."

"Look, I get that you're upset, and I agree that you have a right to be angry. You do not belong to me," he said. The word "yet" hung in the air between them, unspoken. "I had no business sharing that information about you with Veronica. I should have asked you for permission or, better yet, waited until it was mine to share. I'm sorry."

Athena hesitated, and it gave Nathan the encouragement he needed. He took a few steps closer. "You're important to me, Athena. Your feelings matter to me, and I will always take them into consideration. But you have to feel the connection that we have. You do feel it, right?"

The horrible thing was that she did feel it. When he touched her, it was like electricity shooting through her veins. When he used that deep, demanding voice, she wanted to throw her panties at his face and straddle him, regardless of where they were at the time. The thought of him behind her, with a fistful of hair, smacking her ass as he thrust into her... it was too much.

She pushed her lips against his, claiming him as her own, at least for the moment. He reached down to cup her ass and pulled her legs around his waist until she was completely off the floor.

Athena sucked on his bottom lip, biting it gently. He rumbled approval and carried her to the bedroom, dropping her onto the bare mattress.

He scowled at the sheetless mattress protector. "You took away our love nest."

"Um..." The kissing had emptied her brain. "You weren't supposed to come back here again."

"And yet, here I am," he said, settling between her legs. "Are you ready for me to taste you, Athena?"

"Yes," she breathed.

"Good." He slapped her thigh and stood up. His rumpled hair made him look reckless, the absolute opposite of what he truly was. Nathan was calculated as fuck, as he was about to remind her. "When you're ready to commit to me, I'll be more than happy to oblige. For now, I'm going to have to pass."

Athena shot up. "What the fuck? What do you mean 'commit to you'?"

"You're right. I should be more clear. When you are ready to give me everything, every part of you, so that I can know without question that sharing what you like in bed with my wife is not something that will cross a boundary, I will fuck you again. Until then, we'll talk. You can ask questions about the lifestyle, about Veronica. About anything, really. And then you can choose."

"Choose? Choose what?"

Nathan sighed. "If you want me to own you, Athena. Like how I own Veronica."

"You can't actually own people, Nathan. Slavery is frowned upon these days." It felt like she was talking to a child, explaining that they couldn't have a real pet dragon.

"Not by me," he said with an evil grin. "I'm not talking about historical slavery or human trafficking or anything like that, Athena. I'm talking about a consensual BDSM relationship where one person owns the other person. Some people might call that fake or role play because it's not legally enforceable or some nonsense like that, but I don't need the law to keep my women in line when they belong to me. I'm surprised you found nothing about that during your research."

"Your women? As in plural?" Athena screeched. "Jesus, how many times have you done this, Nathan?" Why had that never crossed her mind? Just how many other people was he seeing?

"Women, as in plural, once you agree to be mine. Veronica was my first and only owned submissive, until now."

"And how does that make her feel, exactly? Or do you even care?" Athena couldn't help feeling sorry for her, waiting at home for her husband to return, having to share him at all. "And why can't she date other people if you get to?"

"One question at a time," Nathan sighed. "She feels alright about it. She even likes that I have the freedom and option to do anything I want while she is restricted to only being with me. It's part of her submission to me. Yes, I care about her feelings a lot. I take them into consideration when I make a decision, but the decision is still mine to make. That's probably the most important understanding that we have in our relationship."

Athena chewed on her lip, unsure what else to ask or even what to say. Nathan stood, running a hand through his hair. He was going to leave, and she wasn't going to stop him. She needed space to think. She needed time.

Her body screamed that she didn't need any of those things that badly, but her brain was adamant. Nathan paused at the door, dug out her house key, and tossed it onto the bed.

"When you agree to be mine, the same rules will apply to you. I'd want you at my house, living by my will, every day for the rest of your life. Let me know if you want to talk about it more or when you come to a decision."

*Chapter 8*

*Now*

Things weren't working out the way she planned. Not one bit. Athena's goal was to totally ignore whatever Donovan told her to do, but so far, he wasn't giving her the opportunity to ignore him at all. It turned out he was a little too good at ignoring her first.

She thought that changing jobs and working at the sketchy convenience store would send him into a dominant tailspin. Lord knows it would have caused Nathan to completely lose his shit. But once again, there was nothing but radio silence from Donovan.

That meant the only express orders he had given her were (1) not to move out of the apartment and (2) to wait for him to grace her with his presence again. As it stood, those were the only ways she could use to show her defiant nature and dissuade him from wanting to keep her as a sub. But it was fine. She could work with that.

The first thing she needed to do was finish moving out of Nathan's apartment. She had paid the deposit and first month's rent on a space about five minutes away. It wasn't nearly as nice as the apartment Nathan had arranged for her, but she didn't need anything that fancy. As long as the door locked and she had a survival baseball bat to lean against the wall, she'd be fine. God knows she'd lived in worse places when she was in college.

What wasn't fine was the moving company situation. Athena had all but given up on trying to hire professionals and instead was soliciting the help of friends, both current and former, to help with the move. Basically, she was texting every number she had in her phone to help her pack up a U-Haul in exchange for pizza, beer, and as much money as the ATM across from the park would allow her to withdraw until then, split evenly amongst all the volunteers.

If it wasn't for Donovan's uppity demands, if there were really just no moving trucks available, she would've stayed in the apartment and just waited for the lease to run out. Nathan had already paid rent for the year anyway, on top of her stipend allowance. Moving was a stupid move financially. But after Donovan swooped in and forbade her from leaving, there was nothing for her to do other than find a way to make it happen.

Athena's heart fell a little when only three people responded that they would be able to help her out. Maybe it was a sign that she was getting older, or maybe it was the fact that she had gone AWOL socially for too long when she was with Nathan. Whatever the reason, her impromptu moving squad had fallen by the wayside since the last time she needed to call upon them.

Harper was the first to say yes to helping. Her former roommate had gotten married early last spring, and Athena had been one of her bridesmaids. They hadn't spoken much since then, but it felt good to know she could still count on her. Jared, whom she hadn't seen since that horrible open-mic night, said he was available for a few hours, and then Jessie, an old friend from art school, said he could also help if the beer was good enough.

Athena had to smile when she read that comment. Jessie was known for drinking pretty much anything short of battery acid back in college, but now he was drawing the line at "good beer." How times had changed.

Athena bundled up against the cold and snow, stepping out into the street to begin her walk to the convenience store. She was assigned to work the overnight shift, 9 PM until 5 AM, and in the dead of winter, that meant she was going to work in the dark and coming home from work in the dark.

While it didn't make for the best commute on foot, hailing a cab would draw too much attention, and walking gave her a better chance of ditching the driver Donovan had sent to tail her. It had only taken the man a few hours to find her during her first shift at the convenience store, and since then, he had followed behind her most nights. Every once in a while, Athena was able to sneak out and walk by herself, a small feat that made her feel a little bit more triumphant over Donovan.

Hmmmm. Donovan. Once again, she found herself comparing him to Nathan. Her former master would have insisted that she quit her job or, at the very least, change her schedule. Donovan's silence communicated that he was totally unbothered by her choices.

She frowned, for the first time wondering if being owned by Donovan O'Malley was really such a bad thing. He seemed to think that he already owned her, that her submission was a bygone conclusion given Nathan's wishes, and if that was the case, his approach was so hands-off that belonging to him might not even impact her daily life. Athena could essentially continue living however she wanted and just know to expect a periodic visit from Donovan to check-in.

She had been so focused on finding a way out of belonging to him that she never stopped to consider how little his owning her changed anything. Maybe he'd even be alright with her finding another dominant guy at some point. Someone who could do wicked things to her body, just like—

She slowed to a stop, the snow collecting on her jacket. Athena blinked back unexpected tears, suddenly emotional. Why was she tempted to cry at the thought of being owned by another dom? For some reason, the idea felt like a huge betrayal of Nathan's memory. She hadn't felt the same kind of shame about being given to Donovan O'Malley, oddly enough. That man brought her a lot of frustration but never any guilt. But then, Nathan had wanted her to be with Donovan. Submitting to him would be the same thing as following Nathan's orders, right?

It wasn't even the idea of kinky sex with someone else that made her tear up, either. If Athena were able to work up the nerve, she would absolutely entertain the idea of going back to the BDSM club, Safeword, on her own, just to experiment and nothing more. But could she really separate the pleasure of rough sex with the need to be owned? She wasn't sure. She had never had to do that before.

The look of the beautiful woman on the spanking bench flitted across her mind. The one Athena had seen that night she went to Safeword with Nathan. He only took her a handful of times, often preferring to bring one of the others instead. But that first night she was there, Athena had witnessed probably the hottest display of dominance she had ever encountered.

A man in a mask stood behind the woman, pounding into her, and holding her down tight... she had felt so many things watching them that night. Too many to unpack, especially with Nathan standing right there beside her. Even now, her instant desire to be dominated by the stranger felt like a betrayal to his memory. She would never admit it, but as she watched the woman being ravished in front of the crowd, she had wanted nothing more than to switch places with her and experience the masked man for herself.

Maybe if Athena ever worked up the nerve to return, the masked man would be there. Maybe he could fuck the grief right out of her system.

Athena took a deep breath to steady herself and walked into the small store, blinking against the harsh fluorescent lights. Simon was by the cash register, his thin frame propped up against the counter, wearing a lazy smile. He straightened and offered a greeting as she dusted the excess snow off herself.

"Do you really just love walking in the snow at night or something? It's horrible out there, Athena. Take a cab next time," he said, removing the cash drawer from the register.

Each shift had a different one, which was intended to help prevent employee theft. Athena had never met the owners of the convenience store, but they clearly were not as trusting as the ones who owned the coffee shop. She never had to even count the drawer there; it was just assumed that everyone they hired was honest.

"When I win the lottery, there will be signs, Simon. Taking cabs every day will be one of them."

Simon scoffed and followed her into the dimly lit backroom. He used to give her a hard time about living in the pricey apartment and not having a car, but all the humor had dashed from his face when she said her dead husband had left her the place. She wasn't actually married to Nathan, of course, but the white lie was enough to get him to drop the teasing about her apartment. It didn't appear to prevent him from commenting about anything else, though. Walking to work was still fair game, apparently.

Maybe she should tell him that her husband had died in a snowstorm on Twenty-third Street. That might shut him up.

"Can't win the lottery if you're too busy getting mugged and murdered," he argued. "Seriously, this isn't the best neighborhood, Athena. I could spot you some cash for a ride if you need it."

Athena shook her head. "It's really fine. I'll grab a cab on the way home. I needed to walk after being inside all day."

Simon shrugged but dropped the issue. He handed Athena the keys to the store and left. Athena watched him get into his old sedan and drive away. The only thing left to keep her company was the hum of the commercial lighting.

The keys weren't anything that she usually needed to use, as the store didn't typically close. From what she could gather, from time to time there was an emergency (usually some kind of violent outburst) right outside the store, and the cashier on duty had to lock the door to keep themselves and any innocent customers safe. The bars on the windows wouldn't stop a stray bullet, but at least no one could force their way inside by breaking one of the glass panels.

Hooray for small blessings, Athena supposed.

No one said it outright, but the dangerous side of the job was the reason Simon was the most senior employee, having worked there for about nine months. It wasn't a place known for its ambiance, to put it nicely. Athena had to admit she was morbidly curious about what her first "situation" would be like.

So far, all the customers seemed fairly nice, if not indifferent to her. Most of them were teenagers or young parents looking to pick up some emergency diapers or cheap last-minute groceries for dinner. Nothing too interesting.

That said, the pay was much higher than any other cashier job in the area for a reason, too. Athena was taking home an extra five hundred bucks a week since she left the coffee shop, which would go a long way to paying some bills when she moved out of her pre-paid apartment.

Maybe soon she would even have enough for a down payment on a car of her own, as the move was draining pretty much all the extra money already sitting in her account.

Athena busied herself restocking and rotating the snacks next to the register. She changed the coffee in the oversized self-service dispenser, then picked a steamy- looking book off the rack and started reading.

The book was so engrossing that she didn't look up again until she heard the front door bell ring, indicating that a customer was walking in. As soon as she looked up, her blood ran cold.

"Hello, Athena," Donovan said. He stomped his boots

on the doormat and carefully removed his gloves. His coat only had a few flakes on it, likely due to him driving the expensive car that was parked out front. It was silver, probably terribly pricey, and she had to suppress an eye roll at how cliche it was for him to drive something like it. Of course, he would have a ridiculous car that went way too fast and cost way too much money. Nathan had a fleet of them, too.

"Donovan," she said evenly. "Can I interest you in some gross convenience store coffee?"

"Tempting, but not this time," he said, walking to

the counter. His eyes flickered to the book in her hands, then back to Athena's face. Her cheeks reddened. Of course, he would catch her reading some smutty romance novel off the rack. Why couldn't he stop by when she was reading some award-winning title from home? Or at least a book on her phone?

A better question was why she felt the need to prove herself to him at all. So what if he judged her for reading literary pornography? His opinion didn't matter.

"Then how can I help you? Are you all out of pork rinds? Is there a crossword puzzle shortage in the trust fund part of town?"

Athena groaned inwardly at her mistake, and Donovan's eyes lit up with humor. Of course, she was part of that crowd now, too. She'd have to remember to stop making fun of people with trust funds.

"This is an interesting change of employment. What happened to the job at the coffee shop?" he asked, changing the subject.

"This is more money," she said, shrugging.

"Hmmm," he said. "And you think taking a job here would piss me off, or is that just a bonus?"

Athena hesitated. She wasn't expecting him to be that direct or to necessarily even care. "If it bothered you, I'm sure I would have heard from you before now. I've been working here for—"

"Three weeks, four days, and two hours," he said, interrupting her. "Just because I choose not to address an issue immediately, don't think for one second that I'm unaware of the game you're playing."

"Game? What game?" Athena demanded. "I'm working a job, just like most people. Sorry it's not as fancy as the one you have, but at least I have the time to call people back."

She wished like hell he would take the bait and explain why he wouldn't return her messages, but he ignored her jab entirely.

"Don't play dumb, Athena. You know what game I'm talking about. You do something crazy to get my attention, so I drop everything to give you attention and punish you, then you get off on being punished, and we wind up right back here the next time you're bored or horny. I'll deal with every misbehavior you have; make no mistake of that, but it will be on my terms, in my time."

"Then why are you even here? If you think I'm trying to get your attention, aren't you playing into the game?" Athena's cheeks flamed. He was flattering himself if he thought for one second she wanted anything from him other than her freedom.

"Hardly. I wrote today's date on my calendar weeks ago, just like I did before visiting you at your apartment the first day we met. You tried your best to manipulate me into calling back before I was ready, but it didn't work out for you, did it, princess?" Donovan smirked, the twisted smile not reaching his eyes. "Your petty actions have nothing to do with me being here, although this conversation would have been totally different if you weren't such a--."

"Great. It's good to know that I wouldn't have been able to contact you if I actually needed something. You must be such a great dom to your other subs. They mean so little to you, they can't even reach you in an emergency," she spat. "Nathan was always available. He always answered his phone right away when I called, no matter what he was doing or who he was with. What kind of owner sits on the sidelines, sticking to some schedule on his calendar to contact a person he's in a relationship with?"

The more she learned about Donovan O'Malley, the less impressed she was with him. If facial expressions were any indication, it seemed like Donovan felt the same way about her. She could feel the disapproval radiating off him, and the look in his eyes could probably murder someone with a less hearty constitution.

He could go ahead and be pissed for all Athena cared. She was mad, too.

When he finally spoke again, his voice was eerily calm. "I told you to have your head on straight when I came back. I gave you some time, but apparently, it wasn't long enough." Donovan leaned in closer. "Let me make something clear to you, Athena. I take my responsibilities to my submissive very seriously, but my sub does not control my life. It doesn't work that way, babe. If that's how Nathan ran things, that he came running anytime you called, that was his weakness. But now you're mine, and I'm the one calling the shots. You need to get used to saying 'yes, sir' more often. Understand?"

Athena glared at him, daring him to say more. She wanted to claw his eyes out for speaking poorly of Nathan, for implying that Nathan was weak.

"Nathan was ten times the master you'll ever be. I'd never call you anything other than 'asshole,' and you'll have to wait for hell to freeze over before I'll be somewhere waiting for you to fit me into your schedule."

Donovan sighed and unwrapped the scarf around his neck. He set it on the counter, along with his gloves, and unbuttoned his coat. He placed the expensive garment next to the rest of his clothes before turning to leave. He paused at the door, lingering as though something was stopping him from walking away.

"Otto will be waiting outside for you when you clock out. From now on, he'll drive you where you need to go or follow behind you in the car. He's armed, in case—or rather, when— some crackhead decides to shoot up this place. If you insist on walking home tonight, wear my coat and scarf. It's a fucking blizzard outside, and I'm tired of watching you freeze for no reason, Athena."

She snorted, wishing she could think of something cutting to say back. Her indignation made him smirk, a horribly sexy sight that caused her to shiver despite being in the warm room.

Desire pooled in her belly, tugging low and heavy. How was he doing that to her? By demanding that she wear a coat outside?

"Oh, and Athena?" Donovan paused, hand on the door. "You're not moving, so you might as well forget about all that nonsense, too."

———

In hindsight, Athena could acknowledge that flipping him off had been a bad idea, but when Donovan made a comment about her not moving, it was either that or throwing her book at him, and she reasoned that between the two options, physical violence was worse.

That's not the way Donovan saw it, though. He seemed to be a big fan of taking matters into his own hands when she waved her middle finger in the air.

"Absolutely not!" Donovan slammed the door shut and stalked back to the counter. Athena turned and ran. She scrambled to hide in the employee bathroom, praying that she would be able to lock the door before he reached her, but he was too quick.

Donovan gripped the door, stopping it in midair as she tried to slam it shut. He easily pushed it open, forcing himself inside the small single-occupancy restroom.

"Look at me, Athena." Her eyes snapped upward, reacting instantly to his authoritative tone. She had fucked up. Some line had been crossed, and now she had no idea what he would do. She focused on his chin, not daring to meet his gaze.

Donovan reached for her, tilting her head roughly until she was forced to look at him directly. His pupils were huge, leaving only a sliver of grey. His nostrils flared, making her wonder if he could somehow smell her arousal. The thought filled her with shame, hating that he could cause such a reaction in her. Her pussy was drenched from the chase, and it took everything in her not to clench her thighs together. She wanted relief, but not from him. She'd rather die than admit he was turning her on.

"That's the last time you show me blatant disrespect. Do you understand, Athena?"

The words were a gravelly whisper, carrying a promise and a threat. Donovan meant business. The question was, would she yield to him, or would she put up a fight? This could be her one chance to make it clear she wasn't interested in obeying him, and as terrifying as it was, she had to make her intentions known. Athena took a deep breath and gathered up all her courage.

"Fuck you," she said. "You can go straight to hell, Donovan O'Malley."

Donovan's eyes flashed. He grabbed Athena around the waist, pulling her off the ground until she matched his height. With his other hand, he grasped her throat and squeezed until tears came to her eyes. She tried to squirm away without any success. She was totally suspended in the air, with just the strength of his other arm to keep her from choking to death or falling to the cement floor below.

"Don't you know, silly slave girl? I'm already there," he growled in her ear. "Now it's time to show you what happens when you dance with the devil."

Chapter 9

*Then*

She was stunning. No, stunning wasn't even the right word to describe her. She was a vision. Heavenly. Sent down straight to Earth to torture him in every mortal way possible. Donovan moved through the crowd, trying to catch a glimpse of her again while not making his interest in her totally obvious.

She was with someone; her collar and leash made that clear. In a place like this, clues like that meant everything. One wrong step, and you could have some "dominant" asshole up in your face, causing a scene about you disrespecting their property. Looking was allowed. Unsolicited and apparent interest? Not so much.

For what it was worth, Donovan wasn't worried about holding his own against some prick on an ego trip. That didn't mean he wanted to go looking for trouble, though. He was new and young compared to most of the men strutting around the club. At 32, in some circles, he'd be considered teetering on the brink of middle age, but in the BDSM world, being a dominant under 40 made him stick out like a sore thumb in a lot of places. His height and athletic build didn't help, either. Dominant men could be just as self-conscious about their looks as anyone else.

A couple moved in front of her, blocking the heavenly woman from Donovan's line of sight. He shuffled over a few inches, trying to catch a glimpse of her. Finally, they moved, and he was granted an unobstructed view of the beauty again. She was like an angel, eyes wide and eager to take in all her surroundings. Gauging from her excitement, that had to be her first time at Safeword, too. Donovan would have bet his entire career on it.

"Who are they?" Donovan asked his attendant. The club provided newcomers and prospective members with a guide. This helped not only field common newbie questions but also reduced miscommunications between new and seasoned attendees.

The attendant followed his gaze straight to the woman in white. "That's Nathan Garcia and his sub. One of them, at least. I believe she is his second, though he has expressed an interest in taking on more in the future."

The look the sub gave to her master—Nathan—was pure admiration. Her eyes kept traveling back to him as she took in the space. In return, Nathan smiled at her, holding her leash as well as her hand. The two seemed happy, relaxed, in each other's company.

He hated it. The sight made Donovan burn with jealousy, to be perfectly honest. It wasn't a feeling he was used to, and he didn't like it one bit. The fact that this woman inspired it with just a look was flooring. He could watch her all day, and the emotions building in him would still feel completely novel and baffling.

Even more interesting, though, was witnessing what happened between Nathan Garcia and his submissive. As soon as the woman turned away, Nathan's eyes drifted, too. While she was interested in a BDSM scene that was unfolding near them, Nathan's attention lingered on some of the unaccompanied subs that were waiting along the perimeter of the dungeon. He looked hungry, like a predator, and they were his meal.

There was nothing wrong with him doing that, of course, as long as it didn't make the unowned submissives uncomfortable. Especially as the man's second submissive, the angel in white must have had no qualms about sharing her master with others. Still... the idea of him not being wholly enraptured with her made Donovan uneasy. How could a man, any man, look elsewhere when perfection was standing right in front of him? If she belonged to him, well... capturing Donovan's entire attention wouldn't be a problem.

"Do they come here often?" he probed, wanting to know as much as he could about the woman. "What's her name?"

The attendant's smile faltered. "I'm not sure, Mr. O'Malley. This is the first time I've seen her, as Mr. Garcia usually comes alone or with his wife. Just as a word of caution, I don't mind answering any questions you have, but you should know that taking a special interest in another dominant's submissive is generally frowned upon. Please restrict these kinds of questions to me or one of the other staff members."

Donovan nodded. He guessed as much, but that didn't help his curiosity or the butterflies that took off in his lower stomach when her eyes found him through the crowd.

For a moment, it was like the rest of the club melted away. Donovan's body hummed, electrified by the connection he felt with her. Her eyes widened even more, and Donovan swore he could see her breath hitch in her throat. It was impossible to deny that she, too, felt something drawing them together. By her side, Nathan Garcia frowned and turned to see what had drawn her attention away from him, only to find Donovan unabashedly staring back.

As a non-member, the mask Donovan wore provided him with a level of anonymity that he was immensely grateful for in that moment. He had requested to wear it until he made a decision about pursuing membership. The owners had reluctantly agreed after he gave the club a sizable donation, though he was the only one who seemed to take such precautions.

Nathan wasn't pleased with her looking at another man; that much was apparent even from across the room. He huffed and turned her face back to him with a single finger placed under her chin. The slight correction was enough to break the magical spell between them. The butterflies in Donovan's stomach stilled, and his heart rate settled, but his interest in her didn't change at all.

Donovan had to talk to her. He needed to hear her voice. What did her laugh sound like? Did a dimple appear on her cheek when she smiled? How would she sound calling out his name, in pleasure or pain?

Images of her bent over his knee caused an instant response below the belt. Donovan groaned, hating that he felt so out of control. Usually, he was measured. Intentional in everything. If a woman turned him on, it was on his terms. Yet, here he was, sporting a boner crushed against his stomach like a randy teenager.

"Excuse me, but can you point me to the restroom, Christina?" he asked. The attendant smiled again, probably relieved that he wasn't posing another question about Nathan Garcia's submissive.

"Of course," she said. "Right this way."

Donovan followed her to the single-stall restroom. There was enough sex out on the open floor that at least he didn't have to worry about walking in on a couple in there. Once the door was locked in place, Donovan dropped his pants and fisted his cock, eager to release himself from his unwanted arousal.

He gave himself a few solid strokes, hating that it was his hand running along the length of him and not her sweet, eager mouth. He shut his eyes and imagined that it was her giving him pleasure. He tried to picture her hands on him, but the size of his fingers were too big, the calluses on his hands too rough. Another woman, any woman, would be better than this hell.

Donovan slowed his strokes, a new idea forming. He was in a private, sex-positive BDSM club. Why the hell wasn't he just taking some of this frustration out on an unowned submissive? Why was his first thought to lock himself away and take matters into his own hands when there were willing, single women all around him?

He zipped himself back up and washed in the sink, eager to leave the restroom and find a play partner. It didn't take long to find the attendant in the crowd.

"Christina, can you show me where I can find a

play partner for the evening? I'm looking for someone unowned and open to casual play," Donovan asked her.

"Of course," she said brightly. "We walked past a few of the unowned submissives already. They all wear colored bracelets to indicate their preferences for play and potential partners. If you find someone who matches your interests, you are free to approach them. Of course, they are under no obligation to serve you, and one of the staff members will facilitate your negotiations before you are cleared to do a scene together. Since I am with you for the whole evening, I'm happy to help you with the process."

"Wonderful," he said, following her lead to the dungeon floor. Sure enough, several submissives were wandering the area, and it didn't take long for Donovan to find a woman who bore a passing resemblance to the angel in white. He didn't know her name, and he honestly didn't care. As soon as he saw that her bracelets indicated she was interested in a casual encounter with a dominant male, he was ready to seal the deal.

"Would you be interested in playing with me?" he asked. Her eyes drank him in, and she nodded her consent. For a moment, Donovan thought he was going to cry with relief.

Christina helped them with the logistics. Protected vaginal sex was fine, nothing anal, no toys, light choking, and pain from his hands and mouth were a go. Thank god it didn't take too long. The negotiations were necessary with a new partner, but he was eager to dive into her, imagining for every second that she was his angel.

*His* angel? Where the fuck had that thought come from?

"I've never seen you before," the nameless submissive said. "Are you new?"

"New to this particular club, yes. New to the lifestyle, no," Donovan answered. "Take off the rest of your clothes and sit on the bench."

Delight flooded her features, and she hurried to strip. Once she was naked, with all her curves on display, Donovan approached the bench and traced her outlines with his fingertips. His hands stilled when he reached her nipples, tweaking them gently at first and then twisting harder. The submissive moaned, throwing her hair back and thrusting her chest out for more. Donovan grinned, happy to appease her. He took one into his mouth, suckling it before he bit down on her sensitive skin.

"Harder," she begged. "Please."

Donovan nudged her knees apart, making room for himself between them. He grabbed a fistful of her hair at the roots and pulled her head back so their eyes met. That was the wrong thing to do. There was no energy. The connection he felt with the angel was missing, and it left him feeling numb. For one horrifying moment, he thought it was going to make him lose his erection entirely.

"Turn around," he growled, forcing her face in the other direction. With her ass to him, he was able to regain his hunger. His dick strained against his pants, alive anew at the thought of plunging into the woman. "I'm not going to be gentle with this. I want to just use you. Is that okay?"

"Please," she said. "Please, just fuck me. I've been edging all night, and I just want to cum."

Donovan leaned forward, biting her hard to leave an imprint of his teeth but not enough to break the skin. While Safeword allowed blood play in some restricted areas, that wasn't part of their agreement. Getting to cum at all would help, and Donovan was just thankful he wasn't spilling his seed in the bathroom alone.

He unzipped his pants and grabbed a fist of his cock. The rest of his clothes stayed on; he didn't want to wait another minute longer to feel release. He wrapped himself with a condom from the tray next to them and added a little extra lube to the latex, knowing that it would help her take someone his size. He gripped the sub by her hips and slowly sank into her warmth, allowing her body time to accommodate his length a bit at a time.

"Oh fuck. Oh God!" When he was completely seated in her, the sub started rocking back and forth, moaning and taking him as deep as she could and then pulling out. Donovan slapped her on the ass, causing her bottom to shake seductively.

"Stay still and take it like a good girl," he growled. The sub whimpered her apology and stilled beneath him. Donovan wrapped an arm around her waist, pulling her to him and lifting her feet off the floor. She instinctually wrapped her legs around his waist, crossing her ankles behind his back.

With his spare hand, he worked her ass cheek, pushing her forward just enough to create some delicious friction before releasing it and letting her ass slide back down to meet his torso. The slight, controlled movement felt intimate like they were lovers and she belonged to him.

He closed his eyes, savoring the idea of that being true with the angel in white. Of course, if she were his, he would do this and more. He'd probably already have a finger in her ass and a piercing through her nipple, something for him to run his fingers over as he steadied her on the bench.

He was getting close to finishing. The woman's screams echoed off the walls, drawing a crowd around them. He could hear them murmuring, getting off at the sight of them together. It felt so good, so right, with his eyes screwed shut and his dick deep inside the sub, that the feeling of unease that came over him suddenly was like a punch to the gut. His eyes flew upon just as he felt his cock jerk with ropes of cum, sending his fluid into the condom buried inside the stranger's folds.

The angel in white was there, watching him. Watching them. Her expression gave nothing away, but her eyes told him everything. She was fuming, jealous, outraged at the sight of them together. How? And why? With her standing there in a collar, another man holding the leash, she certainly couldn't cry foul at him taking some comfort in another.

Donovan knew he wasn't in the wrong, but it felt like a betrayal. He imagined for a moment what it would be like to watch her master take her in the club. What would he do? How would he handle that?

He wouldn't be granted a membership at Safeword, that's for sure.

His thrusts slowed, and he pulled out, never once breaking eye contact with the angel as he disposed of the condom and zipped himself back up. He forced his attention back to his partner, helping the submissive sit on the bench and wrapping her in a towel before offering her a drink and her discarded clothing. The woman thanked him and exited the play space. When Donovan turned back to find her in the crowd, the angel was gone. Without a word, she had disappeared as quickly as she appeared, leaving him hard once more and completely unsatisfied.

Donovan groaned. How was his dick already

eager for round two? And not for the other submissive but for the woman entirely out of his reach. A frown creased his brow, and he headed for the door.

"Are you alright, Mr. O'Malley?" Christina jogged after him. "I hope your visit was satisfactory."

"It was great, thanks. You were wonderful, Christina. Very helpful. I'll let management know you went above and beyond."

The club attendant beamed at him, and Donovan made a mental note to have a generous tip for her added to his card on file. But for now, he needed some fresh air and distance from the club. When he returned, if he ever returned, he needed to come prepared for what he might see and who he might see doing it with her.

"Wonderful. Have a great day, Mr. O'Malley!"

Donovan stepped out into the crisp night air and pocketed his mask, grateful to have it off his face. He handed the valet his ticket and waited impatiently for the young man to return with his car.

"You're not very subtle, you know." Donovan didn't even have to turn around to guess who was standing behind him. Sure enough, when the older man appeared at his side, it was none other than Nathan Garcia, owner of the woman Donovan had been lusting after for the better part of the evening.

It wouldn't do him any good to deny his attraction to her. If he had been that obvious, Donovan knew he needed to own up to it and apologize.

"I'm sorry if I made you or your sub uncomfortable, Mr. Garcia. She is striking. You're a lucky man." Donovan offered his hand out to shake. For a moment, it looked like Nathan might ignore it, but then he finally extended his own.

"So, you've asked around and found out my name, Donovan O'Malley. Has anyone told you anything else about me?"

Donovan shrugged. "I asked one of the attendants about you as your submissive caught my eye. They mentioned you having a few women and possibly being interested in owning more."

"I see. Do you consider that a problem?" Nathan pressed. "If so, please spare me the lecture. My women consent to my living a polyamorous lifestyle."

"Not at all," Donovan said. "What you do is your business. Though I did wonder why you would want to have any others, given the beauty of the woman you were with tonight."

Nathan Garcia narrowed his eyes. "That's exactly the type of issue I mean, Mr. O'Malley. Just because you're not polyamorous yourself does not mean there is anything wrong with it. Vanillas would throw that same kind of judgment at everyone inside that building. There's no reason to sling it amongst ourselves."

"Fair enough. I meant no disrespect," he said.

"I'm curious, though. Do your submissives have the same option to take additional lovers? Or is that a privilege you reserve for yourself?"

Nathan's expression hardened. "I don't prescribe to the idea that my subs should be afforded the same privileges as me, Mr. O'Malley. My women are content living with a double standard like that. It makes them feel owned and prevents a situation where I am, in turn, owned by them. The imbalance of power exchange is part of the draw. Don't you agree?"

Donovan nodded. "Yes, I do. I was just curious as to your own personal arrangement. That's all."

The valet pulled up to the curb with Donovan's silver Jaguar. A flicker of approval dashed across Nathan's face as he looked at the car, but it disappeared when he turned back to Donovan.

"Your curiosity is exactly why I followed you out here, Mr. O'Malley. My submissives are not permitted to have any other sexual or romantic relationships. Anyone I own, including Athena, serves only me. In the future, please stop yourself from ogling my property in such an obvious way. Keep your distance, and we'll get along fine."

Nathan clapped Donovan on the shoulder in a fatherly way that caused the younger man to grit his teeth in annoyance. He wanted to brush off the warning and veiled insult, throwing Nathan's words back at him, but he was too distracted to come up with anything cutting to say in return.

Athena. Her name was Athena. It was literally the perfect name for her. She was a goddess walking among men.

*Chapter 10*

*Now*

Athena trembled in his arms, hating how vulnerable she felt pressed against his body. If Donovan thought he was the devil, who was she to argue with him? He was an arrogant, selfish asshole at the very least, and now she was utterly at his mercy in the bathroom of a run-down convenience store.

She shouldn't have flipped him off. That much she'd own up to, but when he announced that she wouldn't be moving out of the apartment as planned, something snapped inside her, and now, she was paying the price. How had he even known that she was still planning to move? The man was infuriating.

"Athena," he whispered. "What am I going to do with you? You don't listen. Your temper is enough to drive a man mad, and yet, it seems to make me want you even more."

As if to prove his point, Donovan ground the lower half of his body against her ass, forcing her to feel every inch of the very hard, very thick length of him. She stilled for a second and then fought against him with renewed energy. She panicked at the thought of what he might try to do to her if she remained in such a compromised position.

Along with her body, her mind struggled to process each bit of what he said. It was like he was speaking in a different language.

Had Athena really gotten everything all wrong? She had intentionally disobeyed him with the goal of making herself unappealing to him. But if he found her acting out arousing, did that mean she had played into his little game instead?

"Shhhh, Athena. Calm down before you hurt yourself. I'm going to put you down on this disgusting countertop, and then we'll talk before anything else happens. There's no way for you to get to the door, so don't even think about making a run for it."

Athena sneered in resignation, huffing, and crossing her arms around her body as he unceremoniously plopped her onto the sticky countertop. She closed her eyes and took a deep breath, trying not to imagine what she was sitting in that made the surface tacky against her jeans.

Between her sudden desperation to go home and

shower, her actively trying not to punch Donovan in the face, and a sharp pang of grief from missing Nathan so much it hurt, Athena could feel all her emotions bubbling to the top.

"I've tried to be patient, Donovan, but you're not giving me a lot of options here," she blurted. *Please don't cry. Please don't cry. Please don't cry*, she told herself.

But it was no use. The hot, heavy tears started falling, and once they began, she couldn't turn them off. Athena dropped her head into her hands and sobbed. For the first time since his death, she gave in and allowed herself to weep over Nathan.

She cried about feeling lost and not having anyone in the world to turn to. She cried about being unowned and not having someone to care for her. She cried about the insensitive jerk who was willing to let her rot alone in that fucking apartment instead of just telling her outright what his intentions were. He wouldn't even answer her fucking messages, for crying out loud. How could Nathan leave her to such an *asshole*?

She cried about all of it. When she was done, and there were no tears left, Athena dry heaved, willing herself to produce more of them to shed. Try as she might, they wouldn't come, and eventually, she gave up trying.

She was vaguely aware of Donovan pulling her back into an embrace. He stroked her hair and whispered some words in her ear that she couldn't even begin to understand. She used his designer shirt as a makeshift Kleenex until she caught herself and stopped, embarrassed.

"It's alright, Athena," he said. "What's one stupid shirt?"

Athena felt an unwelcome laugh bubble up through her. When it passed her lips, she knew it sounded like the cackle of a crazy person, but she was past caring. Past hoping for anything but to get away from this huge, horrible man who made her feel too many awful things all at once.

She scooted off the countertop and pushed away from him. For a second, Athena thought he was going to stop her and try to dole out the punishment he had promised, but instead, he just stood there as she left. She fished the keys out of her pocket and locked the store's front door from the inside. She hit the lights, leaving Donovan alone in the dark, somewhere in the back.

Athena ignored the warm clothes sitting on the counter, leaving without even taking her own coat that she wore to work, and took off running into the night on foot. She didn't know where she was going, but she knew she couldn't bear being with Donovan O'Malley for one more minute.

———

Athena was frozen. That was the worst part of it.

She was also mortified that Donovan had seen her totally come unglued in the bathroom, but that would have been infinitely less horrible if she was stewing over it someplace warm.

She trudged through the slush that filled the sidewalks, where everybody walked during the day, causing mud to mix with the ice until the once-white snow looked soupy and disgusting. After about a half hour of that, the bottoms of her jeans were completely soaked, chilling her to the bone. Athena's teeth chattered as she drew her thin sweater tight around her body. Her nipples were so painfully hard that she could feel them jutting through the flimsy fabric. She should have grabbed her coat before running; that much was apparent. Athena's pride refused to let her consider taking Donovan's things, even though they were objectively a better choice. But not taking her own coat had been a truly stupid move.

One reason for that was the keys to her apartment were still in her coat pocket, so without it, there was no way for her to even let herself back into her home. Instead, she was reduced to wandering around the dimly lit streets of the city, praying that she didn't run into a situation where it would be necessary to call 911. Her phone was, of course, in the other pocket of her coat.

Beating herself up about forgetting to take it with her wouldn't help anything. Athena needed to think positively until enough time passed that she could return to the store without having to face Donovan again.

*Positive thinking. Positive thinking. Hmmmmm.* Well, maybe if Athena caught pneumonia, Donovan would feel so guilty that he would just leave her alone for the rest of her life. Maybe breaking down in front of him was what he needed to see that she wasn't worth the headache of keeping her anymore. Maybe he had already left the store, and she could finally go back and warm up.

That thought was exceptionally positive, and it caused Athena to grin wildly as she turned on her heel and headed back to the convenience store.

Sure enough, when she returned, Donovan's silver car was gone, leaving only a trail of tire tracks in his wake. Her fingers were numb as she fumbled with the keys to unlock the front door. A massive gust of icy wind followed her inside before she could slam the door shut behind her.

The heat inside made her skin prickle, which she took to be a good sign. She could remember something about people with frostbite no longer being able to feel their extremities, and she was feeling all of it.

Donovan's coat, scarf, and gloves remained in the same place on the counter, but otherwise, there was no sign that he had been in the store at all. Athena flipped on the lights and walked over to the coffee dispenser. Her hands shook as she served herself a cup, but the warm liquid helped so much. She savored each sip of the bitter beverage, thankful to finally be warm again.

Athena walked behind the counter and retrieved her phone. It was already after three in the morning. She only had a few more hours of her shift before the next person came to relieve her. With any luck, there wouldn't be any more customers, and she could just relax and try to process what happened.

Those thoughts were dashed to hell as an unknown number lit up her phone's screen. She sent it to voicemail, only for the caller to try again. Athena sighed and answered. "Hello?"

"Don't send me to voicemail ever again, Athena," Donovan barked through the phone. "It's good to know you didn't end up kidnapped or unconscious in a ditch with hypothermia. When I let you walk away, I thought you just needed a minute to compose yourself. I didn't think you'd run out of the fucking building and into the snowstorm wearing a t-shirt. But don't worry; lesson learned."

"It's a sweater."

There was a pause on the other end of the line. Athena cleared her throat. "I'm wearing a sweater," she said. "Not a t-shirt."

"I don't give a fuck if it's a t-shirt or a sweater or a coconut bra! Use some goddamn common sense! I've put up with this charade long enough. You made your point with the new apartment and the shitty job, but now you are literally putting yourself in danger just to get my attention, Athena. Enough is enough!"

"You think I want your attention?" she screeched. "Don't flatter yourself. I was hoping you'd realize I wasn't worth the trouble, and you'd let me go. That way—"

She stopped short of spilling everything to him, but it was too late. She'd shown her hand, and the damage was done.

"That way, you'd be free from your commitment to Nathan, and you could live your life alone guilt-free, is that it?" Donovan asked. "You were trying to manipulate me into releasing you so you wouldn't be the one backing out of being my submissive."

He laughed bitterly, and Athena could almost picture him on the other side of the phone, shaking his head in disbelief.

"Well, sorry to break it to you, sweetheart, but I'm not playing a game of chicken with you. If you back out of your ownership agreement, that's on you, not me. Your master thought I would be good for you, and as hard as you're making this, I happen to agree with him.

"So, the choice is yours. Run or don't run, but if you do, don't think for one minute I won't track you down. He left you to me. You're mine, Athena. You just need to get that through your pretty little head."

Donovan might have gone on to say more, but Athena ended the call before he could. She needed space. She needed to regroup and figure something out. She needed to scream.

"Arrrrggggggahhhh!" Athena threw the cup and the rest of her horrible coffee still inside against the wall. She watched as it ran down the plastic faux wall, knowing she would need to clean it up before the end of her shift.

She didn't care. It felt good to break something.

———

"You don't have a U-Haul for me?"

"You've decided not to rent out the unit? Really?" "The furniture has to stay at the apartment? Since when? I see...."

Athena wanted to bang her head against the wall. Since coming home from work, she had been bombarded with phone calls about things that impeded her ability to move.

The U-Haul location near her was "overbooked" and couldn't get her another truck for at least a month, though the whole interaction with the manager reeked of Donovan. The same feeling shot through her when the new landlord called to say he decided to renovate the apartment before letting it out. Even her current landlord called to say that the furniture was actually part of the unit, a gift to the owner from Nathan, so she wouldn't be able to bring everything with her after all.

It had to be illegal. All of it. There was no way these people could break out of a contract or revoke an understanding without opening themselves to some kind of legal liability. The question was, would she be able to find a better attorney than whoever Donovan would send to represent them if she filed a lawsuit? Probably not. At least not in time for her to move out on schedule.

She slumped onto her sofa, phone in hand. She wasn't going to cry anymore. After her breakdown, there really weren't any tears left in her. Instead, she grit her teeth and made a call of her own.

"Hello?" The voice on the other end was a little groggy, like he was waiting for his morning coffee to brew, and Athena wanted to kick herself for forgetting that most people weren't wide awake at 7 a.m.

"Hey, Jared. It's Athena. Sorry if I'm waking you up. I wanted to let you know that it doesn't look like I'll be moving this weekend after all."

"Oh, that's too bad. I was looking forward to catching up. Is everything okay?"

Athena nodded to herself. "Yeah, it's just that the place I was going to rent isn't available anymore, so it looks like I'm stuck for the time being."

There was a brief pause on the other end, and Athena crossed her fingers and held her breath, hoping beyond hope that he was thinking the same thing she was. The last time they spoke, when he agreed to help her move, Jared had mentioned having trouble with his roommate and needing to find someone new. Now, that bit of information might be her last chance at regaining her independence.

"Got it. Yeah, the rental market is crazy these days. Listen, I have a two-bedroom over near the coffee shop, and my old roommate, Lenny, just moved out. It's not too far away from where you're at now. If you need a place to stay, I'd offer to shack up with you. I mean... not like that, of course, unless..."

"Yes! That would be amazing!" She leaped up from the couch, doing a victory twirl on the hardwood in her socks. "Thank you so much, Jared. I would love to be roommates. I actually rented this space furnished, so not having to buy furniture for a whole apartment on my own is even better."

"Wow, okay. Awesome. So, when do you want to move in?"

Athena grinned into the phone, her heart racing. For once, she had the upper hand, and there was nothing Donovan O'Malley could do about it. "As soon as possible."

*Chapter 11*

*Now*

Donovan swore under his breath, cursing the woman's stubbornness. Keeping her in line was either going to be the greatest accomplishment of his life or put him in an early grave.

"Call Otto," he grumbled, perhaps even more agitated at the man who allowed this to happen. At least Siri knew how to follow directions.

"Yes?" Otto Mendez said, picking up on the first ring. He sounded about as thrilled as Donovan felt about the situation. "I have eyes on her, sir. You can go home if you want."

"Can I, though? Your instructions were pretty damn clear. You were supposed to be trailing her to work every evening, and tonight I had to step in because she was out on her own, again, this time wearing basically nothing in the middle of a snowstorm." Donovan was losing his patience with the new employee. Otto Mendez had come too highly recommended for someone who couldn't follow basic directions. Before his accident, Otto's specialty had been protecting diplomatic internationals, which was what had caught Donovan's eye. Otto had the right background and all the training for the job. All he had to do was follow one young woman around, and he was failing miserably at it.

"She went out the back way. It won't happen again." Otto paused. "Maybe I should keep an extra sweater in the car for her. You know... just in case."

"I'm glad you can see the humor in this because I'm close to terminating your contract, Mendez. You're hardly doing me any favors if I end up having to take matters into my own hands."

There was silence for a moment on the other line. "With all due respect, I honestly don't see why you need me following her, Mr. O'Malley. It's been the both of us out here most days. Why not save yourself the money since you're following her anyway?"

Of course, Otto had noticed him watching. "Just do your job, Mendez."

Donovan ended the call, his attention back on the shitty convenience store doors. He could see Athena through the bars on the windows, cleaning up the coffee she threw with some industrial brown paper towels. They weren't doing very much in terms of absorbing the mess, and she eventually gave up in favor of using a mop.

He could watch her for hours. He had been watching for hours, in fact, from a distance. That was how Donovan knew exactly how many nights she'd ventured out to work in nothing but a thin windbreaker and how he found out about her trip to the nearest U-Haul location.

She was clever; he'd give her that, but that situation would be easy enough to rectify with a few phone calls. He'd already been in touch with her potential future landlord and the owner of the building she was currently at. No, moving wasn't in the cards for Athena Garcia. She'd be right where he left her, waiting for him, just like he said, whether she wanted to or not.

Donovan strummed his fingers on the steering wheel, debating between going back home and keeping watch over his sub. Theoretically, it should be fine for him to leave. Mendez was only a few hundred feet away. But that prick had proven not to be the most reliable babysitter.

Donovan knew why, of course. It was the same reason the rest of his personal security team teased Mendez about being on detail to follow Athena. She was a nobody, an unlikely target for anyone to notice, much less harm. His guys sure as hell couldn't understand him justifying two top-notch guards to sit on their asses all day to watch her front door. But it didn't matter what they understood. Donovan was the boss, and he'd made himself clear at the last debrief when he reenforced the need for her to have constant surveillance.

"I want Mendez with her 14 hours a day," he had insisted. "We'll have Alvarez cover in between. This is only temporary until I move her home, then I'll have a new schedule in place."

His head of security, Chester, had struggled to suppress an eye roll. "Do you really think that's necessary, Donovan? Hiring Mendez was a good call, but we can use his help here. Don't keep wasting his training on a girl no one's ever even heard of."

"Not. Your. Call," Donovan ground out. "Just do what I say, and I'll ask for your opinion if I need it."

That seemed to fix the situation, at least temporarily, but Otto Mendez half-assing the assignment was unacceptable. Donovan would have to rectify that first thing in the morning, even if it meant letting an otherwise good employee go. Mendez would learn to follow orders, or he'd be replaced with someone who could.

Weary from the long day and the situation with Athena, Donovan reversed the car and drove back to his house. He needed some rest. It had been almost 72 hours since the last time he had slept, and even that had been an uncomfortable nap on a plane. His breakneck schedule was catching up with him in more ways than one. Too many people wanted someone dead, which meant a lot of business for him and his guys.

"Hey. Good flight?" Melissa called from the living room as soon as he walked through the door. Officially, Mel was his personal assistant, but in reality, she was much more important to him than that. She would probably love to hear about his run-in with Athena, especially after all the times she had fielded his sub's calls over the past few months, but Donovan didn't have it in him to chat. He needed a few shots of whiskey, a shower, and some sleep.

"It was fine, thanks. I'm heading upstairs for the evening. If I get any calls, just forward them to Chester. Unless—"

"Unless they're about Athena Garcia, then wake you up immediately," she finished. "Yeah, I know the drill. Get some rest. I'm sure you need it almost as much as you need a shower, Nova."

Donovan smiled at her, enjoying the way the nickname rolled off her tongue. They had known each other for years. Had grown up together, in fact. Her parents had worked for his, and when the time came for Donovan to step out on his own, she had inserted herself as his closest friend and confidant, even when she was being a total pain in his ass.

"Thanks, Mel. See you in the morning."

Donovan trudged upstairs, his shoulders and back aching with each step. He cursed his own weakness over confronting Athena at the convenience store. On the one hand, it had been necessary when he was driving by and saw her walking on her own to work, without a coat and Otto nowhere in sight. It had taken everything he had not to pull over, throw her into the car, and take her home right then and there.

Instead, he had made an illegal U-turn and waited for her greasy coworker, Simon Macdemara, to leave. And even after that, he hadn't barged in like his instincts demanded. He enjoyed watching her putter around the store, restocking the shelves, and murmuring to herself. It was only after she settled down and had begun reading that trashy novel that he had made his move.

He had been forced to come up with a stupid lie about already planning on meeting with Athena to save face. If she knew her disobedience was getting to him, getting her to submit would be next to impossible. Next time, he'd need to come up with a better cover story, though. Seriously. Who pencils in meetings on their calendar for the middle of the night?

Donovan undressed quickly and stepped into the shower, turning the hot water all the way up. He closed his eyes and groaned, the heat doing wonders on his muscles. The comfort of the steam caused an almost instant reaction below the belt, which was annoying. Dealing with Athena had stirred up his libido, and now he would have to deal with it alone.

Using the hot water and suds as a lubricant, Donovan fisted his cock and started pumping, making long strokes from the base to the tip. His eyes screwed shut, remembering how it felt when he rubbed his hardness against Athena, rocking to her core. He'd been able to feel her heat even between both sets of their clothes. The smell of her arousal, the look in her eyes... she had felt him, too. If only he had pushed a little more.

"Fuck," he swore. His orgasm took hold quickly, and he watched his seed spill down the shower's drain. He came so fast, so easily, just from imagining her. What would it feel like to actually have Athena writhing underneath him? That sensation alone would probably be his undoing.

Donovan finished washing himself, wrapped a towel around his waist, and stumbled to his bed. The silk sheets felt like heaven when he slid between them, still naked and not interested in wasting any time scrounging up a pair of boxers. Within moments, Donovan's eyes were closed, and he was lost in dreamless sleep.

He awoke in a panic hours later, though with the blackout curtains in the bedroom, it was impossible to guess what time it was. He threw a hand out to the bedside table, fumbling with his phone to check the clock. 11:30 A.M. —way past time to be up for the day.

Grabbing some shorts and a t-shirt on the way, Donovan crept down to the kitchen, where Mel was waiting for him. She smiled from behind her computer across the expansive island, the counter around her cluttered with notes and planners.

"Morning. Coffee's in the pot," she said, gesturing to the machine.

"Morning," Donovan grumbled. "You should have woken me up. I need to be across town in an hour."

Melissa snorted. "Fat chance. When you stay up for three days straight killing people to prevent them from killing other people, you get six hours of uninterrupted sleep. That's just the way it is."

"Must have missed the policy change," he said, wincing as he stifled a yawn. The sleep helped, but some of the bruising on his back went pretty deep. Maybe it would teach him not to turn his back on a certain spoiled mafia prick, but more likely, it would just serve as a reminder to knock the asshole out completely next time before stepping away.

"I rescheduled your meeting for tomorrow, and Chester wants you to call him. He's pretty pissed about how you handled Otto."

Donovan groaned. "If he wants that fucker on the team, he needs to reign him in. Mendez was given one job, and he's blowing it."

Mel chewed on her lip. "Well, there's a whole

separate issue over his assignment, Nova. A lot of people are wondering why we're wasting resources on Athena Garcia when Otto could be put to better use working out in the field. Or better yet, he could be saving your literal ass from taking a beating."

Sighing, Donovan took a long drink from his mug. Of course, Mel already found out about the weasel throwing a couple of cheap shots at him from behind. "It doesn't matter what they think, Melissa. She's important, so she'll have the best security I've got. Maybe everyone should be a little less concerned about how I delegate my resources and a little more invested in the fact that soon he won't be assigned to Ms. Garcia anymore."

"Oh. So, you're going to reassign him, then?"

"Not if he keeps fucking things up," Donovan said, grinning. "I'll be changing her last name way before that happens."

Mel rolled her eyes, as she always did when he spoke about his future with Athena. Normally, Donovan appreciated Mel's level head when it came to... well, just about everything else. But she didn't understand his draw, his certainty, about Athena, so she couldn't appreciate the fact that he knew, without a shadow of a doubt, that Athena was endgame.

"You might want to get the other bitches out of the house before you bring the new model home," she scoffed, eyes turning back to her computer. "I hear that copious amounts of random pussy actually bothers some women. Who knew?"

"Already done, if you must know," Donovan said, shaking his head. "Copious pussy, Mel? Really?"

Donovan had always kept a few no-strings-attached submissives around his house. That much was true. They loved to serve, and the truth was, they grounded him. Having someone count on him, desire him, admire him... that was some pretty addicting shit. The sex was good. Everyone got their needs met, and until recently, there was no reason for him not to pursue a casual relationship or two. But he had ended all that the moment he was able to pursue things with Athena.

Maybe if Melissa had spent more time actually paying attention to her surroundings and less time giving him shit, she'd have noticed they were gone on her own.

He was about to tell her as much but stopped when her eyebrows shot upward. "What is it?" Donovan asked, moving around the counter to look at the screen.

"Looks like the press leaked info about that arms deal," she murmured. "Weren't you around for the brokering of that one yesterday? I thought it fell through."

"It did." Donovan frowned, skimming the Times article. He and a few of the best on his team had played security for the supplier during negotiations, though the buyer's identity hadn't been shared. At least the article didn't mention anyone by name, but that was for a good reason. The editor wouldn't still be alive if it had. Chester would've seen to that.

Donovan never thought he would end up in the private security world, especially for the likes of arms dealers and governmental idiots. His parents had pushed him to join the family business, and while the money was good enough, he eventually had to step away and do something else with his life.

Maybe that's true for anyone working for their dad, or perhaps it was just too much for Donovan personally. Maybe that's just what happens when your family's wealth comes from scamming and cheating people out of their wealth. Who could say?

At least he didn't have to sit through any horrible family dinners during the holidays.

"Contact Chester and see if they know who the leak is," Donovan said, standing and wincing again. Damn, that bruise was already getting old.

"Already on it, dick head," Mel muttered. "Like I haven't done this a thousand times before."

Fair point. She knew the drill.

Donovan finished getting ready and made his way out to the car just as Mendez was pulling into the driveway. Fuck that guy. Donovan didn't have time to listen to him moan about babysitting again.

"Morning," he grumbled.

"Sir." Otto Mendez's voice was clipped, annoyed,

which rubbed Donovan the wrong way.

"I trust she's with Alvarez." It wasn't a question. He just needed Mendez to acknowledge the assignment he was given, preferably without snark.

"Yes, sir. Of course," he agreed like it was the most obvious thing in the world.

"Make sure it stays that way or I'll have you pulling doubles with Alvarez. It seems like it might take both of you working together to keep up with her."

It was just pettiness at that point, but Donovan didn't care. He was sore, pissed off, and now he had to go straight to another meeting after the press leak. He needed a vacation.

Or maybe a honeymoon. That idea helped a little bit until he saw Otto's face.

To his credit, Mendez tried to hide the smug grin but he failed terribly. Donovan narrowed his eyes, ready to demand an explanation.

"Sorry, boss, but you've got bigger problems than that. Seems like your girl's moving out after all."

Oh, well. If that's all, he already handled the potential moving situation on all fronts.

"Don't worry about that," Donovan said, turning back to his car. "I took care of it."

"Really? So, Alvarez trailing her to some guy's house with a cab full of boxes was just a fluke, huh?"

Donovan blinked. "What?"

The blood in his veins began to boil. What the fuck

had happened between last night and this morning? Donovan jerked the car door open and slid behind the wheel. He didn't have to look up to know that Mendez's grin must have bloomed into an all-out smile.

"Call Alvarez," he told Siri through his teeth. Donovan's heart pounded in time with the phone's ringing. "Pick up, goddamn it."

"Hey, boss. I'm guessing Mendez must have—"

"Where is she?" Donovan hissed, punching the car in gear. "Are you with her now?"

"I'm outside the apartment. She and some other guy have been unloading a taxi for a little while. I think they're just about finished."

"Send me the address," he said, ending the call.

Donovan sighed and rolled his shoulders, trying some of the relaxation techniques Mel had recommended. He needed to show up at this place calm and collected. Letting Athena see that she had gotten under his skin, that she had gained any ground at all in getting the upper hand, was out of the question. That would destroy any progress they had made together and would completely undermine the nature of their relationship. No, what Athena needed was a man in control. She needed proof that Donovan wasn't giving up his claim to her, and there was nothing she could do to get out of the situation short of going back on her word to Nathan.

The deep breathing helped if only a little bit. Donovan set the navigation to the address Alvarez texted. It wasn't far from her old apartment, which made him frown. Alvarez had mentioned some other guy. Did Athena have some little boyfriend living nearby? Was that why she was trying to push him away?

No. Not possible. Donovan would have already threatened his life if another man was in the picture. It was highly unlikely that someone like Athena would be interested in a random vanilla anyway. Especially not when she had him, a control freak, willing and waiting for her to get her shit together.

"Hold on, baby girl. I'm coming." The phrase made Donovan smile. He'd be saying those exact words to her soon enough.

*Chapter 12*



*Now*

"You weren't kidding when you said you didn't have much furniture."

Athena laughed and dropped the last of her bags onto Jared's living room sofa. With his help, it had only taken a couple of trips. Now that the taxi was gone (and the meter wasn't running), Athena could finally relax. She had done it. She had moved out of the apartment against the wishes of the all-powerful Donovan O'Malley.

She should be celebrating her freedom and cleverness, but something else was nagging her. What was that small feeling deep down that seemed to ache at the thought of outsmarting Donovan? Regret? Disappointment?

She shook her head at the idea. Whatever it was, she needed to get over it. If anything, being able to move from the apartment so easily only solidified that Donovan wasn't the right guy for her. Sure, he could talk a big game, but he was too busy and distracted to own a sub, even if he wanted to. Nathan would've caught on to her plans much faster. Athena wouldn't have even made it out the door if Nathan was still alive.

"Where's the bedroom?" Athena asked, gathering a few more bags in her arms.

"Right down the hall, last door on the left," Jared said. He picked up a box and tipped his head down the hallway, indicating she should follow him.

It probably wasn't the wisest decision, trying to be roommates with Jared. She still wasn't interested in him romantically, but enough time had passed that he probably wasn't into her anymore, either. He was most likely just happy to have someone to split the rent with after his old roommate left. Speaking of which...

"Hey, here's a check for two months and my half of the deposit," Athena said, handing him an envelope after they set her things on the floor. The room was partially furnished but still lacked a bed. She'd be couch surfing in the living room until one could be delivered.

Jared glanced at the envelope, then shook his head. "Don't worry about it. I was hired to do some freelance stuff, and the money's been really good."

"Seriously, you're doing me a solid here, Jared. I want to pay half the rent and utilities. Just take the money."

"Nope, sorry," he said, leaning back against the wall, arms crossed. "There's one way you can pay me back, though. That is, if you're really interested."

Athena's heart skipped a beat. Was he actually suggesting...?

"Cook for me, and we'll call it even. Seriously, I've been living off takeout since my last breakup. You can cook, right? I can't remember if that was one of your many talents."

Athena nodded slowly, folding the envelope in half, and sticking it in her back pocket. She'd still give the money to the landlord when they added her name to the lease, but she was willing to let the issue go for the time being. She didn't have it in her to argue anymore. "I'm actually a really good cook these days. Let me take a look at the kitchen, and I'll make us some lunch."

Jared smiled. "Great, let's see what I've got in the fridge."

It turned out that he had a lot in the fridge. Athena raised an eyebrow at him over the fresh produce he had stocked up on.

"I forgot what girls eat," he laughed. "I even bought some tofu and vegan cheese because I couldn't remember if you eat meat and dairy."

"I eat everything," Athena said. "But thanks. It was thoughtful of you to get this extra stuff. So, what are you in the mood for? Comfort food? A tofu and vegan cheese omelet?"

"Maybe skip that," Jared said, grimacing. "How about some soup and grilled cheese? Regular grilled cheese."

"I can do that."

They worked together, Athena coaching him on how to prep vegetables for a homemade tomato soup while she sliced the cheese for the sandwiches. Jared grabbed a beer and offered her one, which she took without a second thought until the bottle was pressed to her lips.

Nathan would've never allowed her to have a beer with lunch. But then, Nathan wouldn't have approved of her standing in Jared's kitchen to begin with, much less moving into his spare bedroom.

"You okay?" Jared asked.

"What? Yeah, of course. I was just—"

A loud knock at the door cut Athena off. She jumped, startled at the unexpected banging.

"Are you expecting someone?" Jared asked.

Athena shook her head. She hadn't told anyone where she was going. She'd left the apartment key in the drop box, along with a note for her old landlord explaining that she had moved out. She hadn't even written down her forwarding address.

Jared moved to the door and looked through the lens. "Just some random dude. Think I should answer it? He's huge, but maybe he needs help."

"It's probably Otto," she sighed. "He's... a guy

who follows me around sometimes."

Jared stared at her.

"Not all the time," she rushed to explain. "Just... occasionally."

Well, that was a flat-out lie.

"Um, okay. If you know him, I'll let you answer it, but don't open the door if it isn't him." Jared stepped back, giving her space to look.

"Open up, Athena." Before she could even reach the door, Donovan's voice came through loud and clear. Athena groaned. Of course, Donovan had found out about her move. Otto or Alverez must have said something to him. Snitching bastards.

"So, you know this guy? Why does he sound so pissed off?" Jared whispered, leaning in next to her. They were so close she could smell the beer on his breath.

"He's always pissed off," she whispered back. "Listen, I think this would be a lot better if you weren't around for it. Do you mind going to the bedroom or something until I can get him to leave?"

Jared looked from her to the door. "Is he an ex-boyfriend or something, Athena? Do we need to call the police?"

Yes. "No," she said, shaking her head. "He's harmless, I promise. He's just... difficult. Just give us a few minutes, and I'll come get you when he's gone."

She intentionally omitted the part where calling

the cops probably wouldn't be much help, anyway. Guys like Donovan don't exactly answer to the local police.

"I'm losing my patience, Athena. Open the fucking door." Donovan's words were a little more muffled, probably because he was irritated. She didn't have much time if she was going to defuse the situation without involving Jared.

She shot her new roommate an apologetic look, and he shrugged before walking to his room. Athena waited until she heard the click of his door shutting before she unlocked the deadbolt to face Donovan.

She shimmied outside, closing the door firmly behind her to prevent him from coming inside. It felt like a good plan until she realized it forced her to stand flush against Donovan O'Malley's overbearing frame. Her breasts hit low on his chest, causing them to pucker through her thin shirt.

"You aren't going to invite me in?" Donovan rumbled next to her ear. Athena allowed her eyelids to flutter, intoxicated by the feel of his hard body against hers. Donovan must have felt it, too; Athena could hear the slight catch of his breath as his chest moved against hers.

"What are you doing here, Donovan?"

"I could ask you the same thing, sweetheart. Have you forgotten my instructions so easily?" His voice was strained, but Athena was too focused on her own reaction to him calling her sweetheart.

It took her a second to gather her resolve, but when she did, Athena pushed away from him. She circled back to him, this time with his back to the door.

"I didn't forget. I just didn't care. I wanted to move, so I did. That's what free women do, Donovan."

"Maybe," he agreed. "But you're not a free woman, Athena." His eyes flickered to her neck, where she still wore her collar. Nathan's collar, rather. The scrap of leather and metal lock told every dominant she came across that she was owned property.

"Semantics," she spat.

"Hardly," he countered, taking a step closer, a predator's grin on his face. "That collar and every pretty thought in your head that's been begging me to fuck you says exactly who you belong to. The problem is the collar's giving mixed signals. Not as much as you do, of course, but it's about time that collar was switched out for one of mine. You're not owned by two men, love."

Athena flashed her eyes at him. "Over my dead body."

"Your body knows who you belong to, even if your head and that piece of leather around your neck are stuck in the past."

Athena fumbled, struggling to tell him to fuck off.

She kept backing up until she was flush against the upper- floor railing. Donovan's hands came down on either side of her on the rail, their bodies almost touching but not quite.

"Who's the fucker in the apartment, Athena? Am I going to need to put a bullet in his head?"

"What? Jesus Christ, Donovan. No," she said, horrified. "Are you serious? He's a friend. And my new roommate."

He raised a quizzical brow. "A friend, huh? A person that Nathan approved of?"

"Um... well, not exactly."

"Of course not. At least you're honest about one thing," he said, pushing himself off the railing. "Are you fucking him?"

"No!"

Donovan searched her face. "Make that two things you're honest about, then."

Athena flexed her hand, wanting nothing more than to flip him off but also remembering clearly what happened the last time she gave him the bird. She didn't need a repeat of their bathroom scene at the front door of her new apartment.

"I think you'll agree that I've been patient with you, Athena. I've given you space to mourn. I've allowed you to keep the money from the trust fund without any interference from me. I haven't given you a single rule or restriction outside of what should have been obvious. And yet, you've managed to thwart the extremely low bar I've set. What is it that you want, exactly?"

Athena opened her mouth to answer, but Donovan's hand flew to her lips, silencing her.

"Before you answer, keep in mind that I'm only asking this once, and if you aren't truthful with me, I won't hold back on giving you a well-deserved punishment.

"Don't even think about telling me that you want to be left alone, Athena. You probably still haven't realized this, but I know you too well to believe bullshit like that. You want this. You miss Nathan. You miss being owned, as much as I want to own you. So, I'll ask you now: what do you want?"

When Donovan removed his hand, Athena licked her lips, which seemed to pull his attention to them and lit a fire in his eyes. Her heart pounded in her chest, and heat pooled between her legs as she stood under his gaze.

"I want to be left alone."

Donovan's features tightened, and he smiled, slowly revealing a set of gleaming white teeth. "Wrong answer, baby."

With one firm motion, Donovan picked her up and slung her over his back. He let himself into the apartment and took her straight down the hallway. "I'm guessing your room is the one that fucker isn't hiding in, right?" he grumbled.

"Fucking asshole!" Athena screamed, balling her

fists and pummeling him on the back. She tried to kick her legs and throw him off balance, but the man was built like a mountain. There was literally nothing she could do other than go limp like a rag doll and wait for him to let her go.

Donovan walked through her open door and tossed her unceremoniously onto the floor. A turn of the lock should have been enough to prevent Jared from trying to rescue her, but Donovan swung the empty dresser in front of the door for good measure before turning back to Athena.

"No bed?" The question came first before a shadow passed over his face. "If you were thinking of sharing a bed with that vanilla son-of-a—"

"I'm going to sleep on the couch until my new one's delivered," Athena said, exasperated.

Donovan grunted his understanding but clearly wasn't giving his approval. He sat in the chair next to the window, looking at her with expectation in his eyes.

"Well, let's get on with it."

"Get on with what?" Athena asked. "I think you should go. You've probably scared the living shit out of my roommate, and I don't need him second-guessing if I should be allowed to live here."

Donovan chuckled, the sound low and dangerous. "No, I don't think so. You want to be punished, and I'm going to give you what you need. Now, move closer and spread those cheeks across my lap."

Athena gasped, and her eyes widened in shock. Maybe she shouldn't be that surprised. Nathan had given her his fair share of spankings, but this was entirely different. At least, she thought it was different.

"That's not happening," she said.

He sighed. "Athena, I'm trying to give you a little bit of dignity here. You can come over on your own, or I'll put you across my lap, but you'll only get this option the first time, and it's almost run out. Decide."

Athena resisted as the tears began to form in her eyes. She wanted to scream at Donovan, call him every name in the book, and hit him with every ounce of strength she had, but she stayed rooted in place. Athena had known this was a possibility since the moment he arrived, but now that it was actually happening, her mind was telling her body to do anything but comply.

"Donovan, please," Athena choked out, desperation clinging to every syllable. "This isn't what I want... I don't need this."

He studied her carefully from his chair and shook his head. "I get it," he said. "But you're asking for something that deep down you don't truly want." He pointed towards the ground between his feet. "Now move."

Athena's heart raced faster, and her breathing

became labored as she considered his words. She wanted to scream at him to go away, to leave her alone. But a part of her also wanted this – the punishment, the release that came with it. It was like an addiction, something she couldn't walk away from, and so she reluctantly moved closer and gingerly laid herself across his lap.

Donovan's hand grasped her waist firmly as she braced for the inevitable pain. He shifted in the chair, stroking her ass through the shorts she had on, toying with the edges as if debating whether he should pull them down.

Nathan would've pulled them down.

Donovan did not.

He began to spank her, not too hard at first, but with enough force that she knew he was serious. With each swat, Athena also felt a sense of relief that made her stomach flip-flop.

It was like a cleansing, her worries and fears washing away with every new stinging sensation. She felt herself tense up and then relaxed into the spanking.

She needed more.

"Harder," she said, her voice muffled under her loose curls. "Fucking harder!"

Donovan complied, but not before shoving her shorts down to her ankles. Moments ago, she would have tried to claw his eyes out for doing that, but now she was beyond caring. She just wanted more pain.

With his hand slapping her bare ass, she finally received the sting she was missing. She still needed more, though. She needed to feel the pain overwhelming her, oozing out of her pores.

"Cut me," she pleaded. "I need to bleed."

"No," he said, pulling her upright, pushing her hair from her eyes.

They refused to focus despite her blinking. She was high, too high to come down so quickly.

"Donovan, please. Hurt me."

"Shhhhh. I will, but my knife isn't sterile. Don't worry, baby. I've got you. Hold still."

Donovan pushed her shirt up over her head, removing it along with her sports bra. He hummed with appreciation, drinking in the sight, but it wasn't enough. Athena needed to feel. She needed to not feel. She needed more.

He grabbed her face, his thumb brushing away the tears that had escaped. "It's okay," he said. "You're safe with me. I'm going to give you what you need."

"Please," she whispered.

Donovan tilted her head to the side and latched onto the sweet skin above her breast, breaking the skin with his teeth and sucking.

Athena let out a low moan, leaning into the feeling of him taking from her.

Donovan unlatched only to shift and bite down

again, hard, on the other side of her body.

Athena groaned and moved against him. She was straddling Donovan, but in her mind, she was floating.

The pain, the blood, was intoxicating. She was out of words. There were no more words for him. Still, she needed more to feed the high.

She rolled her hips, hoping that he would take the hint. Then, without warning, Donovan pulled away and slapped her across the face. She breathed deeply, loving how the impact grounded her.

"Again," she said, her voice not entirely her own. Donovan leaned in; his face buried in her hair. "No." Athena would have protested if she were able to, but there was hardly anything she could do besides slump against him and relish in the feeling of the bruise blossoming on her skin. This was what she needed. Impact play. Release. And with Donovan's arms around her, gently running his fingers through her hair, she realized that maybe she could have it all. She could have this without any of the strings attached. She just needed to find someone else to give it to her.

*Chapter 13*

*Now*

"That doesn't explain why you're still here," Athena grumbled, trying to fasten her bra without giving Donovan a show. It wasn't easy to do with him watching her so carefully from his seat on the chair. She wished there was an en suite bathroom or walk-in closet to hide from his prying eyes. "Can you at least look away or something? Maybe pretend that you have some manners?"

He snorted. "You're pretty modest for someone wearing my bite marks all over their body. And you definitely didn't care if I saw your tits when you were begging me to—."

"Stop." Athena's cheeks flamed. She pulled her shirt over her head and pushed the dresser away from the door, using her full body weight to make it budge. "It's time for you to go."

Donovan nodded, standing. "I'll send Alvarez

back for your things."

She sighed, breathing deeply through her nose. "No, Donovan. It's time for you to go. It's time for me to finish unpacking."

"You think you're still staying here? After all that, you need more convincing that I own you, huh?" Athena wanted to throttle both of them: him for not taking a hint and herself for being so damn weak. If only pain wasn't so addicting. If only he didn't do it so well. Her body was still humming happily long after her sense of modesty was back in place.

"Sharing a little bit of kink is hardly the same as asking you to own me," she argued.

He shrugged. "Guess it's a good thing you don't have to ask me to do that, then. It's already a done deal."

Athena rolled her eyes, not sure how to argue with that, especially after he had made the point of her wearing Nathan's collar. "Just leave. Please."

Donovan reached for her cheek, the same one he slapped when she begged for more from him. "Do you have any makeup? That's going to bruise."

"Um... yeah, I guess. I have some concealer in one of my bags."

"Good. You put that on, and I'll get you an icepack from the kitchen."

She opened her mouth to protest, but he was already halfway out the door. Defeated, she started rummaging through her cosmetics bag. The sooner this was done, the sooner he would leave. *Besides, a sudden black eye would be really hard to explain to Jared.*

As soon as that thought crossed her mind, a crash came from the kitchen, followed by an impressive string of expletives. Athena abandoned the makeup on the bed and rushed out to find Jared swearing and clutching his side, the freezer still wide open. Donovan stood nearby, icepack in hand and a look of disgust on his face.

"What happened?" she asked, hurrying over to Jared and helping him up gently. "Jesus. Are you okay?"

"Fine, thanks," Donovan answered dryly. Athena shot daggers at him and turned her attention back to Jared.

He winced as he straightened, looking between Athena and Donovan. "I heard a crash, so I came to investigate. Ended up getting a broken rib for my trouble." He gave Donovan a look that could have melted steel before his gaze softened back on Athena. "What's going on here? Who is this guy?"

"He's... well...." She frowned, and Donovan raised an eyebrow, waiting for her to answer. "He's a friend. Or, just someone I know, I guess. What happened?"

"This asshole here thought he was going to sneak up behind me, and it didn't work out well for him," Donovan said, closing the freezer. "A real fuck-around- and-find-out type of thing."

"Fuck you, man!" Jared hissed. "This is my fucking apartment!"

"Ah. Well, there you have it, Athena. Sounds like this guy wants his space, now if you'll--"

" Holy shit!" Jared gaped, seeing her for the first time. "What happened to your face, Athena? Did he do that?"

"No!"

"Yes."

Athena glared at Donovan, who seemed more than happy to stir the pot and rile Jared up. But, of course, he was. All he needed was for Jared to kick her out, and she'd be back to living at Nathan's apartment.

"It was an accident. I'm fine, but that's why Donovan was getting the ice pack."

"An accident? How? Did you run into his fist?" Jared shook his head. "No, absolutely not. I'm sorry, Athena, but he needs to leave."

"It's fine. I wasn't planning on staying long anyway," Donovan said. He crossed the kitchen, moving around Jared to gently press the ice pack to Athena's cheek. He reached up and brushed the other side of her face with the pad of his thumb, his eyes never leaving hers.

Athena gasped at the sudden and unexpected tenderness of his touch. His cold fingers lingered on her skin, and he looked down at her with an emotion she couldn't quite place. He seemed softer somehow. The moment was broken when Jared coughed awkwardly in the background, reminding Athena where they were. She stepped away from him, breaking their contact.

"You think you're staying, then?"

"Yep," she rasped. Why did she sound like she had swallowed a bucket of nails? "See you around, Donovan."

His eyes flashed, but only for a moment. Donovan went to leave, pausing only as he reached the door. "Every decision has a consequence, Athena."

And then he was gone.

Athena turned to Jared, knowing she might have to plead her case to not be evicted. "Here. Let me help you sit down. Do you really think anything is broken?"

Jared winced, sitting and accepting the ice pack she offered. "I don't know. Probably not. Seriously, Athena, is he going to be coming back? Are you guys... dating?"

"No. We definitely aren't dating." She paused, struggling to find the right words. "He was a friend of Nathan's. You know, my boyfriend who died."

"Your boyfriend?" Jared frowned. "I thought you said he was your husband."

Fuck. That white lie had finally caught up with her. She had forgotten she had told him that. "We weren't legally married, but he was my husband in all the ways that counted," she said. "Not that it matters. Donovan is just.... he's really protective."

"He's so protective that he leaves bruises on your face?" Jared said. When she tried to argue, he raised his hand to stop her. "He admitted to doing it, Athena. I'm not an idiot."

"I mean... okay, he did cause the bruise, but it was consensual. You know... like, rough, but not forced?"

Jared's jaw went slack. "Wait. Like... kinky shit? That's what you're into?"

She groaned, wanting to die. "Can we not go into that right now? Let's focus on whether I need to call someone to take us to the hospital."

Her joke fell flat, as the hospital might be a real concern.

"I'm fine, but seriously, Athena. I can't have him back at the apartment, okay? Your love life is your own business, but don't bring him here. I'll call the cops next time. I mean it."

Athena nodded. "Yeah, of course. That's totally fair."

She hugged Jared, careful not to press against his ribs. Thank god Donovan hadn't screwed this up for her. She was taking control of her life, one step at a time. But that didn't mean she couldn't have fun doing the other stuff.

Her smile spread, causing the bruise on her cheek to prickle, and the wheels started turning in her head. No, she was going to enjoy all the wonderful parts of being an unowned sub. That's how she'd get Donovan to know she really meant she was unowned. He might be able to ignore her job and living with Jared, but knowing she was playing with other men would change his mind about her fast. She could practically guarantee it.

---

Donovan flexed his hand against the leather on his steering wheel. Of course, Athena was probably celebrating what she took as a victory. Still, it was his marks that she wore on her body. His teeth that had broken the skin on her breasts and shoulders. The thought made him smile.

Regardless, there was no way in hell he was letting her blatant disobedience go. He had given her plenty of chances, too many chances, really, to fix her attitude and go back to her apartment. It had taken every ounce of self-control not to hoist her over his shoulder and throw her into the passenger seat of his car. He probably would have, too, if she wasn't rooming with that boy. Not that it mattered too much. She wouldn't be staying there for long.

He dialed Alvarez. "Keep eyes on her," he said as soon as he picked up. "She might be leaving with the roommate to get his ribs looked at. The fucker tried to sneak up on me, and I knocked the wind out of him."

Alvarez chuckled. "I could've told him that was a

bad idea. At least, it'll only happen once, huh?"

"Once is probably his limit. I might have put the fear of god into him for a moment, but I still don't like Athena being there. She won't be able to afford her end of the rent soon, though. I'm on my way to that fucking convenience store to put an end to that right now."

"Hmmm. Well, that might work, or it might not, boss."

"What do you mean?" Donovan growled. He didn't have the patience for word games. "Spit it out, Alvarez." "Well, I was listening in through the wire I planted in her luggage, and he isn't taking rent money from her. He's letting her stay there for free."

Donovan cursed. "What are you saying?" There was a pause on the other line. "I'm saying he isn't charging her rent. That's it. It's all I heard before they moved to another room and the mic cut out."

Donovan cursed again under his breath. If that fucker wasn't accepting money from Athena, he damn sure was expecting to receive something else in return. Young guys like him didn't do things for pretty girls without expecting payment of some kind.

The idea of them together in bed was enough to make Donovan see red. Athena was his. His property. His sub. He had to wonder how naive Athena actually was. If she thought for two seconds that her friend wasn't charging her rent to be kind, she wasn't as clever as he gave her credit for.

No. She had to be smarter than that, right?

At least they weren't already fucking. Athena had been adamant that they weren't sleeping together, and so far, Donovan was convinced that his girl wasn't a liar. She might be naive as hell, but he'd take that over hearing lies any day. She wore the truth plain as day on her face, so he doubted her honesty would ever be an issue for them.

"The wire was a smart idea" he said. "I'm going to need more surveillance inside the apartment, too."

Alvarez grunted. "Yes, sir. I figured as much. I'm just waiting for them to leave, and I'll pop in to plant some audio and visual in each room."

"Good. Send the feed directly to my account. I want access 24/7." Donovan forced himself to remove the tension in his shoulders. This was still okay. He would work it out. One day, he would tease Athena about the fight she put up. With enough time, all of this would seem like a distant nightmare.

"Yes, sir. Will do."

Donovan cut off the call and pulled out of the alley, tires squealing. He kept his foot pressed to the gas until he reached the convenience store where Athena worked. His jaw was clenched so tightly he thought his teeth might break. He parked, took a settling breath, and rotated his shoulders, urging himself to calm down. He was used to high-pressure situations, things that would drive a typical person to an early grave. But somehow, anything related to Athena kept him balancing on an emotional tight wire.

He sauntered into the store, projected a calm exterior that effectively hid the rage he felt just below the surface. He startled a worker stocking shelves in back, causing a bunch of soda to fall from a display. Donovan's eyes scanned the room until he found the schedule tacked to the wall behind the counter. He reached over and ripped it down.

Athena's name was clearly listed as working that night, as well as a few other days that week. Simon, the worker from yesterday evening, shrank away from him, his wide eyes darting between Donovan and the alarm hidden beneath the register. Did he think he was being subtle?

"Relax," Donovan said evenly. "Tell your manager that Athena Garcia doesn't work here anymore. Got it?"

Simon nodded, too terrified to speak. For someone who worked on the rough side of town, Simon looked ready to shit himself over a simple ripped page. Though, to be fair, Donovan had almost a foot of height on him, and was obviously someone who packed a weapon or two at all times.

Donovan gave a sharp nod of his own and strode out of the store, glad to have put an end to that particular problem.

Satisfaction allowed him to calm down for real, this time. He grinned imagining what Athena's reaction would be when she tried to show up for work that night. Donovan would need to clear his schedule. He had to see the look on her face when she realized that he had won that battle, too.

He called Mel and pushed the last meeting of the day until tomorrow. She was less than thrilled when she learned what he was missing work to do, but he didn't need her approval. For now, Donovan would go home, relax, watch some surveillance of Athena's apartment, and then tonight he'd come back to see everything unravel for her.

He was setting the trap, bit by bit. Soon, Athena would be caught in his web, and she'd have no choice but to surrender. Until then, he'd savor the feel of her skin under his teeth and the sound of her begging for more. One day, he'd experience that whenever he wanted. The thought alone made it all worth it.

———

Athena took a cab to work. There was too much ice, and she was too exhausted from what happened with Donovan to walk. She paid the driver and gladly stepped into the warmth of the convenience store.

It was empty, except for Simon standing behind

the counter. That wasn't so strange given the time of night, but she instantly knew something was up when he was surprised to see her. Simon quickly schooled his expression into one of indifference as he continued to count the money laid out in the drawer in front of him.

She waited for him to finish. Finally, he shoved the cash back inside and met her eyes. "Cynthia's working tonight," he said.

Athena scoffed. "Sure, she is, Simon. Cynthia would rather have us close than come in for the night shift. Just get me my drawer so you can get out of here."

"No, I'm serious, Athena. There was some issue with the owner, and Cynthia's covering tonight. They couldn't find coverage in time."

Simon might have continued talking, but Athena wasn't listening. Instead, her eyes were glued to the schedule posted behind the counter.

"Why am I off tonight?" she asked, leaning over the glass to get a better look. She always worked a handful of weeknights. Her heart sank as she realized her name had been taken out of the rotation entirely. "What the fuck, Simon?"

"Um, yeah...uh," he began hesitantly. "The thing is...you've been let go." He spoke quickly, looking away as if he was afraid of Athena's reaction. "Cynthia's coming in to cover your shift last minute. Sorry. It was cool working with you and everything."

Athena felt like she'd just been punched in the gut. She'd never been fired from anything in her life.

"Let go?" she asked, her voice barely above a whisper. "Why? What did I do wrong?"

"Nothing," he said, a little too quickly. "Um. I guess it was the owner's call."

He was lying, Athena was sure about that.

"It was Donovan, wasn't it?"

Simon swallowed hard. "If you mean the terrifying guy who stormed in here earlier? Yeah... that was it, to be perfectly honest. Listen, Athena, I don't know how you know him, but he seemed like he's got some real issues. Are you safe? I mean, if you need somewhere to stay, I can spot you for a hotel room."

No," she said firmly as she untied her apron and dumped it onto the counter. "I'll be alright. Thanks, anyway."

She gave Simon a small smile and headed outside to order an Uber home. As she stepped out into the parking lot, she saw Donovan's car. He must have pulled up as soon as she walked inside.

For a brief, terrible moment, she thought he was going to get out of the car and walk towards her. To do what, exactly? Gloat? Brag about how he had gotten her fired, just like he had stopped her from moving into a new place of her own?

Athena wanted to be mad. She wanted to scream

and curse Donovan O'Malley. She wanted to scratch that smug look right off his beautiful, stupid face and gouge out the eyes that drew her in against her will.

She wanted to, but Athena's only card now was to be totally unbothered. She needed him to lose his shit, to be pushed too far so he would surrender. Her losing control would make him the winner by default.

Athena pocketed her phone and began the walk back to Jared's apartment. Obviously, losing the job was her punishment for not leaving with Donovan. Every choice had a price, he'd said.

The cold was enough to freeze her to the bone, but it barely even registered for Athena. She had other things on her mind, like how she was going to make Donovan O'Malley eat his own words.

*Chapter 14*

*Now*

"Let me get this straight," Jared said, trying and failing to suppress a grin. "Not only are you a super kinky freak, but you're going to a BDSM club to actively seek out a partner to do that shit with? Just tell me what to do and I can help you out here, in-house. Free of charge."

Athena laughed, shaking her head. "Needing to coach someone through it kind of defeats the purpose for me. Besides, I know for a fact that it would put you even higher up on Donovan's shit list. It's a better idea if you just sit this one out."

Jared crooked an eyebrow and folded his arms. "Let me get this straight. You're doing this, knowing it will make him mad? Why?"

"Lots of reasons," she said, shrugging on her coat. "One, as much as he thinks I belong with him, I don't. Two, I'm fully capable of making my own decisions. And three, I guess I haven't been clear enough that I want him to leave me alone. Knowing that I was with someone else in *that way* could do the trick." She grimaced, thinking about how much it sucked being fired from the convenience store. She needed that job to begin rebuilding her independence. Whatever Donovan had done to get her taken off the schedule was enough to give Athena the last push she needed. No more waiting around and playing games with him.

"Okay. Just, you know... be careful." Jared glanced out the window, frowning. "Is your best friend out there going with you?"

Athena shrugged. The answer to that probably depended on which guy was on duty at the moment. "Maybe. I'll have to ask him."

She left the apartment, taking the stairs down to the parking lot in quick succession. Safeword opened at seven, and her nerves urged her to get there before it became too crowded.

The bodyguard that Donovan had sent was easy to pick out amongst the other cars in the lot. It was always the same newer model black sedan, though the two men behind the wheel changed on a rotation. At the moment, it was Mendez. Perfect. He was the more laid back of them, at least. For some reason, Alverez seemed genuinely concerned over the things she did.

"Hey, Otto," she said, as he rolled down his

window for her. The look on his face was tired and suspicious. Fair enough; other than a few angry words, they didn't interact too much.

"Athena," he said evenly. "What can I do for you?"

"You don't have to do anything for me. I just wanted to let you know my plans for the evening. I'll be at a club called Safeword. Do you moonlight as a taxi service or should I get my own ride?"

"I don't get paid enough to deal with this shit," he grumbled. "Listen, whatever you're playing at, O'Malley isn't the guy to mess with. I don't know too much about this situation, and I don't want to, but you're playing a dangerous game here."

Athena nodded. "Okay. I'll just see you there, then?"

———

Safeword was packed, and the energy was off the charts. Athena took a sip of her drink, enjoying the bubbles in the complimentary champagne. She was lucky to make it past security at the door. If a nearby waitress hadn't remembered her from one of her visits with Nathan, she would still be standing outside with Mendez, where she assumed he was waiting with the car.

It had taken the weary bodyguard less than five seconds to change his tune about taking her to Safeword. A quick call to his boss, who must have given him the green light to take her, and she was riding in the leather encased front seat of whatever fancy car he drove.

"Be good," was Otto's only advice to her when she left. Athena had rolled her eyes at him, not wanting to listen to yet another man's opinion, but the tone of his voice had caused her some pause. She was playing with fire, but that was kind of the point.

"Hey, baby." A stranger with a deep voice slid onto the stool next to her. "I think you're just my type. Would you be interested in going out to the floor? Or maybe visiting one of the private rooms?"

Athena fiddled with her collection of bracelets that indicated her preferences for a partner. She was single, looking for something casual with a man, into pain, and submissive. It didn't leave much to the imagination, and putting that much information out there made her feel horribly exposed, despite still being fully clothed, even after removing her winter coat.

She was going to turn him down, but before she could work up an excuse, the man's attention shifted away from her. He frowned, then nodded his understanding to someone behind her. Athena turned, trying to see what he was looking at, but there was no one there.

"Eh, sorry, love. My mistake. Have a good evening." The man pushed away from the bar and disappeared into the growing crowd. Athena sighed in relief, grateful that she didn't have to turn him down. The goal was to find someone to play with, but the best way to do that would be to see a dominant in action and ask them to do a scene with her later that evening.

At least, that's the scenario she had dreamt up when she planned the night in her head.

Athena downed the rest of the drink and set it back on the bar. The sip of alcohol didn't do anything to help with her nerves, but her curiosity was getting the better of her. When Athena came to Safeword with Nathan, he hadn't let her have a real look around. She'd been glued to his side, focused mainly on him during those evenings. Now, she was finally free to explore the space at her leisure. She wanted to take it all in.

Around her, there were men and women both on the giving and receiving end of play and punishment. Most of the bottoms were scantily dressed, while some of the dominant partners wore full sets of clothes. A few of them were in dark suits, like the ones Nathan wore when he visited. Athena toyed with the hem of her plain shirt, wondering if she should show more skin, too. She had put on a particularly seductive set of underwear beneath her regular street clothes. The bralette dipped low on her ribs, covering part of her stomach with black lace. The panties were a boy short cut that showed off the curve of her hips in a way that would give her an extra dose of confidence.

Before she could second guess herself and completely chicken out, Athena walked back to the locker space where her coat was stored and began undressing. When her jeans and shirt were securely tucked away, she ran her fingers through her hair and slid her heels back on her feet. She walked back to the open floor, this time catching more than a few appreciative glances from men and women nearby. Athena leaned into each step, allowing her hips to sway as she walked.

On one side of her, a couple played with some wax candles. The sub purred with delight as the dominant partner covered her breasts with splashes of different neon colors. On the other side, two men were fucking the same woman, one on either end, while a third smacked her ass with a paddle. Athena stared at the scene, trying to force away the memory of the last group sex situation she had engaged in with Nathan. It had been so painful, too painful, but all the partners on the bed in front of her seemed to be enjoying themselves. Good for them.

She felt him before he said anything. A shiver went down her spine. Here we go, she thought.

"Anything in particular interest you, sweetheart?"

Athena sighed. "It's amazing how quickly you can get to a place when you're motivated. I'm guessing Mendez didn't have to leave a message with your secretary."

Donovan chuckled low at her side, his hand reaching around and skimming her lace-edged waist. "Melissa's my personal assistant, and she's really more of a friend than anything else. And I happened to be nearby."

"Hmmm." Athena turned to face him, feeling a rush of heat travel through her body. Donovan had opted for a formal look, his dark features meshing well with the crisp tailored shirt, his jacket already discarded. With the long sleeves rolled up to his elbows, he looked like a man ready to work. Or play, as the case may be.

Donovan's eyes swept over her body, the heat from them causing Athena to flush. "What did you have in mind for tonight, Athena?"

"Something that doesn't involve you," she said sweetly. Donovan's eyes flashed, but he gestured at her to take the lead. No doubt, he would be following close behind.

Athena set off towards the play spaces in the back of the large room, which were filled with more intimate scenes than the open floor provided. Each one was partitioned off on three sides, allowing observers a glimpse of play as they walked by. As she got closer, she could hear soft moans reach out to her from within each area, making her heart beat faster in anticipation. The first room held a woman tying up a man with some intricate rope bondage.

"Have you ever tried anything like that, Athena?"

"Of course," she said. "Have you?"

"As the one doing the tying, yes. As the one being tied, no."

"Maybe you should give it a try. Who knows? You might like it." She meant it as a tease, but Donovan seemed to consider the suggestion.

"I'd be willing to try pretty much anything with you. If you want to tie me up, just say the words."

"What? Are you serious?" She spun around to look at him, walking backwards as she continued down the crowded aisle.

"Sure, why not?" He shrugged like it was no big deal. "I trust you. If tying me up would do something for you, then let's give it a try. Of course, I'll give you lots of pointers to make sure we're safe as you learn how to do it properly."

Her shock must have been written on her face. Donovan laughed it off, shaking his head. "I take it Nathan wouldn't have been okay with a little topping from the bottom?"

Athena shook her head. No, he would've tanned her hide just for suggesting she might tie him up.

Donovan reached out, stopping her right before she tumbled into a couple watching another scene. "I'm different than your former master in a lot of ways, Athena. To me, play is play. It's meant for us to have fun together. Whether I'm on the top or the bottom, giving or receiving, it has nothing to do with who's in charge in our relationship. The two things, play and real life, are separate. Does that make sense?"

"I guess," she said, wetting her lips nervously . Donovan's gaze heated as he took in the sight of her tongue peeking out. Her stomach flipped over and the throbbing between her legs returned. Getting turned on by Donovan wasn't part of the plan. She was here for her own pleasure. She needed to focus on something else, anything else, and direct her arousal towards that. She shook off his hand and held up her collection of bracelets.

"Since I'm sure you've been here before, you probably noticed that I'm here for casual play with another partner."

Donovan's jaw ticked and he swallowed hard. "It's been handled."

"What the fuck does that mean?" Athena asked wearily. She was getting tired of hearing that phrase.

He shrugged. "What do you think it means, Athena?"

Her eyes flared with a new burst of anger. "I don't know what it means today, but it sounds similar to finding out that I've been fired from my job, Donovan. Would you know anything about that?"

"I told you decisions have consequences. You should have gone back to your apartment."

Donovan somehow scraped together the audacity

to look irritated with her. Athena gaped at him. How was he possibly turning that around and making it her fault? She wanted to argue her point, but she already knew he wasn't going to budge. Anything else she had to say would be wasted on deaf ears.

She sighed, frustrated and resigned, then turned to watch the scene near them that was coming to a close. The dominant was untying the sub, as she sipped a bottle of chilled water. When he was finished cleaning up the space and wiping down the bench, he wrapped her in a large blanket, whispered something in her ear, and she nodded with a smile before leaving on her own.

"Maybe I'm in the mood from some rope play tonight," Athena said, gesturing to the man who was coiling up his bondage tools. "Do you think he'd be interested in playing with me?"

"I suppose you could ask, if you're really interested in having him as a partner."

Well, that wasn't what Athena expected to hear, but now it felt like a challenge. She squared her shoulders and turned, leaving Donovan behind. The dominant with the ropes stood to greet her as she came closer.

"Hey, I'm new to playing here, and I saw your amazing rope scene. Would you be interested in doing some rope play with me?" The words spilled out of her quickly, causing the dominant to smile, until his eyes flickered back to see Donovan standing behind her.

"Sorry. I'm taking a break. Maybe I could take a raincheck for another time?"

Athena's confidence circled the drain, but she smiled and nodded. "Absolutely. Thanks, anyway."

Getting turned down with an audience sucked enough but getting turned down in front of Donovan was a thousand times worse. He was probably gloating, relishing that other dominant wasn't interested in her. It took everything in her to turn and face him.

"You're scaring them away," Athena hissed. "You need to give me some space. Go and play with someone else or something."

Donovan looked surprised. "You would be alright with me playing with someone else?"

"Of course," she said, frowning. "Why would that bother me?"

But for some reason, as much as she hated to admit it, jealousy started bubbling up at the thought of Donovan playing with another sub. What would it be like to watch him walk away with someone else? Would it feel like it had with Nathan? That last time... it had almost broken her to see him with the others.

"Shhhh. Come here," Donovan said, wrapping her in an unexpected hug. If her head was in the right place, she would have pushed him away, but instead, she wrapped her arms around his waist and buried her face in his shirt, breathing in the fresh scent of his laundry.

"I hate you," she whispered.

"I know. At least, I know you do for now," he said. "We'll work on that, but it's going to take time. The first step is me getting past that barrier you have built up around yourself."

Donovan pulled away a little bit, tilting her head up so they were looking at each other. "You had to be tough living in that house with him. With all of them. That's where we're going to start."

Athena let out a shaky breath and let him lead her through the crowd and into one of the private rooms in the back. She had visited a similar room with Nathan during all their visits. He loved to play with her at the club but hated the idea of other people watching her bleed and whimper and cum, so the private rooms were the only place she ever experienced anything fun.

Donovan brought her to the sheet-covered padded bench that was pushed against the wall. She allowed him to gather her in his arms and relaxed as he ran his fingers through her hair, massaging her scalp. The screams from the play floor sounded far away, almost like they were in a different reality.

In the private room, it was like they were in a world all alone.

"Tell me about it, Athena. I want to understand

everything about you. Why do you love him so much? Why is there so much pain?"

Athena let out a shaky breath. She hadn't gotten into anything deep with her therapist other than trying to solve practical issues like learning how to clothe and feed herself after Nathan's death. She didn't want to talk about the jealousy and the pain or any of the negative stuff that she had to live with when Nathan was alive. It felt pointless to rehash all of it. He was gone, after all. If the good stuff was over, the bad stuff was, too.

"You'll try to use anything I say against him. You'll just say he was horrible because of this or that, and I don't want to hear it, Donovan. Nathan was a good master. He was a good partner. No one's perfect."

Donovan frowned. "I'm not looking to use any information against you, Athena. I think you're avoiding being with anyone new, including me, because you don't want to hurt like you did before. I already know so many things about you. You're loyal, beautiful, and intoxicating... but I don't know everything, and I think I could help you if you're able to open up a little. If nothing else, it might feel good to talk about it."

Athena chewed on her lip, debating what to do. Finally, she spoke.

Chapter 15

*Then*

Athena dropped her bags down on the kitchen counter, cringing when a loaf of bread smashed against the box of apples. Nathan was gonna be pissed if the bread was smooshed and deformed, but there was nothing she could do about it now. Maybe she could toss it out and order another one before he noticed.

Veronica always ordered grocery delivery for the house anyway. Athena usually just tacked on whatever she wanted to Nathan's wife's list, but she had some serious cabin fever after quitting her job at the coffee shop. Taking a trip to the store had felt like an escape from the walls that were slowly closing in on her.

Athena opened the freezer to put away the frozen bags of vegetables when she heard a loud moan coming from down the hallway. She paused, wondering if Nathan had come home while she was out. It wasn't unheard of that he would take a long lunch, especially if he knew that she or Veronica would be around for some fun.

If he was home, that left Athena with some decisions to make. Either she could go and join them, or she could pretend that she hadn't heard anything and finish putting away the food. She could even slip back out and take a walk around the neighborhood if she wanted. There was no rule that she had to join them in bed every time they fucked each other. At least she didn't have to if Nathan didn't even know she was there.

Athena debated this for a few minutes as she finished putting away the perishable groceries. Was she horny for sex? Sure. Especially now that things in the room were heating up. Nathan's grunts and the sounds of the headboard smacking the wall were practically vibrating through the apartment.

Her pussy clenched, imagining how it would feel to have Nathan behind her, railing her with his thick cock. He might make her eat Veronica out as he did it, pushing Athena's face further into the other woman's pussy with each thrust. They had done it enough times that Athena could recall the exact taste and feel of his wife coming on her tongue. Or maybe Veronica wouldn't be in the mood for that. Maybe Nathan's wife would just want to watch them together, masturbating from across the room in her chair as they fucked.

Athena smiled. She could handle doing a round or two of that.

Decision made, she lifted her shirt over her head and began to undress. She paused as she reached for the button on her jeans when Veronica entered the kitchen from the living room.

"Oh, I didn't hear you come in," she said, glancing down the hallway, which led to the bedroom where the sounds of sex continued in full force. "Nathan came home... and, well..."

"Yeah, obviously he's home, Veronica. What the fuck's going on in there if you're out here?"

She hesitated. "Um... I'm not sure what conversations Nathan had with you about this, but you know that things are open on his end, obviously. And he... well, he found someone."

Athena's heart stopped beating. "What do you mean he found someone?"

"I mean that, like what happened with you, he found someone. Another woman that he wants to add to the family."

"What?" Athena shrieked. Her mind raced, trying to think back to every conversation they had. Had she missed it? Was there any indication that adding more women was a possibility? She couldn't think of anything specific that he had said. Did he say he wouldn't do that, though?

No. She had assumed he wouldn't want anyone

else. She just thought that she would be it. That between her and Veronica, they were enough for him.

It was the urgency in Veronica's voice that snapped her back to reality.

"I know you're different than me with all this, Athena. I get off on the idea of sharing him, and you... you kind of put up with it in exchange for having him." Veronica leaned against the counter. Her eyes were full of something— regret? Sympathy?

"If you get off on it, what are you doing out here?" Athena snapped. "You don't want him fucking anyone else any more than I do. You just won't admit it."

Veronica looked surprised. "Um... no, I'm out here because I was enjoying the sounds. You know... hearing everything and imagining what's going on. I don't have to be in there to get off on it."

Tears threatened her as the feeling of betrayal really sank in. Why hadn't he even told her about another woman? He obviously told Veronica. Why would he let her think that she was special to him?

Veronica crossed the kitchen, arms outstretched. "I'm sorry, Athena. I hate that you're feeling this way. Let's go out together. We'll come back after they're gone."

"No!" she shouted, pushing her away. "He can't get away with this. It's total bullshit."

"You're not thinking clearly, Athena. Look," Veronica said, pointing to her collar. "You said you'd do whatever he wants. You agreed to live this way. If he decides to take other women, well, then that's part of the deal."

"That's not... I mean, I didn't..." Athena sputtered. "I agreed to be with him when he had you. I didn't agree to an endless list of other women coming and going. I didn't agree to share him with anyone else!"

"He didn't say that you'd be the last," Veronica said gently.

"He didn't say that I wouldn't be, either!" Athena pushed past her, fumbling to get down the hall. "Athena, I'm telling you. You don't want to go in there." But it was too late; she was already at the bedroom door, the same bedroom she shared every night with Veronica and Nathan since moving into their home. As soon as she opened the door, Athena knew that she would never sleep in there again.

On the bed laid two beautiful women rubbing their pussies together, legs scissored. Nathan stood, fucking one of them in the face until he pulled out and moved to the other. He shoved his dick into her mouth, treating her throat like a cunt, just as he did with the other girl moments before.

Nathan reached down to where they were joined and shoved his fingers between them, teasing their folds as they humped his hand.

"Fuck," one of the women said breathlessly. "I'm

going to cum. Don't stop!"

"You'll come when I say you can come," Nathan grunted. He had said the same thing to Athena so many times. "Then again, I think I'd rather you come with my cock in your ass. Move."

The women pulled apart, and one grabbed the lube from the bedside table. Nathan turned, hand outstretched so he could apply some to his glistening dick. His eyes scanned the room, stopping at the open door when he saw Athena standing there.

Nathan swore, muttering under his breath. He stumbled away from the bed, leaving the two women to stare at each other and then at Athena.

"Fuck you, Nathan." Athena slammed the door shut and ran back to the kitchen, fumbling with the empty grocery bags to find her purse. Veronica was gone, probably hiding somewhere to avoid whatever the fallout from the situation was going to be.

*Fuck her, too,* Athena thought. That bitch could have at least warned her that there were two women in there.

"Athena, stop," Nathan huffed. He had paused to put on some shorts but had finally caught up with her. His words didn't mean anything to her; it was the look on his face that made Athena pause. The fucker had the nerve to be angry at her. Like she was the problem here.

"Go to hell, Nathan. I'm done," she said, purse in hand.

Nathan laughed, but there was no humor in his voice. "No, you're not. Sit down." He pulled out a stool for her.

"Fuck you." Athena left the kitchen and was only steps from the door when Nathan grabbed her around the middle and threw her over his shoulder. He carried her, legs and arms flailing, into the office and shut the door behind them. It was the same office that Veronica had led her into on her first visit, which had to be poetic in some way, seeing as this would be her last night with them. Athena pushed Nathan away, wishing like hell she never came back after that first night.

"Let me out," she said through clenched teeth. "I swear to god, Nathan. Let me out of here."

"Not going to happen," he said, arms crossed. His body was effectively blocking her from running out of the door, and there was no other exit. Athena began pacing, feeling very much like a caged animal.

"You have to let me out of here at some point, and the second you do, I'm calling the police."

"I'm sure once you've had a chance to calm down, you'll feel differently," he said. "Have a seat, and let's talk about this."

Athena thought about telling him to go to hell again or at least shouting for help. Maybe the neighbors would hear her and send the police to Nathan's door. But then she remembered about the soundproofing he had installed throughout the whole apartment, and her shoulders slumped in defeat. She was stuck in that room until Nathan decided to let her out.

"Much better," he said as she sat in the oversized leather armchair. "Alright, let's do this. What the hell were you thinking, barging in on us and causing a scene?"

Athena's jaw dropped open. "What? Are you fucking kidding me? You cheat on me and Veronica, and I'm the one who's at fault? What kind of twisted logic—"

"Wrong," he said, cutting her off. "Try again."

"What the fuck do you mean 'wrong?' Veronica might have known about this, but there is no way I consented to any of that. You never told me—"

"I didn't have to tell you anyway! I don't tell you everything, Athena. That's not how this works."

"The hell it doesn't," she argued. "We're in a relationship, right? A consensual relationship? That means you have to be honest with me. We have to negotiate things like adding other people."

Nathan sighed. "I think there's been a misunderstanding, Athena. My perspective is that when you agreed to be owned by me, you agreed to live under my direction in everything. Property doesn't have a say in what happens unless the owner says so. Do you understand?"

Athena stared at him. "That's the most abusive bullshit I've ever heard in my life. So, you're saying that when I agreed to be owned by you, I also agreed to be fine with anything you decide to do, even if it impacts me in awful ways?"

"Not exactly. I mean, as a human, you're going to have emotional reactions to things. Hopefully, they don't include outbursts and yelling, as that is a little juvenile. But I thought you understood that even if you feel negatively about something, it doesn't mean that I'm not going to do it. Does that make sense?"

"Yeah, it makes perfect sense," she said, standing again. "You want to do whatever you feel like, and Veronica and I just have to live with whatever decision you make. Whether it's adding other women to the family or fucking two strangers in our bed."

"I mean.... Yeah, kinda," he said sheepishly. "That's the lifestyle I want. It's what we agreed to."

"It's not what I agreed to," Athena said. "Now, move out of the way. I'm leaving."

Nathan rolled his eyes. "Stop being so dramatic. Sit down."

"I mean it, Nathan. I'm done. I don't want this. I don't want you anymore."

He moved across the room quickly until they were nearly touching. Nathan raised his hand, and for a second, Athena thought he was going to hit her. But instead, he gently touched the leather collar around her neck.

"Do you remember your vows from the collaring ceremony?"

Of course, she did, but she sure as fuck wasn't going to repeat them at that moment. Not that it mattered. Of course, Nathan remembered them, too.

"'I promise to obey you in all things, Nathan Garcia, for the rest of my life. I hereby consent to all decisions you make about me, my care, and our family,'" he recited, his eyes never leaving hers. "That's what you promised to me, Athena. You can be upset. That's fine. Scream and shout and get it out of your system if you need to. I'll sit in here working it out with you for as long as it takes. But none of that will change my mind about taking another submissive or fucking other women whenever I feel like it. You gave up making the rules here when you accepted my collar."

Athena laughed, then reeled back and slapped him across the face. "Fuck you, Nathan."

Nathan worked his jaw, her handprint an angry red outline on his skin. He slowly turned his eyes back to her. From the low light, they looked almost completely blacked out. This time, he was pissed. "No, Athena. Fuck you."

———

Veronica wasn't entirely correct about Nathan's plans for adding an additional submissive to the family. She was right about him wanting Denise; Nathan collared her a few weeks later.

Athena later found out that Denise was the one sucking his cock when she first opened the door, and she had a hard time not reliving that moment whenever their eyes met for days afterward. A bonus surprise for everyone was when Nathan collared the other women in that room, Teresa, a month later.

"How many of them are there going to be?" Athena asked one night, after the rest of the house was in bed.

"I'm satisfied with our family as it is, Athena," Nathan answered wearily. No doubt he thought she was going to yell or threaten him if he gave any other answer, but Athena's spirit and desire to argue about any of it was already broken.

She forced herself to feel nothing when he announced Teresa would be joining them permanently. If Veronica felt any negativity about the situation, she hid her reactions from everyone. Denise seemed to be excited, which made sense, as Athena learned later on that they were actually good friends who had known each other for years.

At first, Nathan tried to promote whole group sex between them, with him fucking one woman while the rest of them fingered and ate each other out. The last time Athena participated, Nathan was balls-deep in Teresa when he ordered Athena to get beneath her and lick where they were joined together.

"Taste her juice on my dick, slave girl. Make me cum, and drink everything that runs out of her pussy," he said. Athena had obliged, ducking below the panting woman who was receiving her master's cock. She sucked and licked his dick as it plunged into Teresa's hole, wiping tears from her face the whole time.

When he finally came, Athena swallowed as much as she could, choking when he transferred his dick to her mouth, and Teresa relaxed, nearly smothering her. The only person to recognize her panic was Veronica, who stepped in to stop the scene.

From that point on, she was excluded from the orgies and group sex. Nathan stopped taking her to Safeword, where she knew he picked up other women. Athena moved into one of the spare rooms, and Nathan visited her on his own for sex on a fairly consistent basis.

She hated herself for it, but Athena still enjoyed fucking him. She'd be lying if she tried to deny it. Nathan had a way of making her body sing and weep at the same time. That didn't mean that things were back to normal between them, though. She could still hear him getting off one room over, emptying himself into Denise or Teresa or one of the other nameless women he would bring home for casual sex. She could hear the bed banging against the wall, the women screaming his name as they climaxed. She imagined them cuddling afterwards when she wasn't even a footnote on his mind.

"Were you always fucking other women? Was I just not paying attention?" Athena hated asking these questions. They made her feel weak. Stupid.

Nathan never answered them anyway, but he didn't really have to. Yes, there had always been others. Yes, she really hadn't been paying any attention.

Athena forced herself to bottle it all up. She buried the feelings deep inside, telling herself it didn't matter. She'd remind herself of her promise to Nathan. She agreed to put up with it, and that he technically wasn't breaking any rules by stepping outside their relationship. She hardly had room to complain, right? The man was already married when she started screwing him, after all. And yet, none of that mattered when he came to visit her, shoving his cum covered dick in her face, his body smelling like another woman.

Athena would just close her eyes and lick it clean, swallowing every last drop.

*Chapter 16*

*Now*

When Athena was finally done, she was sure that Donovan was going to make fun of her, or worse, pity her. She was the dumb one, after all, agreeing to have someone else own her, then expecting him to never want another person sexually. Of course, a man with total control would use it to hunt down more pussy. But just thinking about it made Athena ache all over again.

Try as she might to deny it, she hated sharing. She hated every fucking thing about it.

The icy exterior, the persona of indifference, that she had created to protect herself after Nathan took the other subs was cracking. *She* was cracking, actually, and she probably wasn't going to be able to put herself back together the same way ever again.

"You probably think I'm a total idiot," she scoffed quietly. Donovan's hands had stilled in her hair a long time ago, and he was just holding her instead.

"Not at all. I think you've been through a lot with your former master. Some people are fine with sharing their partners. Like his first sub. She found an aspect of his polyamory that really worked for her, and it made sharing worth it. But other people can't handle it, and there's nothing wrong with that. Everyone's wired differently," he said, then paused, hesitating. "Is that why you don't want another relationship with a master, Athena? Do you think that all dominant men want multiple submissives?"

Athena looked at him like he was a total moron. "Of course, men want other women. We're sitting in a place that is basically dedicated to that purpose. How many of the male dominants out there do you think already own someone? Half of them? And yet, they're here to play with someone else. Or at least, they're here to look at them."

She added the last part quietly, almost as a whisper, and it made Donovan's heart sink. So, she had noticed Nathan gawking at all the other women in the club. He should have known that. Athena was too clever to miss something so obvious.

"If that's the case, then why not just settle down with some vanilla guy? Someone... like the guy you're staying with, maybe?" Donovan held his breath, waiting for her to answer. He didn't actually think anything was going on between them, but his own jealousy clouded his judgment and made it impossible for him to know for sure. Jared certainly seemed to be interested in Athena, even if his feelings only went one way.

She laughed, like the idea was totally ridiculous, and Donovan allowed himself to relax into a smile, too. "Jared was the only person I could turn to when you were a total ass about me moving, and I feel like I owe him big time, but I'm not attracted to him. I need... something different."

"I know," Donovan whispered. He started massaging her scalp again, this time grabbing and pulling her hair at the roots to make his point.

It felt so good that Athena was tempted to shift on his lap and straddle him, but she forced herself to stay put. "Since I can't do vanilla, and I can't do another full ownership relationship with all the emotions involved, I think I might want to do some no-strings-attached play. You know... the way you do."

Donovan flinched. "Someone told you about that, huh?"

He wanted to tell her that she was wrong, and he was different. Donovan wished that he could say he had always been staunchly monogamous, but that would be a lie. The best he could do was to explain that he didn't want anyone other than her anymore. He was about ready to say as much, but Athena spoke first.

"They didn't have to tell me," she whispered.

Athena reached up to cover part of Donovan's face, the same portion that was hidden with a mask the first time they met. His eyes widened above her hand. "You thought I didn't know. It took me a little while, but I'd remember those eyes anywhere. Why didn't you say something?" "I thought about it. But you were already owned... and I was a little ashamed that you affected me so much," Donovan confessed, still stunned that she had pieced together a small part of their history. Would he ever feel ready to share the full extent of his obsession with her? No, probably not. Athena scared easily.

She raised a skeptical brow. "Affected you so much that you fucked another woman in front of me? I have to admit, I haven't heard that one before."

"Well, it's true. I found someone who looked a little like you, at least from behind, and used her to get some relief."

Athena studied him, trying to weigh his words for honesty, but even without a face mask, Donovan never gave anything away.

It didn't matter, though. He had other submissives around according to Nathan's will. And while Nathan didn't tell Athena everything, what he did say to her was always the truth.

Donovan cleared his throat and looked away. "So, how's the hunt for casual kinky stuff going?"

Athena rolled her eyes and gestured to the empty

room around them. "As you can see, it's going very well. Dominant men are practically falling over themselves to play with me. The one I approached definitely didn't turn me down flat."

"Ha!" Donovan shook his head and grinned at her. "Well, if they weren't scared of approaching you, I'm sure you'd have a lot more assholes banging on the door, eager for their turn."

"Wait... what? Why would they be scared about approaching me?"

Athena glared at Donovan, watching as he tried to come up with an excuse for his slip of tongue. Eventually, he just sighed. "Fine. I made a few calls before you arrived, and management let all the male doms know you're off limits, despite what the bracelets say."

"For fuck's sake, Donovan! You've got to be the biggest cock-blocking, pain-in-the-ass, selfish—"

Donovan put his finger to her lips, silencing her rant. "One day, Athena, you'll realize there is nothing you can do to change the fact that you're mine. If you don't want a 'cock-blocking, pain-in-the-ass, selfish' type of situation, feel free to surrender at any time. Once I get my hands on you, you'll have more dick than you know what to do with. Until then, I'll enjoy showing you exactly how many options you have."

"Let me guess," she said. "I have exactly—"

"None," he finished. "Yep. No other options,

baby. But take your time really understanding what that means. I'm enjoying the chase in the meantime."

———

Donovan pulled up in front of Jared's apartment, scowling as he put the car in park. "Explain it to me one more time. How, exactly, did you convince me to bring you back here and not to the apartment you should be living in?"

Athena grinned. "It didn't help that you admitted to liking the chase. Or that I agreed to allow your goons to drive me everywhere in exchange for staying here. Plus, if you took me there, I'd just leave again."

He sighed, pinching the bridge of his nose. Athena was already an expert at pushing his buttons. "Keep up the sassy attitude and I'm putting you over my knee."

"Where?" she asked, glancing at the non-existent backseat.

"You know where. I've already done plenty to you up in that bedroom."

"Jared said you couldn't come back in the apartment," she warned him.

Donovan snorted. "It's a good thing I don't give a fuck what Jared thinks. Change the attitude, and you won't have to worry about it. Otherwise, you might have no choice but to go back to the dreaded apartment. Or..." he leaned forward, his voice dropping a few octaves, "you could come back to my house."

Athena's pulse sped up and she did her best not to squirm as his words worked their magic. "Got it," she said quickly.

"Mmmmm. I think I like obedient Athena. Maybe I'll even hear a 'yes, sir' one day soon."

The longing in his eyes basically undid her. She wanted him. Or, at least, her body did.

"Yes, sir," she whispered, testing the words to see what they would do.

"Fuck," Donovan growled, grabbing the back of her head, and pulling her into his lap. His lips captured hers, and she instantly felt his tongue running along the seam of her mouth, asking her to open for him. She did without any hesitation, and he angled his head, deepening the kiss with a satisfied moan.

Athena unintentionally squirmed in his lap, seeking to create friction against the hardness in his pants. "Goddamn it, Athena," Donovan gasped. He wrapped a thick arm around her waist and pulled her down firmly against him, so that he could set the pace of her movement.

She whimpered when he ground her ass against his lap, his entire length hard as steel. She wanted more; no, she needed more.

"Please." She broke the kiss long enough to beg,

but all Donovan did was lean in, their foreheads touching.

"I'm not giving you more until you yield, Athena. You think that you want something casual, no-strings- attached, but that's the last thing you need. Especially with me. We're it, baby. You and me. Say the words, and I'll take you to my home, fuck you in my bed, and keep you there as my prisoner for the rest of your life."

She gulped for air, her brain finally clearing enough to form words. "Why does it matter what I think or say? You think you own me... so go ahead and think that. I don't care."

She really didn't; at least not right then. She had a single thought racing through her mind, and it didn't have anything to do with arguing over hypothetical ownership situations.

Donovan chuckled. "Tempting, but no. I don't think that I own you, Athena. I know it. I know it with everything inside of me. But you need to know it, too, and you need to acknowledge it, or this will never work out."

Athena moaned, frustrated that he wasn't already getting her off. "Fine, you own me. Happy?"

His body stiffened beneath her, and he snatched her face, forcing her to look at him. The rage in his eyes sobered her sex-starved mind. Holy fuck, he was pissed.

"Don't you ever say anything like that again if you

don't mean it," Donovan snarled. "Now get the fuck out of my car so I don't do something I'll regret."

Athena pushed his hand away, angry, too, but mainly at herself. Ownership was a big deal to her. Saying those words totally disrespected her relationship with Nathan. Why had she done that? So that he'd fuck her? Holy hell. How desperate was she?

She opened the door hastily, eager to put some distance between them. She was ready to slam it shut behind her and make a run for Jared's apartment, but Donovan caught the door instead.

"It's alright, Athena," he said softly. "Don't beat yourself up over making a mistake, okay? You've had a really emotional day. We both have. I believe that you take your ownership promises seriously. If you didn't you wouldn't still be here. But next time you say something like that to me, I am taking it at face value, do you understand?"

Athena bit back a snarky remark. He was letting her off easy, and it was more than she deserved. So, instead of starting a new debate, she just nodded.

He studied her for a moment. "Tell you what. I'm going to make this really easy for you. I'll know when you're ready to acknowledge that you're mine when you move back into the apartment. You won't have to say a word, okay? You move back in, and then we'll move forward."

Donovan didn't wait for her to agree. He shut the

door and turned on the engine. She thought he was going to speed out of the parking lot, but after a few seconds she realized he was waiting for her to go into the apartment.

It was pointless for him to wait, as either Mendez or Alvarez was parked only a few spaces away, but she didn't care to point that out. She just wanted space to think. And some sleep. She hadn't realized it was so late.

"How was it?" Jared asked as soon as she walked inside. He was texting on the couch and didn't bother to look up.

"It was fine. You know, just a bunch of kinky people doing kinky stuff."

Jared shook his head, setting his phone face down on the coffee table. He hesitated a moment. "I saw you get out of that guy's car, though. Are you... um, still *friends*?"

Athena sighed. "It's complicated. Sorry, but I don't really feel like talking about it right now. I'm going to bed."

"Yeah, cool. How's the new mattress, by the way?"

"Fucking wonderful," she said, meaning every word. The mattress she purchased was delivered the day before, and it was infinitely better than sleeping on the couch. She trudged down the hall, eager to change into something comfy and get some rest.

She pulled out some pajama bottoms but hated

the idea of slipping into them without taking a shower. Even if she hadn't played at Safeword, just being around all the people and sweat made her feel like she needed to bathe.

Athena grumbled and padded to the hallway, over to the bathroom for a quick shower.

"Yeah, they're still together, I think. No.... yes. Fuck, I don't know. She just got back, but the guard dog is in the parking lot. Are you even sure you need her?"

Athena paused. Jared was on the phone. It sounded private, but his door was open, so she could hear everything. At least, she could hear everything he was saying. Athena stood there, frozen, not sure if she should go back in her room. Something told her to wait.

"She said it was complicated. No. Fuck if I know. Look, I need to go... yeah, I think I heard her in the hallway."

Fuck. Athena scurried back to her room, not daring to close the door behind her as he might hear it shut.

"Didn't you hear me? The fucker's car's downstairs. I can't do it tonight." There was a long pause. "Fine, Pete. Fine. We'll do it your way. But if it doesn't work, it's all on you."

*Pete?* Athena's stomach dropped. She remembered Pete. She remembered Pete a little too well, actually. She scrambled to open her dresser and made a show of searching for something, anything, so it wouldn't look like she was snooping in the hallway. Whatever he was talking about... it didn't sound good. She needed to get out of the apartment. She needed help.

"Athena?" Jared appeared in her doorway, blocking her only way out of the room. "Are you alright? I thought I heard you in the hallway."

"Yeah, no... I was thinking about taking a shower, but then I remembered that I left a few of my favorite products at the other apartment. I might just swing by and pick them up."

Jared looked skeptical. "It's literally two in the morning. Why don't you just wait and get whatever it is tomorrow?"

"Um... yeah, but I also need to pick up my last check. Simon said he'd leave it out for me, and I want to get it before the morning shift change." Lies. All lies, but Athena was grasping for straws. She needed to get out of there. If she could get to Mendez or Alvarez... whichever one was currently waiting outside and watching, she'd be safe.

A flood of relief filled her as she remembered that the other apartment had multiple forms of security— dual door codes and an alarm system. She could just stay there, and never come back to find out what Jared was talking about with Pete. Yeah, that'd work.

She tried to hide the adrenaline and relief

coursing through her now that she had a plan. Jared was studying her, probably trying to determine if she'd heard any of the phone call.

"I guess I can't stop you," he said slowly. "But you'll just go to the store and then to your apartment, right? Nowhere else?"

"Duh," she laughed hollowly. "I'm so tired. I'll pick everything up, come back to crash in this new bed. Then make us breakfast tomorrow morning. Deal?"

Jared loved her pancakes. In any normal circumstance, the promise of food would be enough to appease him. "Do you need a ride?"

Athena shook her head. "Nah, there's a guy waiting outside 24/7, remember? I'll just get him to take me."

"Yeah, about that... maybe have him take the night off, okay? It gives me the creeps that he parks out there all the time. Seriously. If you're going to stay here, I need him to leave."

Of course, he needed the car gone. It was getting in the way of his plans, whatever he was talking to Pete about on the phone. As much as she hated having the car following her around, it was probably the only thing that had kept her safe up until that point. The irony of it all was not lost on Athena.

"Sure, I'll let him know. Be back soon."

She inched around him and grabbed her shoes

and purse. As soon as the front door was shut behind her, she took off in a run. Once downstairs, she forced herself to walk calmly over to the black car. No doubt, Jared was watching her from above. His living room window had an unobstructed view of the parking lot.

Athena rapped on the widow, causing the man inside to stir. It was Mendez, with a groggy glare that said she had just woke him up. "Hey, I need a favor. Can you drive me over to the apartment? The other apartment, I mean."

"Does O'Malley know about this?"

"He... well, no, but—"

"Then we're staying here," he said curtly. "Go back upstairs and get some sleep."

"You don't understand," she said. "Donovan said—" "Fuck what Donovan said," he spat. "I'm sick and tired of having to play babysitter and chauffeur for you. Either call him and he'll tell me you need a ride, or just go back upstairs and leave me alone. Christ."

He rolled up the window, ignoring Athena's protests. She beat on the glass a few times for good measure, but she couldn't even see him behind the dark tint.

"Fucking asshole!" she yelled, kicking the tire. Athena glanced up at the apartment and saw Jared's outline in the window. He was watching, waiting for her to come back up.

If Jared knew that her own fucking bodyguard wasn't going to help her, he'd probably be able to do whatever it was that Pete wanted with her.

Time was running out for her to do something. She didn't have time to make a phone call and wait around in the parking lot for Donovan to come back. She'd call him once she was back at the Brownstone, safe behind a locked door and security system.

Athena turned and took off running to the main road. It wasn't that far, but she was out of shape now that she wasn't following Nathan's strict exercise regimen anymore.

She kept going long after the pain started in the side of her chest. That's what she got for not working out. Finally, she made it to the front door of the Brownstone apartment. She dug through her purse, only to remember that she had given the key back to the landlord.

She cursed, searching for her phone instead to call Donovan. Maybe he'd answer. Maybe he could get there in time.

It rang briefly and someone picked up. Athena took a breath, but before she could say anything, a heavy blow snapped against the back of her head, causing her to stumble forward and crash to the ground. Her phone went flying, and the contents of her purse spilled onto the sidewalk. The only thing keeping the purse on her body was the way she was carrying it: slung across her midsection and over the shoulder. She turned to confront the attacker, but before she could see who it was everything went dark.

*Chapter 17*

*Then*

Something was wrong; Donovan was sure of it. At first, it had been painful seeing Athena at Safeword with her master. The way she looked at him, respected him, acted so happy to serve him was too much to take. It made Donovan burn with jealousy that she shared the same air as that fucking cunt, but he forced himself to watch it all. Whatever he could learn from observing her would help him win Athena over in the end.

What he learned so far: Garcia didn't deserve to share the air she breathed. Every time she turned away, he was ogling a new, young submissive nearby. When she left for the restroom, his hands were all over any girl who allowed him to fondle her. He was smooth, Donovan had to give him that. The second Athena returned, his hands were back in his pockets and he was on his best behavior.

All of that would've been bearable, if it wasn't for the fact that at some point in the evening Garcia would, without fail, lead Athena back to one of the private rooms and do god knows what to her behind closed doors. It made Donovan see red every time, knowing that the fucker was touching what should belong only to him.

Sickeningly, Donovan couldn't even pretend his concern was about Garcia doing anything nonconsensual. No, it was clear that Athena went back to that room with him eagerly. Donovan's feelings were entirely selfish. She belonged to *him*.

It was further illogical because he used other women to take the edge off his own needs. Whenever they left for a private room, he found himself reaching for someone, anyone, that he could tie up or cut or slap or fuck and pretend that he was doing all those things to her.

Then, one day, Garcia stopped bringing Athena with him and started showing up with two other submissives. "Who are they?" he demanded from one of the attendants the first time they arrived with Garcia.

She glanced at the trio, then turned back to him. "That's Mr. Garcia with his newest submissives, sir. He collared them both fairly recently, I believe."

Donovan's heart pounded. He was torn between wanting to stay and watch what Garcia did with them and wanting to call Alvarez to make sure

Athena was alright. Was she upset about him taking on more women? Was she indifferent? Would Alvarez even be able to tell from outside the Garcia home?

Of course, Alvarez wouldn't be able to. But logic and Athena never went together for Donovan. He had been trailing her ever since she had showed up at the club with her asshole of a master. Completely disregarding Garcia's request to give them space, Donovan's obsession with Athena had only grown since that night, and he had Alvarez keeping tabs on her whenever he could spare him, just to help put his mind at ease in between her visits to Safeword.

A few minutes wouldn't make a difference to Athena, though. Not if Garcia had already had collaring ceremonies for both of the women hanging on his arms. Donovan settled into a chair on the outer rim of the play space, his eyes locked on the man he hated most in the world.

Donovan wasn't sure what he was expecting, but it wasn't for Garcia to choose a spot out in the open to play. He never played in public with Athena or his wife when they joined him at the club. The rumor was that he didn't like other people seeing his property in compromised positions. Clearly, that rule didn't apply to all his submissives, as Donovan watched the scene unfold.

The women took spots on the bench, asses exposed and up in the air. Garcia removed his jacket, taking his time to select one of the riding crops from his case. With all the other scenes going on, Donovan couldn't hear anything that was being said between him and the women. He was tempted to move closer, but he also didn't want to draw attention to himself.

It didn't matter, though. Garcia slapped the crop against the girls' backsides and raised his hand to land another shot, locking eyes with Donovan from across the room, a smile on his face.

Donovan burned inside. Garcia knew he was watching. No doubt, this entire display was for his benefit. Had he brought the other submissives just to rub it in Donovan's face?

Donovan tried his best to school his features and remain fully in his seat. He reached for the gin and tonic the waitress had placed on the side table for him and raised it to toast Garcia from across the room.

"Congratulations, motherfucker," he mumbled. "You've sealed your own fate."

His Athena wouldn't have to put up with that bullshit forever. He'd see to that soon enough.

Finally, after what felt like hours, Garcia cleaned the blood off his crop. He called for a first aid attendant to bandage up the superficial wounds he had left, then he handed the women each a water bottle. Donovan would have thought that he would have stayed with them, offering praise and comfort, but instead, Garcia left them with the attendant and started walking Donovan's way.

God, why did that man have to be the absolute worst human being?

"Mr. O'Malley," he said, reaching out his hand. "How have you been?"

Donovan forced himself to shake it. "I've been well, thanks. Congratulations on acquiring the two new submissives."

Nathan practically beamed looking back at them. "Thank you, I'm very pleased with them. Though, the transition hasn't been without issue if you know what I mean."

The look on Donovan's face said that he didn't, causing Nathan to grin.

"I forget how young you are. Despite agreeing to full ownership, some submissives have a difficult time sharing their master with others. I'm sure you'll encounter that situation at some point, too."

"Doubt it," Donovan grunted. "I'm guessing that's why you brought your new girls here and not one of the others tonight?"

"Aw, yes, I had forgotten your infatuation with Athena," Nathan said, though his tone betrayed him. He had never forgotten how taken Donovan was with the woman. He never would, either. "She's resting at home. The transition has been particularly rough on her."

Donovan trained his features to reflect a boredom

he didn't actually feel. "Maybe she just needs to feel special to you," he suggested.

"That's exactly the problem, though. A master shouldn't need to constantly reassure his women that they matter to him, right? Why not just go vanilla if you want to be whipped?" When Donovan didn't answer, Nathan posed another question. "How many subs do you own, O'Malley?"

"None," he answered. "I play with some women casually, but I've never had the desire to own any of them permanently."

"Interesting. Too bad Athena's already taken." Donovan grasped the glass so hard he was amazed it didn't break in his hands. "Is there something I can do for you, Garcia?"

"There is, actually. I came over here to discuss a business matter I'm involved with. Do you mind talking shop tonight?"

"I don't discuss my work in a public venue."

"Of course," Garcia agreed. "I meant, would you like to come to my home this evening and discuss it there?"

Donovan felt instantly torn over the idea. As a rule, he didn't discuss business in client homes, either. There was too great of a chance that he was being recorded or that a meeting would turn into an ambush. He didn't succeed in his line of work by being sloppy.

On the other hand, the possibility of seeing

Athena in her home, outside of the club, was difficult to pass up. He scowled, realizing that Garcia was toying with him and probably already anticipated the conflict he was feeling over the invite.

"Well?"

"I don't make house calls for business matters, and I'm enjoying my evening off tonight. If you think I can be of help, please call my assistant to set up an appointment." Donovan handed him a card and turned his attention back to the play floor.

Garcia flipped the card over in his hand, pondering the response. "I'll do that, Mr. O'Malley. Enjoy your evening watching."

As soon as Garcia was out of sight, Donovan collected his jacket and walked out to the valet. He dialed Alvarez when he was back in the car.

"Good evening, sir," he said, answering on the first ring.

"Hey, Alvarez. I just found out Athena Garcia's home alone tonight. Can you swing by her apartment and stake it out for an hour or two?"

The best part about owning a surveillance business was that his team knew better than to ask questions. Of course, Alvarez was willing to go to the Garcia family home. He'd camp out there for days if Donovan told him to.

"Of course, sir. Anything I should be looking for in particular?"

Donovan sighed. "No, not at the moment. Just make sure if she leaves the building, that she looks alright. Don't approach her; just call me if you happen to see her."

"You got it, boss," he said before hanging up.

Donovan caught a reflection of himself in the rearview mirror. His face held the same cold indifference he must have shown to Nathan Garcia.

Good, he thought. He needed to keep that fucker guessing.

————

"Any calls for me?" Donovan asked Melissa the next morning. It was early, but Garcia could have reached out the night before. He didn't seem like the kind of man who slept much.

Melissa nodded. "We received a tip about another missing girl," she said. "And there was a request for a consult meeting from Mr. Nathan Garcia, but since you're asking, and you never ask, I'm guessing you already anticipated that one."

"Yeah, guilty," Donovan said, pouring himself a glass of orange juice.

"Well, who is he? Google says some business guy. Old money?"

"A little bit, but mainly self-made. I'm not sure what kind of a consult he needs, but he's Athena's owner. You know... from Safeword."

Melissa groaned. "Are you fucking kidding me?

Haven't I heard enough about the latest piece of ass you're chasing."

"Get it out of your system now, Mel. I'm not going to allow that shit when she moves in here and has my babies."

"Barf," Melissa said, pretending to gag. "As for the meeting, I told him that ten would work. You're not due for your flight until three this afternoon. Sound good?"

"Yeah, that's fine. Tell me more about the kidnapping tip."

Organized crime, especially trafficking, had become a type of pro bono work for Donovan over the past few years. He hadn't intended to become some kind of vigilante, but the nature of his surveillance and bodyguard work meant that he had access to a lot of information. Much more than, say, a typical police station. For that reason, he had started dedicating time each week to looking into some of the missing women and children in the area. He usually turned over his findings to the police anonymously, which typically led to an arrest within a few hours.

But if they didn't work fast enough, Donovan sometimes had to do the legwork on his own, too. Hence, the need for more employees like Mendez.

He wasn't stupid. Doing that work didn't negate the fact that he was a murderer or that he had done some really shitty things over the years, but it felt good to offer something positive to the community. It had to make all the difference to those families who had their loved ones back home, at least.

At five till ten, Nathan Garcia arrived on his doorstep, a bottle of scotch in hand. Donovan's housekeeper greeted him and brought him to Donovan's study, where he was pouring over some intel on his computer.

"Mr. Garcia," he said, standing and offering a hand. "Good to see you this morning. What can I do to help?"

Nathan shook his hand and offered the scotch. The housekeeper came back with glasses on a tray, as well as a selection of cigars.

Somehow, the meeting had turned into an old boy's club situation and Donovan was already tired of it. Who drank hard liquor before noon, anyway? Still, he took the glass when offered, but he left the cigar smoking to Nathan.

"Thanks for clearing your schedule. As you probably already know, I'm a businessman here in the city. While most of the people I work with are on the up and up, I'm sure you, more than most, can understand that things can get a little...muddled now and then."

Donovan wasn't going to answer that. The detecting wand and body search that his security team conducted before allowing Garcia to enter the room meant he wasn't wearing a wire, but that didn't mean Donovan was going to blab about illegal activity.

"Yes, well. I'm here because I've been working with someone. A group, actually, and they are trying to find a way to get to me. They tried my business, but I keep the books spotless. My next concern was my family. As you can imagine, having four women who all essentially act as my wives leaves me open to a lot of scrutiny. If it were just them threatening my reputation, I wouldn't care as much, but I am worried that they could actually present harm to my girls."

Donovan blinked. "Are you saying... Athena and the others could be in danger?"

"*Athena and the others?* Could you be any more obvious in your interest for her, O'Malley?" Garcia sneered. "Yes, that's what I mean. I am concerned that they may be in danger. If there was anyone else I could go to about this, you know I wouldn't be knocking on your door. But you're the best there is, and I need the best. They deserve the best."

At least they could agree on that.

"Tell me everything. Why do you suspect they're in danger? Who do you think might be behind it?" Donovan flipped on his voice recorder, causing Garcia to hesitate.

"I need the recording for my notes. I'll share what I need to with my team, but it will be destroyed once the job is done," Donovan said.

Nathan paused for a moment, weighing his options, then continued. "Fine. Just ensure that this remains strictly confidential."

"Of course." Donovan didn't want the information getting out any more than Nathan did, but that should be obvious. Being able to keep client secrets was the only way he stayed in business.

"Well, it started years ago. I, or my wife, rather, was targeted a few times. It caused us to move from our house into a highly secure apartment building. After the move, the attacks stopped for a little while. Likely only because she was never alone."

"What do you mean by 'attacks,' Garcia?" Donovan asked.

"It was small things at first. A note left on the counter. A door wide open when she came home from an outing. The security system was always disarmed. It came to a head when someone broke in at night while I was out of town on business. I couldn't let us stay there anymore, not if I was going to protect my wife."

*But can you protect her from yourself?* Donovan wanted to ask. Surely, she had some emotional fallout over her husband taking on the other women in the home. Instead, the only thing he said was, "Go on."

"Well, we lived in the new, more secure, apartment for a few years, and then I met Athena. That first day I met her, there was another attack."

———

Donovan missed his flight, but it had been worth it. The information Garcia had shared with him was upsetting, especially because it did sound like Athena was in trouble. His first reaction was to set up a car to watch the building 24/7, but Nathan had shut that idea down. Supposedly, he already had bodyguards on staff, and he didn't want to worry his women by having more security added unnecessarily.

Donovan almost snorted at the mention of the puny half-wit that Garcia hired to watch the building. Alvarez had spotted him almost instantly, and the idiot was usually sleeping or watching television on his phone.

Adding a car would be necessary, but there was no reason Garcia had to know about it. Donovan could just start a rotation between Alvarez and another one of the guys. He had been tempted to do that anyway, after the news of the other submissives entering Athena's family. He needed to know that she was alright, that she was happy or something close to it.

As for the other stuff... it was going to take more digging to get to the bottom of who was targeting Athena's family. Nathan provided limited insight, something about a man he used to know from some business dealings, but it wasn't terribly helpful. One quick search of city records showed that whatever name he gave to Nathan was fake.

Donovan reluctantly slept for most of the hours-long flight. He knew that as soon as the plane landed and he had a secure internet connection, he'd be back to working on Athena's case full-time, in addition to whatever the client he was meeting needed from him. Hopefully, none of it would take too long and he'd be back home soon. He needed to lay eyes on Athena for himself to believe she was safe.

*Chapter 18*

*Now*

"Athena?" Donovan answered. "Hello?"

There was some muffled rustling in the background, but Athena didn't answer. Donovan sat up straighter, closing the laptop and listening carefully. A glance at the clock told him it was after four in the morning. It wasn't a great habit, but pulling an all-nighter was typical for him, especially when he was so close to finishing a long project. But according to the conversations Donovan had overheard from the bugs he had planted all over the apartment, Athena usually went to bed much earlier. *What is she doing up so late?*

"Athena? Can you hear me?" Donovan gathered his keys and wallet, pressing the phone to his ear as he moved around the room. He was so distracted that he ran straight into Chester in the hallway.

Donovan's home doubled as extra office space

and a general hangout for the surveillance team, despite each of them having their own offices and houses, too. Apparently, Donovan wasn't the only one burning the midnight oil that night. It wasn't too surprising, though. Donovan might work long hours, but Chester just didn't seem to sleep, period.

"What's up?" Chester asked, taking a huge bite of Mel's expensive Greek yogurt. She'd probably skin him alive for it in the morning.

Donovan muted his phone, unsure if someone was listening in. "Athena dialed me, but she's not responding. It's still an active call, so see if you can trace it. Give me a location for the tracker that was placed in the lining of her purse, too. And then pull up the surveillance from the Brownstone apartment and the place she's been staying on West 130th."

"Got it," Chester said. He moved out of the way, allowing Donovan a clear shot down the hall and out of the house.

In the car, Donovan pulled out a second phone and called Mendez. He was on duty with Athena overnight, and should be able to tell him if anything unusual was happening. Donovan tried to remain calm, reminding himself that she could've just dialed him by mistake.

But then why wasn't she answering? And if nothing was wrong, why was her call still active?

"Hello," Mendez said.

Donovan froze. Why did he sound groggy, like he

was just waking up? If he had fallen asleep while on duty, Donovan was going to kill him.

"Where is she?" he demanded. "Is she alright?" "What? Yes, sir. I think she's inside. Like always." "You think? Why the fuck wouldn't you know for sure?" Donovan sped out of the driveway quickly, tires burning.

"I mean, of course she's up in the apartment. Where else would she be?" Mendez wasn't inspiring any confidence.

"It's not my job to know. That's your fucking job, Mendez. You get the hell out of that car and go check. Right now," Donovan growled. "I'll be there soon, and you better have good news for me."

Chester called back as soon as Donovan hung up.

"So... don't freak out, but the call is coming from the Brownstone apartment on West 152nd. We don't have any visuals because the cameras were compromised a while ago. We weren't monitoring that address anymore, and the data that would've caught the cameras being vandalized is gone. Too much time has passed.

"The tracker in her purse is still on the move. Looks like it's in a car, but she might've just accidentally left the purse in a taxi or something since her call is still active at the apartment. My guess is that she's there at the Brownstone. Maybe she forgot something at the old apartment?"

"No, she's waiting there for me," Donovan said, a

grin slowly reaching his face. That was quick. He told her to go back to the apartment when she was ready to acknowledge his ownership of her. The fact that she didn't have Mendez drive her, though... she better hope that there's a record of an Uber or something dropping her off. If she walked there in the middle of the night... well, they'd be starting out this new chapter of their life together with a serious punishment.

He worked his jaw, thinking about the fact that Mendez thought she was still at the other apartment. That son of a bitch would regret letting Athena slip by him again, even if she was unharmed.

Donovan shifted gears and took the offramp to the Brownstone.

His phone rang again. Mendez.

"Sir, she's not at the apartment, and neither is the roommate."

The smile slipped from his face. Why would they both be gone? No, something wasn't right. Donovan ended the call and stomped on the accelerator.

He parked illegally in front of the Brownstone apartment and raced to the front door, keys in hand. He sucked in a breath upon seeing the discarded phone and what looked like some makeup but didn't bother collecting them. Donovan's priority was getting inside the apartment.

He forced the key, cursing the fact that he would

need to get through another set of doors. But none of that mattered when he was finally inside the studio apartment. Athena wasn't there.

In a matter of minutes, Mendez scurried through the door, eyes wide. It was about fucking time he showed up.

Mendez was out of chances, and it was time to pay up for being sloppy.

Without a word, Donovan pulled out a handgun and shot him in the head. Mendez didn't even have time to react. He was dead almost instantly, blood and brain matter splattered on the wall behind him. Donovan stepped around the body as it crumbled to the floor and locked the door behind him. Chester would have to deal with cleaning up that mess. At least his gun had a silencer on it, sparing them questions from the neighbors.

Donovan hurried back to his car, dialing the head of security as he went.

"She's not here. Her phone and some other items are scattered outside the apartment. Do you have any updates on her tracking device in her purse?"

"Yep, it looks like the purse is all the way across town, traveling fast."

Donovan revved the engine and put the car in gear. "Stay with me and navigate until I can reach her, Chester. Send a message for backup to anyone not currently working another job. And when all this is over, send a crew to clean up Mendez's body at the Brownstone."

Chester swore under his breath. It wasn't the first body he had to make disappear but taking care of one of their own hit differently.

"He should have done his job," Donovan said through gritted teeth. "If he hadn't been a whiny bitch about watching her, she wouldn't be missing right now."

"Just get her and bring her back, preferably without killing any more of our people," Chester sighed. "I can't exactly find replacements for them by placing an ad on Indeed."

———

He'll run out of gas soon. That's what Donovan kept telling himself. Chances were that whoever was driving that car didn't start with a full tank, making Donovan insanely grateful that his team refueled all the company cars every night. He wouldn't be the first one who needed to stop, most likely. He just needed to be calm. Patient. Just keep driving, but not too fast to catch the attention of some rookie, snot-nosed cop who might not recognize his car and try to pull him over for speeding. Donovan really didn't have time to deal with making a phone call to a newbie's superior.

Donovan's pro bono work for local law enforcement wasn't done for the sake of perks like speeding without consequences, but in a pinch, he was glad they just tended to look the other way. Bribes were effective to an extent, but nothing worked as well as making the cops think you were on their side.

Better still, that shit was untraceable. No investigations, no lawsuits; just the police looking the other way whenever they might have otherwise stepped in and caused a problem.

Chester was in his ear, on and off, alternating between cracking jokes to break the tension and navigating so Donovan could follow the tracker they installed in the lining of Athena's purse. It was pure luck that she had managed to keep it on her... at least, he hoped she had. There was every possibility that Donovan was chasing a moving target that housed her purse and not his submissive, too, but he wasn't allowing himself to go there just yet.

Donovan was banking on the likelihood that whoever took her wasn't very good at this shit. After all, they had left her cell phone calling him in front of her old building. Fucking amateurs.

"The tracker stopped moving, over on East 233. A gas station."

"Got it," Donovan growled. He was closing in on the bastard. No one would get away with stealing from him, especially not the most prized piece of property he owned. Donovan would burn everything down before he allowed that to happen.

*Chapter 19*

*Now*

Athena moaned, clutching the side of her head as she sat up in the backseat of a car. It hurt like hell, and when she pulled her hand away, there was blood. Most of it was dried and matted to her hair, but some of it was still fresh.

The car wasn't moving. Wherever she was, it looked like a secluded, extra shitty gas station. She struggled to remember what was even going on. Finally, it started to come back to her.

Jared's suspicious call, the argument with Mendez, the person attacking her at the old apartment. But why would someone want her? Did Donovan suspect someone might try to harm her? Athena had assumed that the two bodyguards had been his way of keeping tabs on her, but maybe they were there for a more practical purpose.

She frowned, realizing a little too late that she

didn't know very much about Donovan at all. Was he involved in something that could cause her harm?

The front door creaked open, but it didn't take long for her to recognize the driver.

"Hey," she said, testing the waters. "Um... where are we going?"

Pete glanced back at her. "Well, good morning to you, too. Glad to see I didn't totally brain you. Hungry?"

Athena blinked and stared at the microwavable gas station burrito he offered to her.

"C'mon. We've got a long trip, and you'll need your strength." He held out the food again. This time, not accepting it didn't feel like an option.

Athena took the burrito, but instead of eating it, she held it in her hands as she studied Pete. She wanted to ask why he had kidnapped her, but something in his expression made her hesitate; he wouldn't be answering any questions.

She shivered a little, remembering how quickly his demeanor had changed the last time they were together. At least then she had the Uber driver in the car with her, and Nathan there when he tried to grope her outside of her apartment building. Now there was no one stopping him from attacking her again. Nathan wasn't there. Donovan wasn't there. She glanced at the gas station attendant still in the building; the one who had sold him the food. Maybe she could make a scene and cause them to call the police.

"Don't even think about it, Athena," Pete said, between bites of his own burrito. "We'll be leaving in just a minute, and the backseat has child-proof locks. There's no way for you to get out, short of crawling over me to open the front door. Just eat your food and play nice. You're welcome for that, by the way."

"Yeah. Thanks. So, uh... where are we going?" It was worth a shot to ask, she decided.

Pete looked at her like she was an idiot. Okay, next question.

"Jared's probably worried about me. Do you think I should give him a call? You know, just to let him know I'm alright."

Pete rolled his eyes. "Really, Athena? That's the game you want to play? Should I just pretend you didn't run from his apartment as soon as you overheard our conversation?"

"What conversation? I was at my old apartment because I forgot something," she argued. "After that, I was going to pick up my last check from work. I told Jared about it."

"Sure, sure," he said, waving his hand dismissively. "Makes perfect sense why you'd need to do all that in the middle of the fucking night."

Athena didn't respond. She wasn't going to win that argument. Mainly because, as Pete pointed out, her story was total bullshit.

Suddenly, she heard a car pull up, its tires crunching on the gravel that covered the edge of the gas station. It was dark and it parked nearby without any lights, making it impossible to see who was driving.

Pete adjusted in his seat, quickly locking all the doors. He slowly reached for a gun stashed in the glovebox. Athena's eyes widened as the steel caught the light from the gas station sign.

"Whatever you do, keep quiet and don't try anything stupid," Pete whispered. The click of the safety being disabled was the only sound in the car, besides Athena's heart beating like a drum.

The car's door swung open wide, but something else drew her attention away from it: two other dark cars maneuvering around them. The blood drained from Pete's face as he realized the same thing. They were completely boxed in.

Athena whipped around to look at the first car, this time, greeted by the outline of the driver. She squinted, trying to see him better, but in her heart, she knew who it was. Donovan had found her, somehow. She was going to be alright.

Pete cursed, then turned to her, gun in hand. "Listen to me right now, Athena. You need to leave that fucking psycho. You think you know who Donovan O'Malley is? You don't know shit."

"That's hilarious coming from you," Athena said.

It took all her courage to say it, but it felt so good to finally be able to confront him. "That night outside my apartment? Fuck you for that, Pete. If Nathan wasn't there... well, I guess the same thing might have happened tonight if Donovan hadn't shown up, huh? You're a creep. A fuckin' creep!"

An eerie smile crossed his face. His eyes were hollow, unfeeling. "Ah, yes. You were also close to Nathan Garcia, weren't you? Just remember me when you finally wake up to the truth, Athena."

Without warning, Pete brought the gun to his head and pulled the trigger. Athena screamed and covered her ears, a little too late. Between the ringing and the shock of being covered in Pete's blood, her mind scrambled. She opened her mouth to scream again but started gagging when she tasted his blood in her mouth. She tried to spit it out, praying that she hadn't swallowed any of it.

Someone was banging on the window, trying hard to jiggle the handle open. Of course, the backseat door was locked, and like Pete said, she couldn't even open it from the inside. Athena looked at Pete's slumped-over body, half of his head blown away, and she threw up. All over herself, all over the seat.

"Athena, move over so I can break the window." The voice was muffled, but she recognized it right away. She scooted over, sobbing and covered in vomit.

She didn't bother to turn her face away when the window shattered, resulting in what was probably several small cuts on her hands and face. It didn't matter. She couldn't feel anything anyway.

She was vaguely aware of Donovan throwing his coat over the glass and reaching for her.

"Come on, baby. I've got you," he said. What sounded like a whisper to Athena was probably him yelling. Being in the car when the trigger was pulled had all but wiped out her hearing.

Donovan wrapped his arms around her, lifting her off the backseat. Athena stared wordlessly at what was left of Pete. Or not Pete; what was it Nathan had called him that night? Leo? Or Leon? It was so hard to remember. Trying to think about anything other than what had just happened, what was still happening, made the world tilt sideways.

Athena felt herself land gently on the fresh leather seats of another car.

Donovan must have seen the state of shock take over. He grabbed a water bottle from the front seat and placed it in her hands. She gripped it like it was a lifeline but didn't try to open it.

Then Donovan pulled out a spare black shirt from the glove compartment. He used some of the water from the bottle to get the fabric wet and began wiping away the vomit that was still on her face. She couldn't register the difference in temperature, but the methodical way he tended to her was soothing.

When he spoke, his voice was gentle but firm.

"You're going to be alright, Athena. I'm here. Shhhhhh. I'm here."

She didn't move; all she could see were images of Pete's arms lying limp on the passenger seat. The gun in his hand. His eyes open forever, or at least until someone forced them shut. Would anyone do that? Were the police coming? She couldn't understand how everything had changed so quickly. Tears streamed down her face, blurring her vision as hard sobs bubbled up from her chest.

Donovan's arms were around her again. He brushed away the tears from her face, and he kept repeating that she was safe, saying it over and over until she finally started to hear the words.

When she did, Athena clung to them and to him like her life depended on it. Somehow, Donovan managed to pry himself loose from her long enough to take her into the backseat with him. Alvarez slid into the driver's seat without a word.

"We're going home, Athena," Donovan crooned. "I'm so sorry you had to see that. I promise I'll keep you safe. I'm here now, baby."

Athena felt a burst of energy come over her. She started shaking and fidgeting against him.

"It's the adrenaline," Donovan said, refusing to let her go. "Shhhh. It'll pass soon. Just stay here with me, Athena."

Her jitters continued to pop up on their drive to

the outskirts of town. Athena frowned when she realized that she wasn't even sure where they were anymore. She'd lived in the city for almost a decade but had never ventured out into the suburbs. She'd assumed Donovan lived somewhere close by, but his profiles online gave hardly any information about his personal life.

The sun was peeking out over the trees when they pulled into the long driveway of the largest house Athena had ever seen.

Nathan had been very wealthy, too, but he used his money for show. The things he bought weren't for comfort or even for a purpose a lot of times.

This place was different. Even from the outside, this house felt like a home, like every inch of the space was used and needed. Nathan's apartment, the one Athena had lived in with everyone else, was sterile. The extra rooms and closets held seasonal decorations or clothes and, in some cases, nothing at all.

"Is this where you live?" she asked, speaking to Donovan for the first time since they started driving. He smiled a little at the question and threaded his hand through her hair.

"It's where we live, Athena."

Under any normal circumstances, she would have batted his hand away, but she was too tired to bother with that or even to argue. She just needed a safe place to sleep, and it took all of three seconds for her to realize that every other place she could go wasn't an option anyway. Jared had some relationship with Pete, and the Brownstone apartment... Athena wanted to throw up at the thought of going back there.

She had never seen anyone die, but she couldn't say that anymore. The weight of what happened was crushing.

"I'm exhausted," she admitted. "Can I... I'll stay here tonight if that's alright with you."

Donovan gave her an exasperated look but didn't argue. "Come on. Let's get you settled in."

Athena scooted with him out of the car, only for Donovan to gather her back in his arms and carry her to the door. Now that she was more aware of herself, it felt completely ridiculous not to walk on her own.

"For fuck's sake, Donovan! Put me down!"

She tried to shift out of his grasp, but his hold on her was strong. "Relax," he hissed. "Just chill, Athena."

Fine. She was out of energy, and fighting with him wasn't working, anyway.

———

"I'm not sharing a bed with you, Donovan."

Athena stepped out of the bathroom, wearing the pajamas he had handed her when she left to take a shower. She had hoped that the warm water would be soothing to her. God knows she needed to get clean, at the very least, but she hadn't expected how horrible cleaning up would be.

Athena tried, and failed, to block out how it felt finding pieces of Pete embedded in her hair and on her clothes. She had expected a lot of blood. She was covered in it, both hers and his. The shower water had run red for several seconds before it finally started to clear up.

Equally hard to block out was the giant man making himself comfortable on the bed in her room.

"I'm not leaving you alone right now. It's difficult to witness your first death, Athena. I want to be here if you have nightmares later on."

Athena frowned. "How do you know that was my first death? Maybe it was my hundredth."

Donovan gave her a look. Yeah, she wasn't used to any of this. It was impossible to pretend otherwise.

"Fine," she said, fidgeting. "Some of us aren't indifferent to carnage. But I guess you're telling me that wasn't your first encounter with a dead body?"

"It wasn't even my first one of the day," Donovan snorted.

"What?" Athena crashed into the dresser. "What exactly is it that you do? Your website said something about security services."

"You Googled me," Donovan said, grinning. "Just couldn't wait to find out more about me, huh, slave girl?" Athena rolled her eyes, trying to pretend that those words didn't do anything to her. Even in her trauma- ridden, sleep-deprived state, it only took two words for her to be instantly horny. "I'm serious. What kind of lifestyle would put you in contact with two dead bodies in twenty-four hours?"

"The website was right. I'm in the security business," he said, patting the mattress next to him. "Come to bed, and I'll answer whatever questions you have. At least until you fall asleep. I can tell from here that you're dead on your feet, Athena."

Athena nodded slowly and moved to the bed. She was exhausted, but even more than that, she wanted answers. "Who was the other body?" She pulled the covers over her, which oddly provided a degree of modesty, as Donovan was on top of the bedding. Still, he was close enough that Athena had to fight the urge to lean into him. It was like her body was a magnet for his.

"Otto Mendez," he said simply.

"What?!" Athena shot up, gaping at him. "My Mendez?"

Donovan glowered at her. "I don't especially care to have you call another man 'yours,' but for lack of a better word, yes. It was the same Mendez."

"Why? Jesus Christ, Donovan!"

"He put you in danger by not doing his job." He said it slowly like he was explaining something to a child. Well, fuck that.

"You killed him because he refused to drive me to the apartment? Look, he wasn't my favorite person, but—"

"Hold on. You're saying that he knew you wanted to go somewhere, and he let you leave the apartment by yourself?"

Athena could feel the room turn colder as his anger settled in the air. She paused, not sure how to answer that without making things worse. Then again, the man was already dead. How much more harm could telling the truth cause?

"Yes," she said slowly. "I told him I wanted to go because I overheard Jared on the phone. He was talking to Pete about doing something with me, and... well, Pete and I had a history, so—"

Donovan cut her off again. He turned to look at her head-on, watching her as she spoke. "What the fuck does that mean? You had a history with Leon? Explain."

Athena's eyebrows shot up. Donovan tried not to show it, but he was clearly unnerved that she knew the dead man. "I'm sorry if I scared you, Athena, but I need to know how you knew Leon. This is important."

"Well, he was Jared's friend. I met them at a bar one night a long time ago. It was the same day I met Nathan, actually." Athena stopped and searched his face. "Wait... how did you know his name was

Leon? Everyone introduced him to me as Pete. The only one who called him Leon was Nathan when he… well, when he was pulling him off of me outside my apartment."

Donovan's eyes flashed, and then he forced the emotion away. "Working in security puts you in contact with a lot of bad people, Athena. 'Pete' or 'Leon' wasn't a very nice guy, as it sounds like you are aware. The fact that Nathan knew him as Leon is telling, too. That was the name Pete used to conduct his… business. Unfortunately, he isn't the guy we really need. We've

been searching for the leader of the ring, and Leon's suicide complicates things. The fucker knew we'd get too much information out of him if we brought him in alive, so he took the easy way out."

Donovan paused and looked far away like he was trying to solve a puzzle that only he could see. Athena needed answers, but she also wanted to stop talking about Pete/Leon. The look on his face before he pulled the trigger would already be haunting her dreams. She didn't want to think about it while she was awake, too. She nudged Donovan playfully, hoping to break him out of the trance.

"You know the stuff I really want to know, and you're avoiding it," Athena teased, though there was truth to that, too.

"You'll have to ask questions, then." Donovan laughed, reaching around and pulling her closer.

Her heart hammered when he leaned over, mere inches from her. "You're mine now, Athena, and I won't have secrets between us. Whatever you want to know, just ask."

"Alright," she whispered. "Tell me how you knew Nathan. You must have been close for him to give me to you. And yet, he never even mentioned you. Even Veronica didn't seem to know your name."

Donovan chuckled. "I was wondering how long it would take for you to ask me about that," he said. Then, true to his word, he told her everything.

Chapter 20

*Then*

Nathan Garcia's surveillance recordings were monotonous. There were hours upon hours of footage that revealed nothing about a potential attacker. It certainly wasn't worth the money he was paying Donovan's team to monitor the footage, but Donovan wasn't going to complain. Working with that dumb fuck was his lifeline to Athena.

Not only did he always have eyes on their apartment, but he had even gone as far as to install some cameras in the living areas of the Garcia residence. Nathan had agreed to that surprisingly fast, which made Donovan uneasy. The man was scared of something; there was more to this than he was sharing. That's the only reason someone would allow invasive monitoring like that.

It was just one more reason to keep Alvarez trailing Athena whenever she left home. Having one of his guys there gave Donovan the reassurance he needed to take on other projects and travel out of town for work. It was enough to feed his obsession of controlling her without having to drop all his other obligations. If he was going to keep working, those things would be necessary, even after she was living in Donovan's home full-time. God, just thinking about that made him ready to pull the trigger and take her now.

From a completely objective standpoint, things were going well, but it wasn't moving fast enough. He needed Athena to wake up already. She wasn't happy there with Nathan. Her jealous nature got her in trouble with her master on a regular basis, enough so that they were often fighting or cold toward each other on camera.

The two of them were incompatible. It was really that simple, but she needed to figure it out herself. Donovan barging into her home as a complete stranger and essentially abducting her wouldn't help her see the light, that's for sure.

Too bad. He'd be more than willing to swoop in; consequences be damned, if he thought it would help. One thing's for sure, though: once she belonged to him, he'd revel in her jealousy. He'd feed it just enough to get them both drunk on the feeling, then ground her with a reminder that she belonged to him and that he didn't need anyone else, either. Her fiery jealousy deserved to be treasured. Teased and protected. Just like the woman herself.

But at the moment, he wasn't dealing with Athena. Instead, he was once again playing host to the man standing in the way of their happiness. From across the room, Nathan Garcia sipped his drink, gazing at the fire in the hearth of Donovan's office.

Donovan sat behind his desk, working on his computer and sending some emails with one eye watching Athena through the live feed in her kitchen as she prepared dinner. Since putting him on retainer, Garcia had stopped by unannounced a few times. At first, he came with the pretense of wanting an update on the surveillance project, but more recently, he didn't even try to come up with a good reason. Any updates could be given over the phone or through emails. What Nathan really wanted was a friend. A confidante he saw as an equal and who would talk him off of a ledge of paranoia.

Donovan could do that for Athena's sake. The stakes were high enough to make the odious task of listening to him ramble on and on worth it.

"I think I'm being followed," Nathan said, swirling the liquor in his glass.

"You're not being followed," Donovan said. It wasn't the first time he'd had to say it, either. He would listen to the man's delusions, albeit reluctantly, but he wasn't going to join in on a game of make-believe. "And from what you've told me, there's no reason for anyone to follow you."

Garcia nodded slowly, eyes still on the amber liquid. "I guess there's more that I haven't shared. Some minor stuff, really, but it might be helpful to your surveillance."

Donovan glanced up. He didn't have to feign interest about getting new information. When it came to Athena's safety, he needed as much intel as possible. "Oh?"

"It's probably nothing, but the business deals that I told you about, specifically the ones that are less than... on the up and up, they involve a character that requires a good deal of money."

Silence hung in the air between them. What the fuck did that mean?

Nathan Garcia sighed. "They have dirt on me. Some information that's pretty damning if it were to get out."

"What evidence?" Donovan asked.

"It's nothing, really. I'm sure it happens to a lot of men, especially men who are used to having women fall all over them," Nathan said, giving a sheepish sideways glance. He cleared his throat when Donovan didn't smile back. "There was a woman. A girl, I guess. She told me she was eighteen, but... well, I found out later that wasn't true."

Donovan grimaced. "How did you meet her?"

"Well, that's the thing. I have a contact who provides women for a price. It's not as bad as it sounds, I promise, but you know how it is. Finding someone in the lifestyle who is willing to d—"

"You have four fucking women living in your home, ready to do whatever the hell you want," Donovan spat. "Give the specifics to Chester on your way out."

Nathan hesitated, shaken by the outburst. He wasn't used to being dismissed, but then again, he was in someone else's home.

"Leave," Donovan growled. "I've got work to do. More now, with this revelation."

"I... understand. Just send my assistant the invoice."

Nathan stood slowly, trying to pretend like he wasn't being thrown out. He puttered around and took a last drink from his glass.

Just as he reached the door to the study, Donovan called out.

"Wait, Garcia," he said. "I've worked with another person in the same... industry. He says a lot of the women test positive for disease, even if they are guaranteed to be clean. When you met with this girl, did you use protection?"

The blood drained from Nathan's face. It was more than enough to give him away.

"Here," Donovan said, grabbing a card and writing down a number. "I have an excellent physician. He's discreet and can give you a complete physical. Blood work. Everything. I'll tell him you'll be giving him a call."

Garcia all but ran over to grab the card, causing Donovan's opinion of him to sink even lower. He was acting like someone afraid of getting caught. Clearly, his women at home didn't know about him seeing the other girls, otherwise he could get a physical from his regular doctor.

Donovan doubted Nathan ever planned on telling them, probably justifying his actions by their agreement to be owned by him. Like that was some excuse to do anything he wanted.

"Thank you!" Nathan said as he snatched the card. But once he had it, he had the wherewithal to look sheepish. "I'm sorry if I'm a little too eager about a referral. You see, I haven't been feeling well. At all. I've been putting off going to my own doctor because I don't want to alarm Veronica. But this is untraceable, right? Completely off insurance and discreet?"

Donavan nodded and flexed his hand as it fell back to his side. He wanted nothing more than to take his anger out on Nathan, but he had to be patient. He had to keep his emotions in check. Even if he murdered the coward right then, his Athena wasn't going to accept another owner just like that. She was loyal to a fault, and Nathan had her wrapped around his finger. What Donovan would give for her to look at him the way she gazed at that worthless prick.

It didn't matter. The greatest revenge Donovan could offer Athena was a lifetime of happiness. Even if she didn't know what that meant yet, she would soon enough.

Garcia prattled on about his health and listed a number of symptoms he was experiencing, but Donovan all but blocked him out. They were more words from a paranoid aging man with way too much money and a severe lack of self-control. He was basically a toddler with a credit card.

When Donovan was finally alone, he dialed his personal physician to confirm Nathan's referral for services and then poured his own celebratory scotch.

———

Donovan received a call from Nathan a few days later while he was driving to meet with another client at his company office about a security breach.

"Thanks for the recommendation, O'Malley," Nathan said. "Your doc gave me a clean bill of health. HIV, the clap; you name it, I don't have it. Those symptoms were just, you know, probably nothing. Just getting older. He wanted to run some additional blood tests, though. I'm guessing he did that for you, too, right?"

"He's pretty thorough," Donovan agreed. "Glad

you're all squared away. What else can I do for you, Garcia?"

"Well, now that I know everything's alright health- wise, I need to talk to you about the rest of that sticky situation. The compromising evidence and all. Are you available later today?"

Donovan rolled his eyes and shifted so he could accelerate. Of course, Garcia assumed he would be able to meet last minute. If it wasn't for Athena, Donovan would tell him to go fuck himself with a request like that, but currently, he didn't have that luxury.

"Of course. Call Mel to set up a time."

When Donovan parked, he pulled out his phone to see if Athena was awake yet. She would usually be getting ready for the day at about that time. Making breakfast or reading in the front room. Sometimes, she'd just be pacing around the kitchen with some kind of nervous energy.

*What are you thinking about, slave girl?* Donovan wanted to ask through the screen. It was happening more often, like her anxiety was building. Now that he was familiar with her schedule, Donovan could spot right away when she missed a meal or fidgeted with her phone. What he didn't know was what it meant or what caused it. Was she just a nervous person by nature? If so, he'd smooth out those edges. Soon, she'd have nothing to worry about at all.

He watched through the screen as Nathan came out of a bedroom and greeted her. They embraced briefly, causing Donovan's anger to prickle. He stared at the two of them as Nathan maneuvered her around to the counter.

Donovan frowned. Was it his imagination, or had Nathan glanced up at the camera?

And then he knew it was no accident. Nathan Garcia knew he was watching. Of course, the fucker was showing off the fact that he had her, and Donovan didn't.

Nathan kissed Athena deeply, hoisting her up onto the island. He grabbed her shirt and threw it over her head, exposing her complete nudity underneath. Donovan closed his eyes, trying to fight the urge to abandon the client he was already late to meet and drive over to pick up Athena right then. He'd throw her over his shoulder and march her out to the car. He'd cage her up in his home and never let her near another man again.

Donovan threw the phone across the car and ran a shaky hand through his hair. He had to keep it together. Soon, Athena would be his. Soon. Soon. Soon.

———

Mel had moved some things around in his schedule to allow for an impromptu meeting with Nathan.

"Why the fuck do you bother with him?" Mel asked when Donovan gave her the green light to pencil him in. "You know he's a garbage person, right?"

"He owns someone, and I'm going to take her from him," Donovan said matter-of-factly.

Melissa groaned. "You are making me reschedule three other clients for a piece of ass. What about her?" Mel gestured vaguely to the kitchen where one of Donovan's submissive playmates had gone to prepare him a drink. "Or one of the others from last week?"

He scowled. "Athena's different."

"Well, she sure as fuck must be, or you need to schedule this shit yourself." Mel reached for one of the open Chinese containers on the counter. "I'm assuming you've at least met her, and she knows her impending fate, correct?"

"Not quite. But I have a live feed from inside her apartment, so you could say things have gotten serious." Mel's jar dropped open. "God damn. That's pretty bad, even for you, Donovan."

"Like I said, she's different." He accepted the drink from the girl with a smile, which pleased her to no end. Donovan couldn't remember her name, but that didn't really matter. They didn't stay long enough for him to put in the effort. More importantly, she was using him just like he was using her. They both wanted some release with no strings attached.

"Anything else, sir?" she asked, eyes downcast.

Donovan tipped her chin until her eyes met his. He kissed her quickly on the lips. "No thanks, babe. Go ahead and get ready for bed. I'll be up soon."

The submissive grinned and scurried out of the room. Mel pretended to gag.

"I know you like them stupid, Nova, but you have to admit it's kind of creepy the way they fall all over themselves for you, right?"

"I don't like them stupid. She's submissive, that's all. And as soon as I can get my hands on her, the revolving door of women ends. I just need a way to blow off some steam. Maybe you should try it some time. I'm sure getting laid would improve your mood a lot and give us all a break."

"Whatever," Mel said, losing all interest in the conversation. "Let me know when the mystery girl arrives so I can warn her about what a freak you are."

Donovan snorted, shaking his head. He could fuck around with Melissa all day, but the bigger problem would be when Nathan arrived, and Donovan would have to face him after seeing the footage of Athena in the kitchen. The image of them together was permanently burned into his mind.

He didn't even have as long as he had hoped to process seeing Athena naked in the other man's arms. Nathan arrived early, and he looked shaken, which made Donovan smile. Chester led him into the office but stayed in the room, just as Donovan had requested.

"Hi, Garcia. I've asked my head of security, Chester, to sit in with us, as it seems like your concern is safety related. Is that correct?"

"Yes, I suppose that's true." Nathan glanced at Chester suspiciously.

Donovan suppressed an eye roll; Garcia was acting like his head of security had the time and inclination to rat him out for cheating on his submissives.

"Chester has the highest clearance to information in the company. If I know something, he does, too. Is there a problem?"

"I suppose not. I just hope he realizes how delicate this topic is. I require complete discretion."

"Of course," Donovan said. Chester shot him a look, silently asking why he needed to be in the room, but Donovan ignored it. Most likely, the man was hoping to leave work a little early to go on a date or play a pickup game of basketball. Those things could wait another hour.

"Please, sit down and explain to us what the security issue is about. From the beginning, if you don't mind." Donovan stood and walked over to the armchairs in front of the fire. He gestured to the other chairs, and all three men took a seat.

Nathan took a deep breath and sighed. "I guess I

just need to come out and say it. You've probably wondered why I chose to come to you with my business, of all people, O'Malley. Especially given your fascination with Athena."

Donovan didn't respond and kept his gaze steady. He waited for Nathan to continue.

"Yes, well. I am aware of the other work you do. The work regarding human trafficking and prostitution. I believe that the people who have damning evidence against me are people you'd be interested in finding, too.

"It's taken me a little while working with you to make sure I could trust you. That you're thorough and... well, competent. I think you're the right person for the job, so I'd like us to work together to take them down."

Donovan nodded slowly, his eyes flickering to Chester. There were several human trafficking rings in the area, and if they had dirt on Garcia, his paranoia might not be totally misplaced. "What makes you think they're after you? What evidence do you think they have?"

Nathan blushed. "Well, it's the girl I was talking about before. I thought she was 18... and she still might be 18. I don't really know. But the contact I used to meet with her said she was a minor after our encounter and that they took photo evidence of us together. They want money to make the pictures go away."

"And you don't want to pay the money, so you want us to make them go away," Chester said, speaking for the first time.

"You're acting like I'm the wrongdoer here. They're the ones who entrapped me. I never would've been with her if they would have said she wasn't 18," Nathan sputtered.

Chester opened his mouth to say something else— most likely that Nathan should have known she was being pimped, making him culpable, too, but snapped it closed when Donovan tapped subtly on the armchair. They had worked together long enough for him to know when to shut up.

"If we help you, what would we get in return, Nathan?" Donovan asked.

Nathan broke into a horrible smile, the panic still etched in his features.

"Why, you'll get what you always wanted, Donovan. I'll give you Athena."

*Chapter 21*

*Then*

"This is a bad idea. He gave us more than enough intel on the group to find them and take them down, but we have to let Garcia take the fall, too. He deserves to be locked up for his part in that girl's suffering."

As soon as Nathan was gone, Chester launched into all the reasons why they couldn't trust him and why he was a horrible person. Chester didn't even bother asking who Athena was, which was fortunate for Donovan. He had always framed the surveillance at her house as part of their service to Garcia and didn't feel like having his balls busted over his obsession with the woman twice in one night.

"We're going to use the information to track the group down, infiltrate to confirm the validity of it, and then hand it over to the police, just like usual," he said evenly. "Don't worry about Garcia."

Chester scowled. "It sounds like you're a little too close to the situation to remain impartial. Maybe you should recuse yourself and let the team handle it."

"Recuse myself? What am I, on the fucking Supreme Court?" Donovan laughed bitterly. "I told you that I'd take care of it. Just do your job, Chester."

He gave a stiff nod and left, likely to begin putting together a team for infiltrating the trafficking ring now that Garcia had given them the name of an organizer.

Leon Romero, the man who had threatened to expose Garcia for fucking a minor, would soon have the best surveillance team in the country on his ass. Even so, Chester was relentless when it came to their pro bono work. Asking him to stand down when a predator, including Nathan, could get away with their crimes was out of the question.

He didn't need to worry. Garcia wasn't getting away with shit.

Donovan checked the live feed, but the only person in the living room was another of Garcia's women. He hadn't bothered to learn all their names. They weren't Athena, and that was all that mattered. He dialed Alvarez.

"Is she at home?" Donovan asked.

"No, sir. She left with another woman a few minutes ago. I've been following them. It looks like they are going out to eat."

"Fine. Keep me posted." Donovan hung up and let out a deep breath. His cock swelled hard against his pants. Just the thought of Athena being out of the house made him want to go and find her. He could pull her into a dark corner and devour her without anyone even knowing. Donovan remembered the look on her face when she watched him fuck the other woman in Safeword. The way her lips had parted in surprise. Her jealousy. Her hunger. He groaned at the thought of sending her back to her master's house with her cunt full of his cum.

Now, that would be the perfect way to deliver some justice to Garcia.

Donovan adjusted himself and logged out of his devices. He had a sub upstairs waiting for him, and he was ready to use her. Fucking a practical stranger was a poor substitution for the woman he truly wanted, but she was here and willing, and he needed an outlet.

———

Chester had an update ready for Donovan first thing in the morning.

"The leadership is hard to trace because they go by several different aliases. It looks like they target women in nearby colleges and high schools to obtain victims and groom recent college graduates for leadership positions within the org. Some of the names are familiar, though the Leon character is new."

Donovan took a long drink from his coffee. The hot shower had done little to wash away the guilt from being with the other girl last night. At first, it had been easy to take out his frustration with someone else, but it was getting more difficult to do so with a clean conscience. . "Nice work. Send someone in with the contact information that Garcia provided. They are expecting some new clientele from him as part of his payment."

Chester nodded, snapping his laptop closed. "Already on it. We should get more info tonight after initial contact is made with the org rep. Obviously, it's going to take some time before the plant meets anyone important."

Donovan nodded, draining the rest of his mug. His schedule was even more packed today after squeezing in the meeting with Garcia the night before. He really needed to get going. "Anything else?"

"What are you going to do about Nathan Garcia?" Chester asked tightly.

Donovan raised an eyebrow. They didn't disagree often, and he had already said that he would take care of Garcia. That should've been enough for Chester to drop the subject.

"Fine. I'll see you later when I have an update."

Donovan nodded, gathering his jacket and

briefcase from the counter. "I'll talk to you this evening, either way."

Outside, Donovan called Alvarez. "What time did she get back?"

"Good morning to you, too," Alvarez joked. "She returned around midnight. They stayed out late for dessert."

"Good. She must be sleeping in this morning." Donovan had checked the live feed but hadn't seen her.

"Probably." There was a pause on the other line. "Listen, Mr. O'Malley, I don't mean to question you about your interest in her, but—"

"Then don't," he said. Donovan hung up before Alvarez could ask anything else. While Chester was still in the dark, he knew that some of the men on his team undoubtedly talked about his obsession with Athena.

A lot of them probably thought he was crazy for monitoring her, tracking her every movement. He couldn't blame them for that. He was crazy about her. But he also didn't feel the need to explain anything to them. They worked for him, not the other way around.

Donovan arrived at his office just as Garcia's name lit up his phone. His lips curled in a smile. This was the call he'd been waiting for.

"Hello? O'Malley here."

"Donovan, I'm glad to reach you directly. I have...

well, I have some terrible news. Some horrible news. I'm not sure what to do. Your physician… well, he found something in my blood, and he just did an ultrasound. I have cancer, Donovan. It doesn't look good, and I have to get things squared away. I need to get things set up for my submissives."

There was desperation and fear in his voice, but it was difficult to tell if he was more worried for his women or for himself. Donovan's skepticism said he was mainly concerned about his own mortality.

"I see. Well, that is terrible news. Have you told your submissives anything yet?"

"No, I want to have everything in place before I tell them," he said. "I need to set up trusts for them. Housing. I promised that I would take care of them for life, and I have the means to do so, but I'll need help."

Donovan frowned, causing confusion to reflect in his voice. "I'm not an attorney, Nathan. I'm not sure how I can help with that."

"I've got an attorney. He's drafting an updated will as we speak. The reason I'm calling you now is that I wanted your opinion on how to handle some other things." Nathan paused. "I mean… being in the lifestyle, I was wondering if there is anything you've heard about that might help with the transition for the girls."

Donovan paused as though considering the request. "Of course, I can help. I'll tell Mel to clear my afternoon."

———

Donovan was going to lose clients over all this rescheduling, but he didn't care. Garcia was at a breaking point. Now was the time for him to act, consequences be damned. Donovan could always send someone else in his place or play clean-up later.

"Thank you for meeting with me again on such short notice," Nathan said. He fumbled with a stack of papers before setting them on Donovan's desk.

Looking at him, you'd have thought the man had aged overnight. His skin was waxy and pale, his clothes wrinkled. He was shaking, panicked over some invisible threat. Had Nathan even been home last night? Donovan had been too busy to watch the feed. He'd have to ask Alvarez about it later.

"Listen, O'Malley, I know that we aren't friends in the traditional sense, but I need your help, and I think you need mine, too. Forget the issue with the trafficking group and blackmail. Soon, none of that will matter, anyway." Nathan shook his head, laughing bitterly. "I'm dying. The doc's given me a month, maybe two. Pancreatic cancer. It's been years since I had a physical, and he said if you hadn't referred me when you did, I might be out of time completely. So, thank you."

Donovan allowed sympathy to color his expression. "I'm sorry to hear that, Nathan. What can I do to help?"

"Here's my will, drawn up by my attorney earlier today. I know you aren't an expert in legal matters, but I'd like another set of eyes on it before I sign. I... well, I trust you, and I don't trust very many people outside of my women."

Nathan nodded and picked up the top sheet. It was all very standard boilerplate stuff. "I'm assuming you also have the trusts established that you mentioned? For the women, I mean."

"Yes, that's all been handled," Nathan said, slumping into a chair. "I just need to designate trustees, and that's where I need your advice. I could ask my attorney, but I would rather have someone more personal handle it. Would you like to be a trustee?"

"For all the women?" Donovan asked carefully. He needed this to work out just right. He couldn't overplay his hand at this last moment.

Nathan shrugged. "I assumed you'd want to for Athena, at least. Do you have another idea?"

Donovan smiled softly. "I believe we can come up with an appropriate arrangement."

It was going to be another all-nighter in the home office for Donovan, but he had never felt so alive. He didn't need sleep, not when he was working on the most important project of his life. He had already drafted sample directives for Nathan to look at, having anticipated the reason for his visit.

Each directive spelled out what Nathan wanted the women to do after his death. He took a little time batting around different names of other dominants in the area before settling on where the other women should go. He called the men, apologetic for interrupting their evening as he explained the situation.

The dominants expressed their condolences but didn't seem to mind being woken up if it meant being deeded one of Nathan's submissives. Of course, Athena would be Donovan's. There was no question about that.

"I think that should take care of everything," Nathan said when the papers were all typed and settled into neat stacks. "I'll take them to the attorney tomorrow. He'll understand the sensitivity of the issue and will absolutely agree to convey all my wishes. I can guarantee it."

Donovan rose from his seat behind the desk and poured them both a drink from his decanter.

Nathan laughed, the sound bitter and hollow. "The doctor said I shouldn't drink alcohol, but I also only have a few months to live. It's not like abstaining is going to help that, right?"

Donovan shook his head and handed Nathan one of the lowball glasses. They clinked them together and took a long sip of the bourbon. Donovan savored the way it burned.

———

A month was too long to wait. Donovan was getting impatient, and it felt like time was moving slowly on purpose. He had to stop himself from picking up the phone and calling Garcia during moments of weakness.

Those occasions had started happening way too often since Donovan wasn't able to monitor Athena like he had before. The fucker had disabled his live feed and hadn't contacted him again since the night they worked on the final directives.

Donovan created all kinds of possible scenarios to explain the radio silence. Had Nathan gone to get a second opinion from another oncologist? Was his doc providing him with enough support? Had he even told Athena that he was dying? And if he hadn't, what would it be like stepping in for Nathan as Athena's owner if she had no warning that her former master was dying? Would that be easier on her, or would it make matters worse?

Luckily, Alvarez was still watching her, though he couldn't do that forever. He had made a comment to Chester that he was itching to get back into the action, so Donovan would need to find a replacement for him, at least most of the time.

The search for a new bodyguard for Athena was something he mainly left to Chester, though Donovan would have the final say over who they hired. The trouble was Donovan wanted the best of the best for Athena. That would mean taking a good person away from Chester, but that's just something he'd have to deal with, especially now that his head of security knew what the woman was to him.

Finally, almost two months later, Donovan's phone vibrated with Garcia's contact information.

He took a few deep breaths to calm himself enough to answer without sounding like a maniac. "Hello? O'Malley here," he said.

"Hi, Donovan. Listen, I have some great news. Do you mind if I stop by today and we can talk?"

Donovan frowned. Great news couldn't be that great for him. "Of course. I'm actually available now. Would that work for you?"

"Absolutely. I've cleared my schedule since... well, you know what? I'll be able to start getting back to work soon enough! Yes, I'll be over in about an hour. Sound good?"

"Of course. I'm looking forward to it." Donovan hung up and made an illegal U-turn, causing some asshole to lay on their horn. He wouldn't be going into the office, after all. He'd let Mel figure out the logistics of his schedule. He had a bigger mess to clean up.

"Monroe isn't going to be happy about this," Melissa grumbled as soon as he walked back in the door. "We're already behind on giving him the report."

"Chester's the one who created the report. Have

him present it. He's already over at the office, isn't he?" Donovan asked, not bothering to stop and talk. He walked straight to the office, loosening his tie. Mel followed behind him, huffing.

"That's not the point. They're a big client, and they were expecting you to be there. What the fuck is so important that you needed to blow them off? And if you say—"

"Athena."

Mel swore and stared at the ceiling as though begging a higher power to grant her more patience.

"Look, Mel, I'm sorry you're stressed. You need to cash in some of your endless vacation days soon. I'll send you anywhere you want to go, but right now, you need to get out of this office because I don't have much time."

"Much time for what?" she asked, narrowing her eyes. Donovan poured a few drinks and brought them to the fireside. It was still mid-morning, but Garcia loved his bourbon, and he sounded like he would be up to celebrate.

"It doesn't matter. Just listen for the doorbell and bring Garcia to me as soon as he arrives."

Melissa chewed on her lip, watching him with mounting suspicion. But then the doorbell rang, and she didn't have a chance to pepper him with more questions.

"Go. I'll explain later. Please."

Slowly, she nodded and turned to leave. "She had

better be worth it, Donovan. It feels like you're losing it. And by 'it,' I don't mean something as simple as your mind. I mean, you're losing yourself. Your morals."

Donovan shook his head as she left. Clearly, Mel was under the impression that he had any of those left. When it came to Athena, there was nothing he wasn't prepared to do.

Moments later, Nathan Garcia rushed in to greet him. If he looked decrepit before, he was a whole new man now. His eyes were bright, filled with life and excitement, and he made Donovan horribly uncomfortable by greeting him with a full-frontal hug.

"Please, sit down, Nathan," Donovan said, arms pinned to his side.

"Forgive me, Donovan. I know you're not one for affection. I'm not, either, but when I called you, it was because I'd just received the best news of my life," Nathan said, moving towards the armchair but not sitting down. He was too filled with energy for that. "I went to get a second opinion because I've been feeling better lately. The oncologist said there's no evidence of pancreatic cancer. He said there must be a mix-up with your physician. Isn't that incredible news?"

"Of course it is, Garcia. I'm happy for you. Truly." Donovan paused as the other man beamed at him. "Have you shared this news with anyone else?"

"Not yet. I plan on taking the girls out tonight to share it with them. I want to tell them all at once so we can celebrate as a family."

"A toast, then. To your health." Donovan raised his glass and offered one to Nathan. They clinked the glasses together, and each took a hearty drink.

"You know I love that stuff," Nathan said. "It burns just enough, but the aftertaste is almost like almonds, wouldn't you say? Send my assistant the contact you use for purchasing it. I'd love to buy a few bottles."

"Let me pour you another glass. I know you're eager to get home, but I'd love to hear the details. Of course, our agreement regarding Athena is still enforceable. I will follow through with the surveillance regarding your blackmail situation, and you will give her to me. Correct?"

It was the right thing to ask. The question deflated Nathan almost instantly, causing him to trade his enthusiasm for feigned embarrassment.

"About that...you see, Donovan, over the past few months, Athena and I have become much closer. The diagnosis helped her put aside some of her jealousy, and we have been able to connect more, like we did before I added more submissives to the family. I don't think giving her to you would make her happy. She has found happiness with me again."

Nathan accepted the second glass eagerly, as

though he wasn't going back on his word to the man handing him the liquor.

"You don't think I would make her happy? Or is this about what would make you happy?" Donovan asked evenly. "Did you even intend to give her to me at all?"

"Now, that's not really a fair question, O'Malley. You helped me draw up the paperwork so that you'd have her when I thought I was dying. Even if I had gone back on my promise regarding your help with the blackmail, you would have gotten her had I died. And I'll still make good on that, by the way. When I die, however that should happen, you'll receive Athena. The paperwork is already filed with my attorney."

"Of course it is, Nathan. I was counting on it."

He frowned, still not understanding. Donovan pushed away from his desk, standing up and moving to block the door. It was the only way out of the room, which acted in part as a security measure. At the moment, it also doubled as a trap.

"What are you doing?" Nathan asked. He had broken out in a sweat and was blinking rapidly, trying to focus his eyes. "What's happening?"

"You're a fucking evil man, Garcia. You lie, steal, and cheat. You support sex trafficking, and you treat the most beautiful woman alive like trash. You think you're suddenly cured, that all this has been a mistake?"

Donovan moved closer, catching Nathan as he struggled to breathe. "You never had cancer, you stupid fuck. I've been poisoning you since you started visiting me. It's amazing how a little cyanide makes someone feel like they're dying, and now we'll get to see what happens when you're finally given a little too much at once. Time's up, Garcia. Looks like Athena will be mine before the sun sets."

Nathan's eyes burned with shock and rage, but the need to breathe became more urgent. Donovan let him fall to the floor and watched as he struggled to survive. Finally, his body stilled, and Donovan drained the last of his bourbon. He hated poison as a rule, but killing the bastard another way would have been too messy for a cancer diagnosis.

Donovan set the glass down and made a few calls. He needed someone to take the body away and to ensure the doctor Nathan visited for a second opinion wasn't going to run his mouth about the misdiagnosis. There was always work to do, but it was worth it. Athena was his for the taking.

*Chapter 22*

*Now*

Athena stared at him. Any plans she had about sleeping were completely out of the question.

"Nathan never had cancer," she said slowly. "Those last few days, we thought... sometimes cancer patients have renewed energy right before the end."

Mentally, she starts trying to piece together the events as they happened. Veronica had insisted on the open casket. His body had given nothing away; it had told them nothing of how he died. Of course, they hadn't requested an autopsy. There was no reason for one; the man had stage four cancer, or so they thought.

The doctor who had signed the death certificate... was that Donovan's physician, too? It must have been. The man deserved to have his license taken away and to be in prison. Donovan deserved that, too.

Athena pushed him away and leaped to her feet. Her body complained, hating her for moving so quickly after being knocked unconscious only hours before. Her head began to spin, threatening to black out again. She needed to sit down.

"That's what you took from all that, huh?" Donovan said, rolling his eyes as he rushed to steady her. "That bastard lied to you, cheated on you, worked with a sex crimes ring, gave you away to someone else without as much as a warning, and you're still upset at me for killing him? Well, don't worry. You have plenty of time to forgive me for that."

"What the fuck does that mean?" Athena allowed him to help her back into the bed, but her words were icy.

"It means that you've acknowledged that I own you, my dear. Our deal was for you to return to Nathan's apartment as a sign that you're mine. I was willing to wait for as long as it took, but you were back there within a few hours."

Athena wanted to argue, and she would argue, but not at the moment. Her body demanded rest. With the last bit of defiance she could muster, Athena shoved him away from her before falling into a deep sleep. "Go to hell," she mumbled before falling asleep to the sound of Donovan's laughter.

———

Was she dead? No, but she definitely wanted to be. The throbbing in her head was enough to make her want to never wake up again. When Athena finally opened her eyes, there was sunlight streaming in from the window and Donovan was gone. Where he was lying on the bed was still made and looked untouched. Thank god for small miracles; she'd still be able to say they hadn't actually slept together.

Athena refused to unpack the images that the thought of them sharing a bed brought to her mind. Nope. Not going there.

The door opened without warning, startling her. The woman peering inside was beautiful, with her brown hair swept up in a messy bun. Athena hated the way she instantly wondered if Donovan had fucked her.

"Good morning, sleepyhead," she grinned. "You've been asleep forever. Are you hungry for breakfast? Or maybe lunch?"

Athena looked at her like she had two heads. "I'm sorry. Who are you?"

The woman laughed and opened the door the rest of the way so she could step into the room. "Sorry. I'm Mel. Donovan's my best friend, unfortunately."

"Unfortunately?" Athena had to smile.

Mel laughed again. "Well, yeah. You've met him. He's a lot," she said, sitting beside Athena on the bed. "I also help him with business stuff. Scheduling and making sure that everything doesn't turn into a giant steaming crater."

Athena nodded slowly. She couldn't help liking Mel, and she seemed more reasonable than Donovan, at least. "Since you're a prisoner here now, how about some food? Donovan made me promise to try and feed you if you woke up while he's out. He's going to be pissed that I talked him into going into the office for a few hours when he finds out that you're awake."

*Or maybe she's just as batshit crazy.* Athena sighed. "I need to leave, actually. I'm not sure how much you know about Donovan and the things that he does, but he's not the person he seems. He's—"

Athena paused and frowned as she reached for the collar around her neck. Where Nathan's leather collar should be, there was another piece of jewelry in its place. This one was made entirely of metal, and it felt oddly cool against her touch. It was sturdy, but without looking at it, it felt almost like a necklace. There was etching on it, but she would need a mirror to read what it said.

The look on her face must have betrayed her panic.

"Oh, fuck," Melissa said. "Yeah. He said you might freak out about the necklace."

―――――

"Glad you could make it," Chester razed him as Donovan stepped into the conference room. "You are required to show up to work every once in a while, you know. In case we need something signed. It's helpful."

Donovan snorted. "Like you haven't been forging my signature on paperwork for years."

"It means more coming from you." Chester gestured to the seat at the head of the table. He didn't need to; it was the only space covered with papers marked for his signature.

"Let's get this done as quickly as possible, okay? Athena will wake up soon."

Chester sighed. "So, you're going through with that, huh? Any more last-minute bodies you need me to move? Other death certificates you need forged?"

"I'll have to get someone else to handle one for you if you don't stop talking."

Donovan clicked his pen and started scanning documents. Hiring forms, tax filings, high-paying contracts. "The business is getting to the point where we need to add an HR department. They could manage at least half of this," he mumbled.

"Agreed. That's one of the forms you need to sign. I hired two people to start a new HR department," Chester said. "Though, I can't imagine they know anything about undercover work or body counts. We should probably keep it that way."

"It's for the best," Donovan agreed. The stacks dwindled until he only had one document left. "What else do you need from me? When Athena wakes up, I'll be busy with her for at least a few weeks."

"If that's your way of announcing you're going on vacation, we're going to have to work on your delivery for HR, too." Chester gave him a thoughtful look. "That's probably all that was really urgent. Lucky for you, this place is a well-oiled machine."

"Yeah, lucky for both of us," Donovan said, glancing at his phone. "Mel just texted that Athena's awake and freaking out, so that's my cue to leave."

Against his better judgment, Donovan didn't rush home. He took his time, obeying all traffic laws, including a yield sign that he typically blew through. Teaching the woman patience would require an opportunity for her to use it. At least, that's what he told himself.

When he walked in on an all-out war between Athena and Mel, he was forced to second-guess that strategy.

"For fuck's sake," he grumbled, picking Athena up and slinging her over his shoulder. He had to smile, savoring the feel of her weight against him. He had dreamed of doing that too many times not to enjoy it.

"Put me down, you mother-fucking—"

"Simmer down, slave girl," he growled. "Mel,

thanks for helping. I'll take it from here."

Mel gave him a mock salute, though her face said she was more than a little pissed about being left in charge of his wayward submissive. Fair enough.

Donovan carried her up the stairs to his own bedroom, a place she hadn't visited yet. She must have been a little curious about it because she temporarily stopped kicking and struggling against him to take in her surroundings. But as soon as he locked the door behind them using his handprint, she began flailing again in earnest.

"You're a fucking sociopath, Donovan. Put me down!"

"Gladly," he lied, letting her fall on his oversized mattress. The room was decorated in dark reds and gold. The windows were covered, totally blacked out, giving the impression that they could be anywhere, even underground. It was intentional. Sometimes, he kept women in here for a while, and part of the mind-fuck was for them to have to guess how long they were captive.

Athena fell into a heap of blankets and pillows, glaring at him as she struggled to sit up. "What the fuck is this, Donovan?"

She grabbed at the collar he had secured around her neck while she slept. Possessive pride bloomed inside him at the sight of her wearing it, regardless of the ire she felt about it.

"You're mine, not Nathan's. It seemed

appropriate, wouldn't you say?"

"Nothing about this is *appropriate*," she sputtered.

Donovan shrugged. "I guess I don't really care."

"Of course, you don't. You don't care about anything or anyone." Athena curled up in the center of the bed, hugging her knees to her chest.

"That's where you're wrong. I care about you very much, Athena. In time, you'll see that's the case."

"And if I don't? What, are you going to keep me locked in here forever?" she demanded. "You've taken away my job. I have no friends, and you've killed my master. How could you ever think I'd want to be with you?"

"I guess you'll find a way." He bent down to kiss her forehead, but she jerked away from his touch. Donovan growled low and grabbed her by the neck to hold her in place. "Don't move away from me, Athena. Lesson one: I'll touch you whenever I damn well please. Now, get some rest. You'll need your strength for what I have planned for us."

———

As questionable as Donovan's threat sounded, what he had planned for them seemed to be for Athena to follow him around all day like a lost puppy. She ate with him, showered with him, slept with him.... though it was literally just sleeping. They shared a bed, causing her body to fight against its baser urges to get close to him.

So, he was sexy. So what? She had been around attractive men before. Nathan, though not as young and fit as Donovan, had been attractive. Every time she thought of her former master, her stomach dropped, and the attraction she felt toward Donovan soured.

Athena knew what she needed to do: she had to find a way to escape and tell the police what had really happened to Nathan. Even if Donovan had the local police in his pocket, as he had suggested more than once, they would have to listen to a solid murder tip, right? That was too serious for them to sweep under the rug. Two murder tips, actually, including what happened with Otto Mendez. Judging from Donovan's nonchalance about the whole thing, those were probably the tip of the iceberg when it came to people he killed. Exactly how many people had Donovan murdered in the name of "business?"

The days dragged on, turning into a week, and then two.

"Don't you need to go to work or something?" Athena asked after spending her fourteenth day at home with Donovan. He had been her sole companion. She hadn't seen Mel or anyone else since that first day.

They were lounging on the bed together, watching a movie on the oversized screen in the bedroom. Donovan had her pulled solidly against his chest, and she was trying desperately not to focus on the way his body felt against hers.

"I'm on vacation," he said, brushing a kiss across her forehead. "I'm fine taking off as much time as you need." He had said the same thing in a variety of ways over the past two weeks, but she still didn't know what it meant.

Athena frowned. "As much time as I need? For what, exactly?"

"Shhhh. This is the good part," he said, eyes back on the screen.

The whole thing was infuriating. Donovan was avoiding answering her questions, which had become the norm. If she only knew what he was waiting for, she'd make it happen. Then, he'd drop his guard, and she'd have a chance to escape.

"I'd be fine being here alone if you did go to work. Mel's here, right? It's not like I could go anywhere."

Donovan paused the movie and looked at her again, surprised. "This hasn't been about making sure you won't leave. I know you can't escape, Athena," he said. "This is about bonding us together. You need to be able to ask the tough questions and work through your feelings. I want to be here for that."

Athena licked her lips, wondering how on Earth she was going to pull off faking something like that. What would a captive working through their anger ask, anyway?

"You're cute when you're plotting my death," Donovan said. He clicked the movie back on and settled against her, his hand drawing circles on her bare skin.

That had been something new over the last few days: Donovan had started requiring her to be naked. She "lost" a piece of clothing every day until she was finally naked, making her wonder if it was all some sick game. Had she done something to trigger the loss of clothes? Was it a punishment? She refused to give him the satisfaction of her asking. Instead, Athena had shed the clothes like it didn't matter either way to her.

Donovan wasn't able to hide his interest so easily. The man walked around with a constant boner since she ditched her top. Every once in a while, she caught him staring at her, but so far, he hadn't tried to do anything beyond an innocent kiss or touch.

It was driving her crazy, which was probably his goal. Fucking sadist.

Athena pulled the blankets up to cover her chest and turned to look at him.

"I'm serious, Donovan. What's the endgame here?" she demanded. "Are you planning on just keeping me locked up in this house for the rest of my life?"

Donovan glanced at her, surprised. "Are you serious? Of course not. I mean, I fucking hope not. I want to take you on vacations and introduce you to the people I work with and my friends. Besides just Melissa, I mean. I want you to be happy, Athena."

She gestured around the dark bedroom. "Then why are you keeping me locked in here? Why am I naked?"

So much for playing it cool about the forced nudity.

"Do you not like being naked for me, Athena?" Donovan asked, his voice dropping a few octaves. He ran a finger across the top of the sheet that concealed her breasts from him. "I love having you nude in my bedroom, honestly. Taking away your clothes was for my benefit."

Athena's breath caught, her eyes dilating. She wanted him, or at least, her body did.

"If I touched you now, Athena, would you be wet for me?"

Donovan didn't wait for an answer. His fingers traveled lower, giving her plenty of time to object. She sat frozen, conflicted, until she felt him stroke her inner thighs. Without a second thought, she squirmed, moving just enough for him to rest his hand against her core.

"So impatient, Athena," Donovan teased. "I would've devoured every inch of you by now. All you had to do was ask."

He bent to capture her mouth with his, coaxing her to open for him. They both moaned in ecstasy when she relented. He devoured her, mimicking the sex act as he claimed every part of her mouth. She grabbed his shoulders, urging him to roll on top of her. His hard body, the way he kissed her like he owned her... it made her head spin.

Donovan readily complied, moving above her and placing his hand firmly against her naked breast. He pinched her nipples, teasing them painfully until she wanted to weep with pleasure. Fuck, yeah. It felt so good.

Athena reached between them to grasp his dick. It pulsed in her hand, making Donovan growl in appreciation. He pushed forward, fucking her hand like a pussy.

"Put it in," she begged. Athena wanted to feel him, how far he would stretch her. She knew it would have to hurt, especially if he didn't take the time to warm her up with fingers or a toy, but that was a huge part of the appeal. She needed it rough.

"Are you sure, Athena?" Donovan asked, kissing her along her jawline and making small bites on her neck. "Are you ready for me, slave girl?"

"Yes!" Athena was trying to keep it together, but it was too much. Too much teasing, too much pent-up desire.

"When I fuck you for the first time, it will be because you beg for it, Athena. Are you begging me to fuck you?" "Please! Jesus Christ, please... please fuck me, Donovan."

"What should you be calling me, slave girl?"

Donovan grasped her throat, applying enough pressure to make her see sparks.

"Master," Athena breathed. "Please fuck me, master."

Donovan nipped at her chest and sunk his teeth into her nipple's sensitive flesh. Athena screamed her release just as he shoved forward, fitting his dick into her pussy in one solid motion.

"Fuck!" It was exactly what she wanted, to feel him there, with the mixture of pain from his bite and taking too much of his dick at once. When he started to move, Athena thought for sure he was going to split her in two.

"You're so fucking wet for me, Athena," Donovan said above her. He slammed deeper, hitting her cervix as he bottomed out. She screamed, but that only turned his eyes dark. They looked feral, like all his humanity was gone. He was getting off on her pain, too.

Donovan pushed forward, seated as deep as he could. He made small thrusts, never removing enough of himself to give her a break. She was going to split in two, the way he hammered into her. The sweet friction of his small strokes hit her clit just right, causing her to build quickly to another orgasm.

"I'm going to cum again," she warned him. If he didn't allow her to cum, she'd simply die.

Thankfully, orgasm denial didn't seem to be a

priority to Donovan. "Cum hard for me. I want to feel you tighten on my cock."

With his permission, Athena clamped down on him, and her self-control shattered. She dug her nails into his back, tearing Donovan to shreds. At the same time, he claimed the sensitive spot under her collarbone, biting and sucking hard enough that her skin bruised purple.

Donovan smiled down at her, but his gaze wasn't on her face. He was looking at the bite mark, which landed close to the collar he placed around her neck. He hooked a finger around the piece of locking jewelry and growled in her face.

"I own you, Athena. And now, everyone knows it. Including you."

Even if she wanted to argue, there was no convincing the man otherwise. He gripped the collar firmly and continued to pound into her until, finally, he came. Athena screamed along with him as he emptied his balls deep into her. She was raw and likely bleeding from his rough thrusts.

In a post-orgasmic haze, Athena pushed aside all the anger and concern about who Donovan was. She threaded her fingers through his hair and allowed herself to float away. Fucking Donovan was a different kind of high. She was instantly addicted and would probably always need more.

*Chapter 23*


*Now*

Donovan was asleep next to her on the bed. Athena wasn't even tired; her mind was too busy going a million miles an hour. Was she a fraud for fucking Donovan? Maybe he was right about Nathan, though could she really call what he did cheating? Nathan had never promised any of them exclusivity. The idea of monogamy was laughable, with the five of them living together.

Of course, that had been a sticking point in their relationship. At her core, Athena had wanted to be the only one. She could admit that now, even though she refused to when Nathan was alive. It felt like a slap in the face to him, and especially to Veronica, to constantly complain about the other women in his life.

Athena knew the deal going into it. And those last few weeks with him had been so good that it was easy to forget the hard times. He had come back to her, or it had felt that way, at least.

But when she remembered the hard times, it made her heart clench painfully. Athena's head spun, thinking about catching Nathan in bed screwing other women. How long would it be until Donovan came to her with the same demands? How long would it take until she was standing in Veronica's shoes, having to accept whatever random woman Donovan decided to bring home?

Athena frowned, realizing that there might even be more women in the house at that very moment. Donovan didn't stray from her side often, but there were times, especially late at night when he thought she was sleeping, that he would leave her alone and go somewhere else in the house.

She had tried to break out of the bedroom during those mysterious blocks of time, but the door only allowed him to come and go, thanks to the palm reader he had installed. The windows didn't open, or they wouldn't open for her, at least. He could very well have other submissive women hidden all over the massive house in different rooms, just like this one.

Athena chewed on her lip, trying to decide what to do.

Realistically, there were two options. She could continue fighting Donovan and live the rest of her life holed up in his bedroom, or she could embrace her role as his submissive while still guarding her heart. Maybe that was the answer all along. She could have the hot sex, all the fun, and still be fine when he inevitably wanted someone else.

At least, that's what she could do until other opportunities presented themselves. Escape would be a possibility eventually. After all, she thought. He can't keep me locked in here forever.

———

"I have to go into the office," he said a few days later. "They need me to sign some things and talk to the new hires. I've met them on Zoom, but it'll be good to see them in person. That sort of thing."

Athena had been glued to his side for the better side of three weeks. She was starting to forget that the man even had a job. "Okayyyy," she said. "What would you like me to do while you're gone?"

She had already taken the kitchen apart and reorganized the garage. She was currently sitting in a pile of books she was alphabetizing for Donovan's office. The weight and smell of the hardcover copies were familiar and comforting.

She had to wonder where her own collection of books was. Maybe still at the family apartment if it hadn't already been sold? She had taken her favorites with her when she moved out, but there had been too many to move them all. Maybe one of the other women had taken a book or two and were keeping them in their new homes.

"You could stay here and finish this," he said, gesturing to the stacks of books. "Mel will be here if you need anything. Or you can come with me and see the actual headquarters and my office. You know... when I'm not working from home here with you."

Athena weighed the options, but she'd be hard-pressed to pass up an outing that involved fresh air and sunlight.

"Aren't you afraid I'm going to run away?" she asked, only half joking.

"No," he said, not offering any more of an explanation. "Get dressed and meet me in the car in thirty minutes."

Well, that gave her hardly any time at all. Ideally, she'd like to shower the sex smell off herself, at the very least, after their daily wake-up call, but she'd have to settle for just styling her hair and putting on some makeup.

Athena hurried up the stairs, well aware that Donovan was laughing at her excitement.

Of course, he was in a position to laugh. He wasn't the one trapped inside the house. He had expanded her world beyond the bedroom, though, which was a huge improvement from being stuck in the same room every day. Since she had begged him to fuck her, he not only kept her satisfied in bed, but he also gave her free rein in the rest of the house. So far, the only woman she had bumped into was Mel, but the house had its secrets; she was sure of it. Donovan certainly did, too.

When Athena was ready, she took a deep breath and stepped outside for the first time in weeks. The sunlight was overly aggressive, almost too bright, and the wind from the breeze tickled her skin. It reminded her of whenever she was home sick for several days. Going back outside had felt foreign, and at the moment, it was like she was seeing trees and grass again for the first time.

Everything smelled so fresh, too. She breathed deeply, enjoying the scent of pine trees and wind.

Donovan rolled down the window and waved at her to hurry up, but he looked amused at her simple joy.

Athena took her time, stalling to soak up the outdoors for another minute. When she finally sat down and buckled herself in, Donovan's expression had changed. He looked remorseful, if such a thing was possible.

"You love being outside, don't you?"

The question surprised Athena, and she shrugged, not sure how to answer. Didn't everyone like being outside? "I didn't realize it... you liked walking to work to be outside, didn't you? I mean...I'm sorry, Athena," he said, looking at her meaningfully. "I wouldn't have kept you inside for so long if I had thought about it that way. Were the last few weeks more difficult being inside all the time?"

"Are you serious?" she asked. The question felt like a trap. Wasn't it painfully obvious how hard it had been? "Of course, it sucks being stuck inside all the time. Isn't that what you wanted? For me to be unhappy?"

Donovan swallowed hard. "Not at all. I wanted you to get to know me better, and I wanted us to bond so you wouldn't feel the need to try and escape the first chance you got. Keeping you at home had nothing to do with trying to make you miserable."

"Hmmm," was all Athena said in response. She wasn't sure if she should believe him. Nathan had totally done things to make her unhappy in the name of punishment. He had never locked her away inside for weeks at a time, but then, she had never given him a reason to.

"From now on, you get outside time. Got it?"

Donovan's tone was so serious that Athena had to laugh. "Yes, sir," she said.

Her cheekiness earned her a slap on the thigh and an evil smile that promised her a good time when they returned to the house.

Athena liked watching Donovan navigate through traffic. You could tell that he enjoyed driving. He kept his hand on her legs whenever he wasn't using it to shift, playing with the frayed holes in her jeans that exposed a little skin. The fresh air was probably boosting his mood, too, whether he realized it or not. Maybe it was the right time to test the waters a little bit more.

"So, are you saying that you aren't going to lock me up for punishment? Or that I won't ever have a punishment?"

Donovan glanced at her. "I think we'd both agree there are times you'll probably need to be punished, Athena," he said. "There's also going to be times you want to be punished. But to answer your question, no. Knowing how much being outside means to you, it's not something I would take from you unless I felt like I had to."

Athena nodded and gazed out her window. As they approached the city, it felt weird seeing familiar places again. She felt like so much time had passed that everything she knew before should have changed, too.

"Keep asking me questions," Donovan prodded. "I really don't mind, Athena. I think it'll help put your mind at ease to know the answers to things."

Alright. If he wanted to open that door, Athena had plenty of questions for him to answer.

"Do you regret what you did to Nathan? Or to Otto?" she asked. "Or anyone else you've killed? How many people is that, by the way?"

"One at a time," he said, giving her a playful glance that turned serious with his answer. "No, I don't regret killing the people I have. Every one of them deserved it, and the world is better because I took care of a problem. I don't know how many people I've killed, Athena. Probably well into the hundreds. I haven't kept track."

Athena's stomach fluttered. Whatever she had expected him to say, it wasn't that. How many people does it take to make someone a serial killer, exactly? She couldn't remember, but surely less than a hundred.

At least he was being honest, though. That's probably the only positive spin she could put on that. Too bad no one would believe her if she went to the police without solid proof.

The weight of Donovan's confession hung between them, but he seemed unbothered by it. It was like he assumed that Athena would be able to reconcile what he'd done and still feel something for him. She had to wonder what that kind of confidence must be like.

"You said you put up cameras in Nathan's house. Did you have cameras inside my Brownstone apartment?

What about Jared's place?"

He nodded. "Yes, to both."

It was such a horrible violation of privacy, but he admitted to it with complete indifference. "Why, exactly, did you need cameras? Was the guy parked outside my home 24/7 not enough for you?"

"No, it wasn't, Athena," Donovan said, not joking

at all. "I'll always be watching you. Owning a company devoted to surveillance definitely comes in handy sometimes."

"But you do more than surveillance," she pointed out.

"Yes, I do," he glanced at her. "We offer protection to people who are wealthy and powerful. We also use the security technology to catch criminals when police can't seem to do so, but that's not something we advertise to the general public. We were able to uncover some local human trafficking rings, which turned into bigger things. We turn the findings over to the police. Usually."

"Usually," Athena scoffed. "But not for Nathan."

"No, not for Nathan," Donovan agreed. "He had wronged you and me, in addition to at least one underage girl. He deserved what he got."

"He said he didn't know she was underaged." At least, according to Donovan's version of what happened, Nathan claimed not to know her age. Athena wasn't going to let that possibility go. It was the only thing that allowed her to believe Nathan wasn't a total monster, and she really needed to hold onto that.

Donovan gave her a look. "He knew."

They drove the rest of the way to his office in silence, but when they parked, Donovan squeezed her leg gently. "You might think that the worst thing Nathan could do is fuck a 17-year-old," he said quietly. "And yeah, that was fucked up. But to me, the worst thing he ever did was beat you down until you thought that you only deserved part of him. I'm telling you right now, Athena. I'm the owner in our relationship, but I don't collect women. You don't have to worry about me sneaking around like he did."

Athena stared at him, not sure how to respond.

Donovan might think that's exactly what she wanted to hear, only to "change his mind" later. Nathan certainly had no problem introducing new ideas after the fact.

"Come on. There's lots of people here who are dying to meet you," he said, opening the car door. "And I probably do need to get a little work done, too."

Athena took a deep breath and unbuckled her seatbelt to follow him inside.

*Chapter 24*

*Now*

Donovan wasn't kidding. From the moment they walked into the building, everyone wanted to meet her, especially the ladies in HR. The entire team seemed to be male-dominated, except for that department, and Athena quickly picked up on the fact that one, if not both, of them had serious crushes on Donovan.

What was even more hilarious was the fact that he seemed completely oblivious to their flirting.

"It's so good to see you in person, Mr. O'Malley," one gushed when they walked in together. "Not that I didn't enjoy the video conferences, of course. Please let me know if there's anything you need."

"Great. Thanks, Janet," he said, hardly looking at her. "By the way, this is my girlfriend, Athena. We've been on vacation together, which is why I haven't been around as much."

"I know," Janet said stiffly. "We processed your leave."

Donovan laughed. "Of course. Well, good to see you." Athena had to contain her laughter when he dismissed Janet from HR. The young blonde clearly wasn't used to rejection.

*Nathan would've drooled all over her.* Athena shook her head. Where had that thought come from?

"Glad you finally decided to put in a half-day of hard work," Chester said, patting Donovan on the back. "Hey, Athena. How are you doing today?"

"Good. How are you, Chester?" She had met him a few days ago after Donovan had lifted her quarantine from the bedroom. She liked that Donovan's employees seemed comfortable enough to give him a hard time.

"Great! Okay, let's do this thing." Chester led them to a conference room that was full of other department heads. Athena looked around, not sure if she should sit at the table with Donovan or wait outside.

"I've got her, boss," Alvarez said from the doorway.

Donovan glanced at Athena, checking to see if she was comfortable, then nodded at Alvarez. She followed him out of the room, closing the door behind her.

"How have you been?" she asked. "It's weird not seeing you every day."

"Believe it or not, I think I miss parking outside of your building, too. I'm back in the action and my feet are killing me. I didn't realize a good thing when I had it."

Athena grinned. He was being kind; Alvarez clearly enjoyed whatever it was he normally did for the company. He must be pretty high up, if he had some of the more exciting work, which gave Athena an idea.

"Hey, I was wondering if you could give me any information about Nathan Garcia. You know... my former boyfriend."

Alvarez sighed and rubbed the back of his neck. "Yeah, I should have seen that one coming. Have you talked to Donovan about him?"

"He told me some things that seem a little farfetched," Athena said carefully. "I was wondering if... well, if there's a file or something on Nathan? Something that would corroborate the things that Donovan claimed about him."

Alverez's friendly charm evaporated, replaced by a mask of indifference. *He must have learned that trick from Donovan,* Athena thought. *Or maybe the other way around.*

"Listen, Athena, I can't get in the middle of a disagreement between my boss and his new girlfriend, especially when it deals with her former boyfriend. All I can say is Garcia was a pretty sick guy, and I've never known Donovan to lie to someone who's important to him."

"Got it. Well, thanks anyway," she said, turning to go. She needed to find a restroom and a vending machine to buy a water bottle. But Athena didn't have to go very far down the hall to realize she was being followed. "What is it? Forget something?"

"No, ma'am. I'm just...staying close. As always." Athena blinked. "Donovan sent you to babysit me, so I don't... do what, exactly? Run out of the building? Hitch a ride to the nearest police station?"

Alvarez shrugged. "I'm just doing my job, Athena."

"Yeah. I got that. Well, don't bother following me into the bathroom stall. Donovan probably already has cameras in there."

Janet from HR gasped as she walked by.

"He doesn't," Alvarez said to Janet. "The bathrooms don't have cameras."

"You never know, Janet. He really does like them everywhere," Athena said, feigning nonchalance. She pushed the bathroom door open and locked it behind her, eager for privacy. A chance to breathe.

Athena studied herself in the mirror. She had lost some weight over the past few weeks at Donovan's house, but that wasn't necessarily a bad thing. He only stocked high-quality organic food, and before moving in with him, Athena had been living off gas station pizza and frozen waffles when she wasn't cooking for Jared.

She bit her lip. *Jared.* Donovan hadn't said anything else about him, and Athena hadn't bothered to ask. With Pete dead, did that mean Jared was gone, too? Did he have any idea about the horrible things Pete was caught up in?

Donovan hadn't shared all the details with her, but Athena was able to piece together that Pete was involved in some human trafficking operation. So, by extension, Jared was, too. And maybe even Nathan, but she couldn't dwell on that. There had to be some misunderstanding.

She finished up in the bathroom and returned to the hallway. Alvarez was waiting for her, of course, and he gave her a guilty smile when their eyes met. A silent apology that said yes, he was still her babysitter.

"Is there a break room or something?" Athena asked. "I need to grab a water bottle from a vending machine."

"Sure thing," Alvarez said. He led her to another room that looked more like a day spa. She was about to ask to borrow some change for the machine but then noticed that all the beverages and snacks were free.

"It's like you work for a shady surveillance version of Google or something," she said, grabbing the water and a bag of chips. She was craving something salty that wasn't grass-fed or high in protein.

"That's exactly why I accepted the position. I wanted the Google amenities and wasn't willing to give up the shady business side of things."

"Really?" Athena asked, taking a sip of water.

"No," Alvarez deadpanned, grabbing a snack for himself.

Athena laughed. A set of heavy footsteps followed the sound, pausing at the doorway. Donovan must have been searching for her, and her laughter had given them away .

"Doing alright?" Donovan asked as he entered the break room. "Sorry, this is taking a little longer than I planned. I told Chester I'd be back in a minute. Do you need anything from me?"

Alvarez looked to Athena for an answer, and she shook her head. "We're fine, thanks. Go ahead and finish whatever you need to do here," she said.

Donovan's eyes softened, causing a pulling sensation in Athena's lower stomach. He approved of her response. He was glad to have her at work. For some reason, those thoughts filled Athena with satisfaction.

"I'll be back in just a little while," he promised. Then, added to Alvarez, "Why don't you take her up to my office? It'll be more comfortable, and she could read or watch TV."

Alvarez nodded, and Athena tried to ignore how good it felt to have Donovan think about her comfort. When Nathan brought her into the office, he had never stopped a meeting to find her, let alone suggest that she hang out in his office.

But none of that changed the truth. Donovan was a murderer, someone she was using for good sex until a better plan came along, and that was the end of it.

Athena followed Alvarez to the elevator and up to the top floor where the leadership suite provided a great view of the city. The suite had another well-stocked kitchen but with the added bonus of a full bar. A glass of wine sounded nice.

"Want some?" she asked Alvarez, holding up a bottle of red.

"Some of us are still on the clock, Ms. Garcia," he said, settling into one of the armchairs and grabbing the nearby newspaper. Athena shrugged and poured herself a glass. She took in the rest of the space as she recorked the bottle.

"This is really fancy," she said. "He's loaded, isn't he? Like, really rich, huh?"

Alvarez grunted, not bothering to look up or give a real answer.

Athena walked to the glass wall, serving as a floor-to- ceiling window. The building wasn't all that tall, but the rent on the space had to be astronomical. Plus, there was the mansion, the fancy cars, the fleet of staff...yeah, Donovan was loaded.

"How much longer do you think he's going to be?" she asked walking back to the lounge area, and taking a seat across from Alvarez. "Is there something I can do to help out? You know, while we wait."

Alvarez glanced at her. "Probably not. All the records he keeps are confidential, and you don't have the clearance."

"Betchya I could get the clearance," she teased. The wine was making her bold. "He said he didn't want any secrets between us, after all."

"You're probably right about that, but you'd have to ask him," he said, turning the page. He handed her a section from the back. "Here. Read this and stay out of trouble."

Athena skimmed the articles without reading any of them. Crime was up. Something about the Olympics next year. Blah, blah, blah.

It was weird that Donovan still had physical copies of the newspaper lying around, right? How many people still had the paper delivered? Didn't everyone just get the news online?

Her eyes landed on a heading at the bottom of the second page. It was a report about a local fire that broke out at Jared's apartment complex. Worse than the property damage, there was a fatality. The article didn't provide a name, and there was no picture or clear description of the extent of the damage, but Athena knew right away that it wasn't a coincidence.

"Would you be able to get my things back soon?"

she asked innocently. "From Jared's apartment, I mean. I had to leave in a hurry, and I still have a lot of clothes over there."

Alvarez didn't answer right away. "I'm sure O'Malley can get you new clothes," he said reluctantly.

Athena shook her head. "It's more than that, though. I have some valuable things that can't be replaced. Maybe I should ask Donovan to take me there after he gets done with work."

Their eyes met over the paper, and Alvarez narrowed his gaze.

"What do you think you know, Athena?"

"Did he do it? Did Donovan do it?" She tossed the paper to him, but Alvarez didn't bother looking at it.

"Your friend was part of something dangerous and evil. Whatever happened to him needed to happen, do you understand?"

"I understand that people who cross Donovan seem to end up dead," she growled. "I'm sure it's a lot easier to justify killing people and destroying their lives if you can say they're evil or whatever, but I haven't seen any proof that Jared even knew what was going on. The only thing I have to go off of is overhearing one side of a phone call, and now he's dead. Just like Pete. Just like Nathan."

Athena stood and wrapped her arms around herself. She wanted to leave, but the only way for that to happen was for Donovan to return and take her away. Being in a car with him at the moment would be even worse than being locked up in the penthouse office space.

"Maybe Donovan should be here to explain this," Alvarez said, sighing. "I'll give him a call. I'm sure he'll be thrilled. Fair warning: you might find yourself banned from reading the newspaper."

"No. Please don't call him," she said, turning quickly. "I'm sorry. No more questions. I just want... I mean, things have just gotten better between us. This is the first time I've been out of the house in a long time, and I don't want to cause trouble with him. I don't want him to punish me."

Alvarez pocketed the phone, assessing her with new eyes. When he finally spoke, it was barely above a whisper. "I work for Donovan, but that doesn't mean I wouldn't stop him if I thought he was harming someone. Donovan is... different, but I assumed your relationship was consensual. Is that still the case?"

"Yes," she said slowly. It was consensual, right? She consented to having sex with him. She called him when she needed help. She wanted to stay at his house after the thing with Pete. But had she really wanted to be cooped in a bedroom for days? Had she actually agreed to have no privacy or life outside of him? He was addicting. And infuriating.

It was complicated, to say the least.

"Alright, then. Let me know if that changes." Alvarez turned his attention back to the paper, and Athena returned to the window. They didn't speak again until Donovan stepped off the elevator.

"Thanks for being patient," he said to both of them by way of greeting. "Looks like I'm just about done here. Anything interesting happen while I was busy?"

"No," they answered in unison.

"That's my cue. I'll see you later, boss. Athena." Alvarez nodded to them as he walked to the elevator.

Donovan didn't respond; his attention was on Athena instead. As soon as the elevator doors closed, Donovan was there, on her, pressing himself against the curves of her body.

"You have been such a good girl," he whispered in her ear. "Waiting patiently for me up here, like I asked you to. I was so hard thinking about it. Do you know that? You obeying me gets me so fucking hard."

Athena's brain scrambled, more than willing to forget anything to do with Jared. Who was Jared? Who cared? Donovan's chest moved against hers, sending delicious friction through her nipples.

Donovan reached between them and hooked a finger in the front of her jeans, pulling her hips to meet his. "I'm going to take you here, Athena. Bent over in my office, panties around your ankles. Next time, I want you to wear a skirt to make it even easier."

"Yes, sir," she whispered. Donovan's eyes darkened, and he bent to claim her mouth with his. He gripped the back of her hair, holding her still as he thrust his tongue into her. The probing, rhythmic kiss felt almost like sex, but it wasn't enough. Athena needed more.

She tried to move down to her knees, but Donovan growled his disapproval, causing her to freeze.

"You're not in charge of how we do this, sweetheart," he warned. "I told you that I wanted you bent over with your panties pulled down. Make it happen."

Athena's heart raced at the words. She wanted this. She needed this.

She spun around and shimmied down her jeans and panties, eager for whatever was to come. Athena placed her hands against the glass window, bracing herself while slightly bent at the waist.

"I can smell you from here," Donovan groaned, eyes roaming over her bare sex. "God, you smell so good. I bet you taste even better."

He knelt behind her, using his fingers to open her entirely. Then, he feasted. Slowly at first, but soon like a starving man. He added two fingers, using the angle to his advantage. His cock lengthened in his pants, but he ignored it. This was exactly where he wanted to be: entirely consumed by Athena. He smiled into her cunt as he felt her legs tremble and her breathing turned erratic. His sweet, obedient sub was close to the edge.

"I want you to be wetter, slave girl. You better make my face drip with your juice."

"I'm going to cum," she panted. "Fuck. I'm coming."

Donovan placed a hand against her stomach, holding her body in place as he fingered her and sucked on her clit. With one final shout, Athena's tunnel closed around him, wringing his fingers as she rode out her orgasm.

"You're so hungry for it, aren't you?" Donovan asked as he pulled her down to him. "That's just another way for me to own you, Athena. You're not going to get this kind of shit from anyone else. No one can make you cum like I can, and I'd kill anyone who'd try."

Athena didn't try to respond, even after her breathing evened out. She allowed herself the freedom to enjoy being in Donovan's embrace, loving the way his hard chest was firm against her own soft curves. What could she even say to that, anyway? That he wouldn't kill someone over her? Of course, he would. He'd done it before, after all.

"Let's go home," he said, helping her up and redressing her in her jeans and panties. Athena stood there, feeling oddly like a life-sized doll. She was grateful when he was done, and she could step away from the awkwardness of being too close to him.

The lights in the city had come on while they were busy, and the streets below them glowed against the night's inky blackness. It was gorgeous, just as beautiful as any landscape in nature.

"It's Friday night and it's barely dark," she argued,

knowing she was pushing her luck. She really didn't want to go back to the same four walls of his bedroom. "Can't we stay out? Please?"

Donovan glanced at her, considering the request.

"I have been very good today. You said so yourself," Athena said, turning and running a finger down his chest.

His breath hitched as she strayed below the belt, directly to the stiff ridge in his pants. Donovan grasped her by the wrist, preventing her from tracing the outline of his erection. He'd be the one deciding when she'd get another taste of his cock, but the fact she clearly wanted more was a good sign. "I think I have the perfect place for a girl like you."

*Chapter 25*

*Now*

"They should give you a punch card or something," Athena said when Donovan tossed his keys to the valet. "Park at Safeword ten times, get one valet service for free."

"Let's pitch that to them another time. We're going to be busy tonight."

Athena swallowed hard, her body already buzzing with anticipation. The physical stuff was easy. Every part of her wanted to submit in that way.

Donovan grabbed her hand and pulled her into him as they walked in. His fingers grazed her collar, reminding her without a word who she belonged to. Her blood pumped, sending endorphins straight to her brain. Yes, she absolutely wanted to belong to him.

He led her past the bar and through the maze of

people getting their kink on. The dominant from before was tying another subject, and he nodded a greeting to her as they walked by. His eyes saw the collar, and he winked. If it wasn't clear enough before, it was now. Donovan had staked his claim.

Donovan must have seen the exchange. His grip tightened in response. "I know how much you've been dying for some rope play. How about we give that a shot tonight?"

"Fuck, yeah!" It had been so long since she had done any rope. Nathan thought it was too much trouble. Most of the time, he liked to focus on the things that got him off, and rope was more of a slow burn. "Do we have time?"

Donovan gave her a funny look. "Of course, we do."

He asked one of the attendants to bring new rope to the scene space in the center of the room. Athena's eyes widened when she realized he wasn't going to make her go to one of the private rooms in the back. "We're doing this here?"

"Get undressed," he ordered, taking the jute from the attendant. He ran his hands over the cords, testing them and making sure they were good quality. He nodded before turning back to the employee. "Can you bring us a suspension frame, too?"

Athena practically threw her clothes off. She had never been suspended. Nathan had promised one day... well, it didn't matter. She was getting a chance to do it now.

Donovan glanced at her, his lips tugging upward despite his serious expression. "Suspension can be dangerous with someone who doesn't know what they're doing. Nerve damage, falling... all sorts of things can happen. I've been tying with a suspension frame for a few years, but I need you to tell me if you'd rather wait for us to do this. I don't mind keeping you on the ground tonight if it would make you feel safer."

Athena blinked, dumbfounded. "You can't tell that I want to do this?"

"I can tell you want to, obviously. But I want you to think about it before you decide to give it a shot. Just take a deep breath and consider if you'd rather leave this particular activity for another day. Like I said, I don't mind waiting."

He had moved on to inspect the suspension frame, feeling along the hardpoints to make sure it would be strong enough to hold Athena's weight. Safeword was known as a safe place to play, but her heart fluttered knowing that he was so invested in shielding her from harm. The idea that it was because he owned her was even more appealing. It made her melt.

"Shut up and tie me, Donovan," she said, stepping up to the mobile suspension frame.

"You're going to regret those words, slave girl,"

he growled in her ear. His teeth grazed against her neck, tracing the vein that was her life source. Fuck. Now, she wanted him again already.

"Turn around," Donovan said. "And put your arms behind your back."

It was a position she knew well for tying, but Athena was so interested to see how it would end with her off the ground. A nearby attendant moved closer to oversee what was happening for her protection and, likely, so the club wouldn't be held liable if the suspension went horribly wrong.

Donovan turned some intricate knots, and Athena lost herself in the rhythm of it. His hands worked quickly, and soon, she wasn't able to move. Euphoria bloomed in her, and her head started feeling light and bubbly. She was floating, even though he had yet to suspend her the rest of the way. Her body was still supported by the block beneath the bar, but not for long.

"Are you ready to fly, baby?" Donovan asked before moving the block away.

The high was too much for her to talk, so she nodded instead. Of course, she wanted this. Donovan supported her weight as he removed the block beneath her, then slowly let her down to hang. One leg was tied back, connecting to the rope that kept her arms in place. Athena closed her eyes and savored the feeling of being tied and weightless. Her body was probably crying out from the effort of being in the tie, but she couldn't feel anything but pleasure. It was a drug, pure and simple.

Donovan pressed himself against her, allowing his fingertips to travel over the rope he had secured.

"Beautiful," he murmured.

All too soon, the block was back in place, and Donovan was untying her. Athena was flushed and warm despite her teeth chattering when he finally unraveled the last knot. Donovan collected her in his arms and sat her on the edge of the play space. He grabbed a blanket and tucked it around her securely, mimicking the intimacy of being tied with the rope. Her skin was red and marked, but she couldn't feel any of it.

"You're amazing," he said, caressing her cheek. "Thank you for letting me tie you. I'm going to clean up the space really fast, then we'll get out of here."

Athena watched with hooded eyes as he collected their supplies and helped the attendant disinfect the area. About 15 minutes later, the high from being tied started to wear off, and she realized that she really needed to pee... and really needed to get her clothes back on.

She was also really, really sore.

"Donovan," she croaked. "I need some water... and a lot of other things."

He glanced at her and grabbed a water bottle from a nearby cooler.

"Sorry. I should've thought about that before I

broke down the scene. What else do you need?"

"Maybe my clothes," she said. "And I have to use the restroom."

"The restroom is fine, but clothes are a no-go. I want to see all the marks on your skin from the rope, at least until we have to leave."

Athena flushed with pleasure. He was proud of her.

"Do you need help to get to the bathroom?" Donovan asked, taking the empty bottle from her.

"What? Um... no, sorry. No." Athena was still a little spacey. It was like she was hearing the questions in slow motion.

Donovan raised an eyebrow, trying to decide if she

was alright to go alone. "Are you sure? There's a single stall that I could take you to—"

"Nope. Not going to happen," Athena said, standing and dropping the blanket. "The women's bathroom is literally right there. I'll be back in a minute."

Donovan gave her a look to address her tone but let her escape to the bathroom by herself. Thank god for that; Athena really needed to go, and having him watch her pee was not a kink she wanted to entertain.

After using the stall, she washed her hands in one of the gorgeous cement sinks and admired the rope marks on her body in the mirror.

"They're gorgeous, Athena. You did beautifully being suspended."

Athena whipped around, recognizing the female voice immediately.

"Veronica! I had no idea you still visited this place. Are you with...? I mean, how are you? How are things going for you?" Athena winced, hating how clumsily her questions came spilling out.

Not only did she want to avoid asking about Veronica's new master directly, she also was still trying to remember how to piece together a sentence in the afterglow of subspace.

Thankfully, Veronica seemed to understand and just smiled back. "Things are going well, actually. I wasn't sure how I'd get on with the new situation, but honestly... we have a good connection," she said, leaning against the wall. "I'm guessing things are going well for you, too, if the tying session I just saw is any indication."

"We have good chemistry," Athena admitted. "But it's complicated. Donovan... he, well...."

Athena's eyes widened. She quickly tried to piece together what to say to Veronica. Did she know the truth about Nathan and the underage girl? Maybe his wife could shed some light on what had happened.

"Actually, I need to talk to you. In private," she said, glancing at the wall of stalls in the restroom. Who knew how many people were listening in on their conversation?

"I see," Veronica said, searching her face. "I moved in with Daniel soon after the reading of Nathan's will. Do you think Mr. O'Malley would allow you to visit at our house? Maybe we could have you both over for lunch, and we could chat then."

Athena shook her head. She needed to do this away from Donovan and fast. If they spent too much time together, she'd have a much harder time doing what needed to be done.

"Could I come by tomorrow? It'd have to be early. Like, probably before dawn. I don't know how I'll do it, exactly, but just give me your address, and I'll find a way to meet you. We need to talk, and I don't think Donovan would approve."

Veronica looked surprised. "You'd go behind your master's back to meet with me? Wow, Athena. Nathan always bragged about your obedience. What changed?" It was a good question. What had changed? Was she less submissive? Was Donovan less dominant than Nathan? No, it wasn't anything like that. Maybe she was just rising to the occasion. Maybe she was defiant because she had to be. It was the only thing she could do to hopefully clear Nathan's name.

———

Something had changed between them at

Safeword. After they returned home, Donovan allowed Athena to stay up late and watch a movie, under the pretense that the suspension tie had given her a huge boost of energy and she couldn't sleep afterward.

It was a huge improvement from being dragged up to the master bedroom, that's for sure.

Athena watched from her place on the couch as Donovan nodded off in front of the movie she had selected for them to watch together. She had pretended to fall asleep first, but Athena was very much still awake. The wheels in her head kept turning, trying desperately to think of any possible way for her to sneak out of the house and come back later without being noticed.

The hardest part would be the security system. Donovan had things locked down tight, and even leaving the house required a code or an alarm would sound. She hadn't been given the code yet, another testimony to how little he trusted her.

Donovan was startled awake when his phone went off in his pocket, destroying any hope of her escaping the room at that moment. She kept still; only her eyes fluttered so it looked as though she was still asleep.

"Hello? Chester?" Donovan answered, the sleep heavy in his voice. Athena felt his eyes on her as he listened to Chester on the other end. "Of course. Yeah, now's fine. I'll be in my office."

Donovan hung up and leaned over to gather her in his arms. She stirred, pushing him away and pretending to wake up.

"What's going on?" Athena grumbled, stretching.

"Sorry, slave girl. Duty calls, and it looks like you're ready for bed. Go on upstairs, and I'll join you after I meet with Chester. He's on his way over now."

Athena nodded, gathering up the spare blanket to take it with her. Donovan's gaze heated as he took the sight of her in. Her hair was tussled, and Athena knew she probably looked a mess. Donovan seemed to find messes appealing, though.

"God, I'll never get tired of seeing you like this," he whispered, grabbing her ass as she walked by.

Athena swatted at him half-heartedly and stumbled to the staircase. She waited at the bottom until she heard Donovan's office door click shut. Now was the time to act. This was her only shot.

Athena felt in her pocket for the phone Veronica had lent to her. They had agreed it was too risky for Athena to borrow a car, so Veronica was coming to meet her instead. The plan was for Athena to slip outside and run to the edge of the property, where Veronica would be waiting. Of course, that was all dependent upon no one monitoring the cameras that were no doubt scattered throughout the house and property. Assuming Athena could even make it outside to begin with, that is.

She moved to the front door and listened. Finally, Chester's headlights shone through the window, and she heard the beep of his car doors locking. She tried to appear nonchalant, as though she were walking by on the way to the kitchen.

"Hey, Chester," she said when he opened the door. "Donovan said you have a meeting tonight. I was just a little hungry before bed. You know... for a midnight snack or whatever."

Chester grunted, walking around her without as much as a hello. Whatever was on his mind helped him not second-guess what she was doing by the front door.

Just as the door was about to shut, Athena placed the edge of the blanket at the bottom. She walked with Chester down the hall. She said goodbye as they parted, him going to the office and her turning towards the kitchen.

She bustled around, knocking jars together in the pantry until she knew he was gone. As soon as the door locked behind him, Athena took off back to the foyer.

Sure enough, the blanket had prevented the door from closing all the way. Athena wadded the blanket up and threw it back in the direction of the living room, hoping that it wouldn't give her away. She dug an old receipt out of her hoodie and shoved it between the lock and the frame of the door. If everything went as planned, Athena would be back in the house before Donovan even knew she was missing.

The motion-sensitive lights were still on from Chester's arrival. They made it impossible to hide from any cameras that could pick up on her escape, but it was less suspicious than them turning on for a second time just for her. Athena just needed to be as quick and quiet as possible.

After several minutes of running, she came upon the edge of the property, marked by the tall fence. It would be hard to scale it, but Chester had left the gate open. On the other side was a car with its engine idling, and behind the wheel sat Veronica.

Athena opened the passenger door hastily. "Drive. Just go anywhere in case someone realizes I'm gone."

Veronica nodded and put the car in gear. She glanced at Athena, asking an unspoken question.

"I'm not being abused or anything. Donovan's been... nice. It's been alright being with him," Athena said. Guilt festered beneath her skin. It was more than alright, if she was being honest, but she didn't need to share that with Veronica. Not when the purpose of their meeting was to bring up shit about her dead husband. "Have you really been okay moving in with... what was his name again?"

"Daniel. And yes, things have been good for me. For us," Veronica said. "Have you spoken to the others? Denise and Teresa, I mean."

Athena shook her head. "No. Just you."

"Good," she said, turning down a dark road and pulling off to the shoulder. "Now. What did you want to tell me?"

Athena licked her lips, suddenly hesitant. "I'm not really sure how to say this. I know that you loved Nathan a lot. You know I did, too, right? More than anything. He was... well, he was..."

Veronica gestured for her to keep going. She was right; there wasn't any time to waste being sentimental.

"Right. Okay. Well, what I wanted to ask is, did you ever hear or see anything about Nathan that was... wrong? I mean... like him being interested in younger girls, or women, who weren't consenting?"

Veronica stared at her.

"See? I knew it was ridiculous. There's no way he would've done anything like that. Look, I'm sorry I bothered you. I just had to know."

"No, you're right. You deserve to know," Veronica said, placing a hand on Athena's. "Yes. Nathan was interested in young girls, and in women who were being trafficked. He was involved with the business side of it, too. His legal business was more of a front for his darker interests than anything else. It lost more money than he could even begin to count. Nathan would've been in big trouble if it wasn't for the trafficking money he received."

The blood drained from Athena's face and her

heart sank. It couldn't be true. Nathan had been everything to her.

Veronica smiled sadly. "It's a hard pill to swallow, I know. I believed in the good in him, too, until I just couldn't anymore."

"He didn't die from cancer," Athena blurted, angry and hurt. "He was murdered. Do you know that? Do you even care?"

"Of course, I know," Veronica said softly. "I helped Donovan O'Malley do it, after all."

Chapter 26

*Now*

"I wanted to kill him in his sleep. I could have strangled him or shot him or something, but Donovan insisted on using poison." Veronica shook her head. "It was the only way he'd help me. I needed a professional like him to keep from winding up in prison, and he needed Nathan to create his final directive before he died so that he could have you. That was his motivation in everything, really. Donovan knew you'd mourn Nathan's death for a long time, and the only way to override that would be for you to follow Nathan's orders. It was quite clever, really."

Athena stared ahead into the darkness as her world tilted on its axis. What was she supposed to say to that? She was going to be sick. "But... he was getting better. You must have stopped poisoning him, at least near the end. You loved him, Veronica.

I know you did."

Veronica looked down at the keys in her hand, fiddling with the chain. "I only stopped poisoning him because Donovan told me to. It was to mimic the temporary improvement that some cancer patients experience before death. He was going to have me finish him off with an extra dose of poison, but after he received a second opinion and realized he didn't actually have cancer, we couldn't wait anymore. Donovan had to take care of him."

Tears flooded Athena's vision. "You murdered him. He gave us everything, and you killed him."

"You think walking in on a threesome was the worst thing I've seen? That some group sex is the worst thing he's made me do?" Veronica snapped. "Please. Listen to me, Athena. Nathan was a classic manipulator. He'd give you just enough good stuff so you wouldn't walk away, and then he'd do what he wanted after you were hooked on him. You, of all people, should know that. He loved hurting you as long as you didn't complain about it too much. It was an ego trip for him to watch you die inside over him."

When she didn't answer, Veronica looked at her pointedly. "Seriously. Did you ever want to share him? Of course not. Yet, you did it because he convinced you it was acceptable for him to have countless women. It's not like he even loved them, either. Oh, he said we were all equal, but did you ever wonder why he was fine playing with them at the club? They got even less of his than you did, Athena. Much less than I did. How is that fair?"

"But you did want to share him," Athena hissed. "So why are you complaining about it?"

Veronica nodded slowly. "Yeah, I did. I liked sharing him with you and even with Denise and Teresa. You don't understand. Nathan liked... other things. Not just consensual relationships. Really twisted stuff. I get it, though. Parts of him were great. He could make you feel like you were the most important person in the world to him. But other parts of him were just evil, and he needed to be stopped."

Neither of them spoke, allowing the weight of Veronica's words to sink in.

"I need to go," Athena said, reaching for the door. "Just..."

She slammed it shut without bothering to finish the sentence. *Just leave me alone. Just go fuck yourself.* Either of those phrases would've worked.

Veronica didn't even try to stop her from leaving. At first, Athena started walking back to Donovan's house, but then she realized being there was just as bad as sitting in the car with Veronica. Both of them were responsible for what happened to Nathan, and neither of them even regretted what they did.

Athena picked up the pace, taking a route that would eventually lead her to the city. Far away from

Veronica. Far away from Donovan.

At least, she was pretty sure it would. Being locked up in a house for most of her time there, Athena hadn't had a chance to explore the suburban neighborhoods.

The cool of the night made her shiver, but the running helped. If she kept up a good stride, she'd warm up and cover a lot of ground. There wasn't anything keeping her there anymore, after all. Maybe she could just disappear and begin a new life somewhere else.

Athena ignored the small voice warning her to turn around and go back to Donovan. He owned her; she could admit to that, and Nathan had given his blessing for them to be together, even if he thought he was dying from cancer. But those weren't the only reasons she felt torn. Despite everything that he had done, Athena was falling for him.

And she hated herself for it.

The houses surrounding her were silent. The people living in them must all be asleep, if they were even staying there at all. The entire area gave off an "I'm visiting my estate in the mountains" vibe.

Headlights turned a corner and pulled up fast beside her, trapping her against a hedge before she could think about hiding or even moving out of the way. It was Donovan. Or maybe Alvarez. Someone who was looking for her, and she'd been found.

"Fuck," she muttered, staring at the tinted windows. She was never going to be allowed to leave the house again.

The door opened, and Athena's eyes widened. She tried to scream, but it was too late. He grabbed her by the throat and made quick work of searching her pocket. Athena clawed at his hand, struggling to breathe as he patted her down.

He found the phone Veronica had lent her and crushed it underfoot. Satisfied, he threw her in the backseat. Athena coughed and sputtered, her hand instantly going to the bruised skin around her neck.

He glanced at her in the rearview mirror.

"Don't even think about trying anything stupid," he said. "I'm not Leon, and this isn't going down the same way."

"It's you," Athena crocked. "Donovan said they were trying to find the one behind all the human trafficking. It was Pete and Jared... I should have known. Of course, it was you."

She was rambling, but it didn't matter. She was going to die. Donovan had no idea where she was. He might not even know she was missing yet.

"Just shut up," Derrick chuckled. "For fuck's sake. There's no need to be dramatic, Athena."

He put the car in drive and eased out of the luxurious neighborhood. Athena tried to steady her breathing and remember the route they were taking, but everything was so dark and unfamiliar. She counted the turns, only to forget the first part of the sequence. There was no way she'd be able to retrace their steps, assuming against all logic that she'd ever have the opportunity to run.

"Why do this, though? You know Donovan's going to freak out," she said. "Seriously, Derrick. If you wanted to stay under the radar, you picked the worst person to fuck with."

"Who says I want to stay under the radar? Besides, no risk, no reward. You're sweet and submissive. Easy to break. That's what kept me thinking about you, Athena; that's why I have to have you." He shifted, and the car sped up. "Messing with Donovan O'Malley? That's just icing on the cake."

Derrick merged onto the freeway, headed in the opposite direction of the city. Wherever he was taking her, they were going North, a part of the state Athena rarely visited and knew practically nothing about.

"You want Donovan's attention?" Her throat burned from being nearly strangled, but she needed to keep him talking. "There are other ways to get it. Ways that don't end with him killing you."

"Don't worry about it," Derrick grunted. "That fucker's been looking for me for ages. We have rings set up all over the state, and Donovan O'Malley already knows about a lot of them. But he hasn't done shit about it. You know why, Athena? Because first, he wants to have me in a corner. He either needs enough proof to put me away for good, or he has to find me to try and kill me himself. And too bad for you, but that's never gonna happen.

Athena stared at him, wondering exactly how she could have been so wrong about him. Hadn't she thought he gave off good vibes? What had she been thinking?

The disgust must have registered on her face because it made Derrick laugh out loud. "You think I'm the monster, but consider the choice your boyfriend's making. He knows where we're keeping some of these women, and he hasn't done a thing about it. He wants me more than he wants to save them. How fucked up is that, right?"

Athena bit down on the inside of her cheek, hard enough to draw blood. She didn't want to give Derrick any satisfaction... even if part of her couldn't help but feel like there was some truth to his words. Donovan was a murderer... and just maybe, he was allowing human trafficking to go on for the sake of catching one person. If what Derrick said was true, that is.

They drove together for hours, ignoring every exit until Derrick pulled off on an unmarked road. It led to a clearing that housed a raggedy motel, though no other cars were parked in the lot. There were no restaurants or even gas stations off the dusty path, either. All Athena could see was the shabby old building and its broken down, partially rotten ancient fence. After he parked, Derrick paused before opening his door.

"There's no one around for miles. No one can hear you scream, I promise. If you try to get away, I'll bury your body in these woods."

Athena shivered, both from the threats and the early morning cold that poured into the backseat when Derrick stepped out. He opened her door and reached inside to pull her out with him. She went easily; there was no point in struggling. She needed to save her energy for when it really mattered. She couldn't give up on getting free.

She just needed one opening. A moment when Derrick would let his guard down enough for her to grab his keys and run back to the car.

The plan might not be the best, but it was all she had.

"Let's go," he said, prodding her to walk toward the building. He had a gun; she could feel the cool metal poking into her side through her hoodie.

Athena walked to the door and tried the handle. It was unlocked, but as soon as she opened it, she turned around and tried to run. Derrick caught her easily and blocked her only means of escape.

She was forced to turn and face the horrific sight.

A few of the women in the lobby looked at them with empty eyes, their barely covered bodies thin and peppered with bruises. Others appeared to be asleep, and some just stared off into space.

Athena screamed, but just as Derrick said, there was no one to hear her.

———

"I think you'll fit in here," Derrick said, dropping her on the bed. "It's about time, anyway. I've wanted to break you in since the night at the bar, Athena. If Nathan hadn't fucked things up... well, it doesn't matter anyway. Leon couldn't even handle that one thing, but he's dead now, too."

"Since... the night at the bar? When I went to Jared's open mic night?" Athena asked. "That was years ago. You've been doing this for years? Kidnapping women... and bringing them here? Or somewhere else?"

He had said something about multiple locations in the car. Athena's stomach lurched, thinking about other

buildings with even more sick and brutalized women. Derrick shrugged. "Like it's hard or something? The police are worthless if you haven't noticed. Even the ones that aren't in my pocket aren't capable of finding out shit. I actually started doing this when we were taking classes at the university, Athena. Art doesn't pay much, but providing goods to consumers? That's always lucrative." Athena hugged her knees, trying to make herself small. "Nathan, though? Did you already know him? He was there at the bar the night I met you and Pete... you and Leon, I mean."

Her head was spinning, trying to remember every detail of that night. Jared had seemed so nervous; Nathan was so mad. Athena had thought he was just jealous of her meeting the other guys, but maybe it was more than that.

Had he already known what they did to women? Was he trying to protect her? Maybe Nathan just didn't want her to be like the women in the foyer. Haunted. Dead inside.

It didn't really matter anymore. She had ended up with them anyway.

"Nathan was a dumb motherfucker. He should've known I'd be adding you to the collection eventually. He couldn't save you forever." Derrick unbuckled his pants and set his gun on the dresser. "He thought you'd be safe with O'Malley. When he found out he was dying, leaving you to that fucker was his only option."

"Donovan's the one who can stop you," Athena whispered. "He's been taking this thing down, bit by bit. It won't be long before he shows up here, and you know that."

Derrick's eyes flashed, and he slapped her hard, sending her sprawling across the bed. "I liked you better when we were in class together, Athena. You knew how to keep that pretty mouth shut back then."

He shed off his pants and boxers, then unbuttoned his shirt before joining her on the bed. Athena clutched her cheek, already feeling the new set of bruises forming.

"It's different, isn't it?" Derrick whispered. "You love to play with rough shit, but the second it gets real, it's too much, huh? You're pathetic."

Athena scooted to the edge of the bed, but there wasn't anywhere else to go. Two goons were outside the door. The window was boarded up, and Derrick was twice her size. But the gun... the gun was on the dresser. Maybe if she could reach it, she'd have a chance.

"Don't even think about it," he said, covering her body with his. "You're not that stupid, are you, Athena?"

There was some loud rustling in the hallway, but Athena couldn't see around Derrick. His face was so close that it took up her entire line of sight. He frowned, then turned back to where the noise was coming from.

One of the men cursed, followed by a string of gunshots echoing on the other side of the door.

"What now?" Derrick was annoyed as he shoved off Athena and knelt to collect his pants.

The door splintered open, revealing streaks of blood, and the bodies of two guards slumped against the wall. Two other men, people Athena instantly recognized from visiting Donovan at work, stepped in with their guns drawn as they scanned the room.

Derrick might have said something else, but he didn't get much out. One of the armed men knocked him out, and Derrick collapsed into a pile on the floor. Athena stood carefully, not sure if they would remember her.

"Let's go," one said to her, offering a hand. "Can you handle this prick, Bryson?"

The other man nodded and slung the gun around his back before hoisting Derrick unceremoniously over his shoulder. Athena walked out with them to the now- deserted foyer.

"Where's Donovan?" Her voice was almost gone between the screaming and Derrick's abuse.

"He's helping the women," Bryson grunted. "Looking for you, too, I would think."

Athena rushed to the door, her eyes wide at the sight of multiple vans and hordes of people in front of the dilapidated building.

Police cars with flashing lights rolled in, along with several ambulances and a firetruck. She scanned the crowd of women wrapped in blankets and members of Donovan's team as they handed over the criminals to the police.

Athena felt his presence before she saw him.

"What am I going to do with you?" Donovan growled as he swept her up into a clumsy hug, her feet dangling off the ground until she instinctually wrapped them around his waist. "I swear to god, Athena... I thought..." His voice cracked, which made her vision blur, too.

There were too many emotions, and Athena felt the overload come down on her. She had been running on adrenaline and fear, but the gravity of everything that happened to her was finally setting in. She had been kidnapped and almost raped. She could have been lost forever. She could have been killed.

"How did you find me?" she croaked.

Donovan stiffened and pulled her away fast, his face darkening as he scanned the bruises on her neck and face. "I'm going to kill him."

He glanced over her head, nodding at someone in the crowd, and then returned his attention to her. Athena didn't want to know what that meant. What did it matter, anyway? So what if he killed Derrick?

But then, maybe she would have thought the same thing about Nathan if she really knew him before he died.

"Take me home," she said.

Donovan cupped her ass, walking them both to the car. "Gladly."

*Chapter 27*

*Now*

Athena's night terrors began the first time she tried to sleep. Donovan had carried her up to their room. He filled the bathtub, washed her, and had her back in bed as soon as possible. He had planned on working on his computer next to her, but her eyes had barely closed when the screaming started.

"Shhhh. I've got you," he said, pulling her into his lap. Her eyes were frantic when she finally pried them open. Donovan made a mental note to schedule a session with her therapist for the next day. Recovery might be a long road for her, but at least his team had arrived before more harm was done.

Still, none of it would stop Donovan from extracting revenge from Derrick. The fucker was being held at a nearby location, waiting for Donovan to have a spare minute to deal with him.

The police hadn't even batted an eye when Donovan's guys shoved him in the back of a van and took off from the crime scene. He should send them a fruit basket or something as a thank you for that one.

"I can't sleep right now. I want you to talk to me instead," she said.

Donovan rubbed small circles on her back. He leaned against the headboard to make more room for her to recline against him. "Sure, sweetheart. What do you want to talk about?"

"Did you have to kill Jared?" she asked quietly. "Was he really the same as Derrick?"

Donovan's hand on her back faltered, then he continued rubbing. The tell was so subtle Athena probably would have missed it if she hadn't paid close attention.

*He didn't know I knew about that*, she thought. Donovan might be an expert at reading her, but she was picking up on his cues, too.

"I didn't kill Jared. A team of traffickers did to keep him from talking," Donovan said. "And no. He was late coming into the business. He only got involved more recently when he needed money. He knew Derrick and Leon already, and they offered him an opportunity for some quick cash when they found out you were moving in with him. Of course, he had bragged to one of them as soon as you agreed, putting the whole thing in motion."

Athena swallowed hard. Knowing that Jared wasn't more involved made her feel even worse that he died. But at least Donovan wasn't involved. "I don't understand how you even found me there. I didn't have my phone or anything with me." Athena frowned and pulled away to look at him. "I swear, if you have some tracking device implanted in me, I'll—"

"You'll do what, exactly?" Donovan smirked. "You're my property, remember, slave girl? If I want to put a tracking device under your skin, I sure as fuck will do it."

Athena tried desperately not to show how much that turned her on. Of course, she failed terribly.

"But, as hot as that sounds, no. You don't have a tracking device embedded anywhere. We knew about that motel and a few other places where they were keeping women, so it was a process of elimination. We only had to stop at one other location first. I was *persuasive*, and a trafficker there told us where you'd be."

"Persuasive, huh?" Athena smiled.

Donovan shrugged, expression innocent. "I guess he preferred to die without additional bones broken."

Athena didn't have a response to that.

"Anyway," Donovan continued. "Derrick was running out of options, and I thought he would probably try and pull some shit with you soon anyway. There was nothing I could take to the police as proof, and I didn't have any good leads on where he was. Even the other traffickers had no idea until recently. Derrick was careful like that. Only a select few ever knew his location. But I knew he'd see you as a pretty good bargaining chip if someone wanted to fuck with me, you know? That's one reason I've kept you so close, Athena. Besides giving us a chance to bond and everything."

She blinked. "You knew he wanted me? But how?"

Oh. Of course. Pete had taken her for Derrick. "He wanted to use me to get to you. For fuck's sake, why wouldn't you tell me?"

Donovan shrugged. "Would you have believed me?"

Athena opened her mouth, then closed it. Good question. She hadn't believed him about Nathan or Jared. She didn't believe him about not wanting other women. She hadn't really believed him about anything.

"It's alright," he said, pulling her close again. "You've had a long line of people being really shitty and lying to you about all sorts of things. It will take time, but we'll get to where you'll believe everything I tell you. You won't have to worry about whether it's a lie. I promise."

"You know, you're not that special. Derrick wanted me for myself, too," Athena said. "I guess he thought me being submissive meant I was malleable and weak or something."

Donovan snorted, shaking his head. "Clearly, he didn't know you very well at all."

They sat like that for a while, enjoying the embrace.

"Did he really know?" Athena asked suddenly. "Nathan, I mean. Veronica said some things, and I need to know if he knew about the trafficking, Donovan."

He sighed. "Yeah, he really knew about all of it. The only thing that made me spare him for so long was that he truly meant to protect you from everything, including that world. I'm sorry."

She nodded and allowed the tears to come with the promise to herself that it would be the last time she cried over Nathan Garcia. He didn't deserve her pain anymore. He could burn in hell.

*Epilogue*

*Now*

Athena groaned as she stepped on the scale. Gaining weight was natural and important to the whole pregnancy process, but that didn't mean she had to enjoy it. Especially when she wasn't even really showing yet. Most of the baby weight seemed to be collecting in her face and boobs.

"I'm going to throw that fucking thing out the window if I see you using it again until long after you've given birth," Donovan said. His eyes raked over her naked body hungrily, letting her know without words that he didn't mind the extra pounds at all.

"So, what I hear you saying is that I can use it, but I need to be sneaky about it, right?" Athena teased.

Donovan rolled his eyes. "Yes, Athena. That's exactly what I meant. Now, hurry up and get dressed."

It was their wedding day, which probably should have been the biggest day of her life. Lots of girls planned out their wedding years in advance, but Athena was fine with a visit to Town Hall and having dinner with their friends and family afterwards. Mel and Alvarez would be their witnesses, and everyone else would meet them at a restaurant downtown.

Overall, Donovan was very accommodating with her low-scale wedding plans. What he wouldn't compromise on was his desire for her to get pregnant right away. His reasoning was that she already wore his collar, so there was no reason to wait for legal red tape to knock her up.

Athena couldn't find any reason to disagree, although her opinion didn't seem necessary. Still, pregnancy and birth, in general, were terrifying.

She had been dreading it until she watched Donovan throw her birth control pills in the trash. Something about that had flipped a switch for her. Maybe it made the idea sexy somehow? She'd never wanted kids with Nathan, but having them with Donovan felt exciting. It was another adventure for them to share; he'd be a great dad. She could already tell.

Her parents would also be there for their reception dinner after the ceremony. They weren't thrilled about her getting pregnant outside of wedlock, but they'd have plenty of time to get over it before the baby was born. Even if they couldn't, their opinion wouldn't impact her life in any meaningful way.

She was finally free, even if that felt like a total oxymoron since she was once again owned by someone. Athena watched Donovan towel his hair dry and walk out of the bathroom. The muscles in his back rippled, making her want him all over again. Pregnancy was turning her into a sex fiend, though Donovan was treating her like some kind of breakable doll. He had tabled all impact play until after the birth just to make sure nothing went wrong.

Athena grabbed her makeup bag and turned to look at herself in the mirror. Her skin was bright and clear, glowing, and not just from the pregnancy. She was happy, just like Nathan had predicted in his final directive.

She allowed herself to feel a moment of gratitude for her first master. Even though he turned out to be a horrible person, she wouldn't have this life without him. After all, Athena had this happy ending only because she was doing as she was told and living by his will.

The End

*Books by Lynne Stewart*

*The True Mate Shifter Series*
- Taming His True Mate (February 2024)
- Tracking His True Mate
- Tempting His True Mate

Living by His Will

## *Author's Note*

I hope you enjoyed Athena and Donovan's story! This is my first dark romance novel, and I had a ton of fun writing it. I'm looking forward to writing more dark romances, as well as additional paranormal romances (including more in the True Mate Shifter Series universe).

Please follow me on Amazon, Facebook, or Goodreads if you are interested in updates. You can also find all my books and other information on my website: www.booksbylynne.com

Thank you for your feedback! Your reviews mean so much.

## About the Author

LYNNE STEWART is an enthusiastic reader and a lover of all things paranormal and interesting. During the day, she works as a librarian and likes spending time with her husband, their children, and pets. By night, she enjoys creating steamy romances with a little bite in them.